I0762847

THE YANKEE SPHINX

Also by Mark Frost

The List of Seven

The Six Messiahs

Before I Wake

The Greatest Game Ever Played

The Grand Slam

The Second Objective

The Match

Game Six

The Paladin Prophecy

The Paladin Prophecy: Alliance

The Paladin Prophecy: Rogue

The Secret History of Twin Peaks

Twin Peaks: The Final Dossier

The Yankee Sphinx

An FDR Novel

MARK FROST

FLATIRON
BOOKS
NEW YORK

This is a work of fiction. All the names, characters, organizations, places, and events portrayed in this work are either products of the author's imagination or used fictitiously.

Printed in the United States of America. For information, address Flatiron Books, 120 Broadway, New York, NY 10271. EU Representative: Macmillan Publishers Ireland Ltd., 1st Floor, The Liffey Trust Centre, 117–126 Sheriff Street Upper, Dublin 1, D01 YC43.

www.flatironbooks.com

Library of Congress Cataloging-in-Publication Data

Names: Frost, Mark, 1953– author.
Title: The Yankee Sphinx : an FDR novel / Mark Frost.
Description: First edition. | New York : Flatiron Books, 2026.
Identifiers: LCCN 2025048710 | ISBN 9781250876898 (hardcover) | ISBN 9781250877048 (ebook)
Subjects: LCSH: Roosevelt, Franklin D. (Franklin Delano), 1882–1945—Fiction | Hassett, William D., 1880–1965—Fiction | World War, 1939–1945—United States—Fiction | LCGFT: Biographical fiction | Historical fiction
Classification: LCC PS3556.R599 Y36 2026
LC record available at https://lccn.loc.gov/2025048710

First Edition: 2026

10 9 8 7 6 5 4 3 2 1

To Uncle Will, Frosty, and Cousin Billy Mac

The greatness of America lies not in being more enlightened than any other nation, but rather in her ability to repair her faults.

ALEXIS DE TOCQUEVILLE

The price of greatness is responsibility.

WINSTON CHURCHILL

THE YANKEE SPHINX

Northfield, Vermont, November 12, 1962

Two days ago, on a rainy, gray afternoon in the Hyde Park Rose Garden, we saw Mrs. Roosevelt to her rest. Those still standing from the old days—only a handful of us now—paid our respects. An air of finality you couldn't help but feel, the end of an era, and an age. Offering welcome consolation, if fleeting, to be in the company again of friends who'd lived it with us.

Modest to the last, she'd asked for a simple, private funeral. She didn't even want her passing announced until the services were over. Not likely for the "First Lady of the World." They did manage, just, to limit the guests to 250, including the current president, two ex-presidents, and the next waiting in the wings. The first gathering of its kind in that regard, to my recollection, in American history.

Seeing my old boss Harry again, and Ike, who joshed that we're all like mirrors to each other now; old, slow, and frayed. Hadn't seen either man since General Marshall's funeral three years ago. Ed Murrow sidled up outside the church, two decades younger than our trio but looking just as careworn.

"We've got to stop meeting like this," he said as he lit another unfiltered Camel. When Ike gestured for one, Ed wagged a finger at him, shaking his head. An old routine between them, and a comfort.

Time plays tricks this way, you'll discover; chances are you have already. Which leaves you and your fellow survivors—if you're "lucky" enough to stick around—shaking your heads, in wonder and befuddlement: How in the world did this happen to us?

I shook Vice President Johnson's hand, although with Secret Service abounding, I missed the pleasure of meeting President Kennedy and his First Lady. The young couple seemed, from my vantage point, dignified, present, sensitive to each moment and the occasion. They were last to enter, and once inside the high hedge that frames the Rose Garden, the graveside service began. They stood apart, aware that all eyes were on them, looking the part and playing their roles in an ageless tale of kings and queens.

I recognized that look in JFK's eye. The Cuban Missile Crisis was on, at a full boil. The president had flown in on his brand-new Air Force One. They'd had to install a special phone box outside the church, just in case news broke. It didn't, as it happened, but presidents never have just one task on their mind; the job demands that—on solemn days like this—they make it seem that way.

• • •

When the eulogies concluded we moved as a slow, milling mass toward the reception. I paid my respects to Eleanor's four sons—all on the outer edge of middle age themselves now—and their extended, complex families, kids and grandkids running off pent-up energy on the lawns.

I stepped inside the old house, Springwood, for the first time in a few years. Suppose this was inevitable, but it felt like the museum it has now become, preserved and spooky. Memories crowding me from all directions, I moved as if in a dream. His fading nautical prints in the entry, the family dining room chock-full of spirits, the wall display of all the local birds he'd hunted—and stuffed himself—as a boy. Moments later, looking in from the ramp down to the Boss's office and library, I heard my name and felt a gentle tap on my shoulder.

Oh my. Dear Anna. She'd grown leaner and tan, sporty even, like a tennis player, her hair cut short and gone salt-and-pepper, but she wore the years, and her grief, I thought, lightly and well. Without a word we embraced, then held each other's hands as I said the usual words and she responded in the usual ways. She whispered something to me as we parted.

My vision blurred, sentimental old fool. Standing in the doorway, memories from his library flooding back, I realized this was about too much for me today. He was born upstairs, for goodness' sake. When I worked for him, Springwood so often became the still point around which the whole world turned. His home is a shrine now, teeming with tourists. The family said goodbye to it seventeen years ago, only seven months after he did. An empty, flawlessly preserved facsimile, yes, but all I could see or hear were ghosts. I turned on my heel and walked outside toward the Rose Garden until I was alone.

The sprawling house, the handsome stone FDR Library I helped curate and grow next door, the profound stillness of these tranquil acres, all so dear to me. Change had hardly touched the estate itself. Only everything else, and all of us.

So Eleanor sleeps beside him now. Bearing only names and dates, the same simple bright white block of marble adorns both their resting places.

"I've kept my promise," I said, or maybe I just thought it.

I wasn't in the room for everything that happened, but I saw more than my share, took part in most of it, and heard about the rest from those who were there when I wasn't, and as you'll see I always paid attention.

I walked to my car, drove slowly down the lane and through the guarded gates. The solemn crowd gathered outside in the rain parted. I turned left, toward Vermont, and a new task for old hands.

I thought of the First Lady's words that had stayed with me through the years:

We must do the things we think we cannot do.

Thursday, February 28, 1935

I was born with a fatal case of life. Learning there's no cure, of course, comes later—not that much later if you're paying attention. I do, always have, which brought me a moment I'll never forget:

My six-year-old self, standing outside a saloon in our small rural village in Vermont. A public house, Blood's Hotel, the only outpost for thirsty sinners in our town of Northfield for miles around. From my first long look at the place when its double doors swung open, and each time since, the pungent scene inside Blood's—sour beer, raucous honky-tonk piano, madcap dancing, and God knows what else going on in rooms upstairs—thrilled and frightened me.

This day upped the ante.

From the street I heard breaking glass, frantic shouts inside, and a woman's piercing scream.

Moments later four men burst out of the joint, hauling something under a grimy white sheet on an unhinged door. The sheet slipped as they lurched down the last step, and from three feet away I came face-to-face with the saloon's oversized proprietor, Big Bill Blood.

Glassy eyes fixed and empty, his open mouth frozen in a gnarled twist exposing yellow, wolfish teeth.

As they moved past me, one of the men's thick fingers pulled the sheet back into place. An inert husk beneath it wobbled like a pudding with each step they took. The bearers were in no hurry, nor did they carry Bill to our doctor's office straight across the street. Then I realized the doctor was one of them. They turned left, in the direction of a place I heard someone close by call the undertaker. Where I assumed the burden they carried would now be, whatever this meant, taken under.

The penny dropped: What I'd just seen used to be a man who shared my name. Full stop. Terror gashed my young soul. Innocence flew the coop, and I realized:

So that's the catch.

The knowledge, it occurred later, must have been lurking, dormant, inside me all along. Until the sight of that dead man tolled a bell in my head that hasn't stopped ringing since.

I felt eyes on me, turned and saw my father outside the saloon doors. If he'd been in his cups when Bill died, he looked rock solid now. Lips taut, holding back emotion, he walked to me, took me by the hand, and turned for home. The hard grip he applied said he was in no mood to talk.

I kept silent because my feelings hadn't found words yet. When they did, in the hours and days that followed, the flood of questions stirred by my face-to-face with a dead man led me to a darker realization; parents and doctors, priests and teachers had no answers.

Worse: Their empty answers convinced me that grown-ups were more spooked about this thing than I was. One moment I'm living the assumption that being "alive" means living has no end . . . and the next Death drops this seventy-two-point headline:

"It's about as eternal as a lit match and there's no way around it, kid."

As I persisted with my quest for answers—you may not see this as a silver lining—I stumbled onto a way of coping that softened the blow: The morbid curiosity aroused by my baptism in mortality turned out, by a fraction, to keep its existential terror at bay. From that day on my one reliable method for finding peace or purpose in life was to keep asking questions.

Which is what led a decade down the road to finding myself in journalism. The only other path I considered was the seminary, but a priest's stock in trade seemed to offer little more than a stare-down with questions one can never answer.

Does this search for unknowable truths also explain why, forty-eight years later, I still drink more than my share? Yes. It's medicinal. Just strong enough to let me consider another failing that gnaws on me on nights like this: Why, at this hour of my life, am I still unattached and alone?

I've made fifty-four trips round the sun. Mostly fair weather, fortune favoring me with my share of smiles. Not lately, but here in the winter of 1935 it's obvious I haven't been singled out. To soft-pedal the lede, times are tough all over, not just here on the outskirts of Wyoming Street. I feel as far removed from the beating heart of our nation's capital—where for so long I had a front row seat—as Wyoming state. But plenty have it worse.

I stare out at a wet winter storm stripping the last leaves off the trees. Passing headlights on Columbia Road flare in the rain and wash across the walls. Rachmaninoff's *Piano Concerto No. 2* murmurs on the radio.

I feel a warning tingle slither down the back of my neck. Something's in the room with me. Nothing I see but only feel; the presence of what my mother used to call the black dog. It's sniffing around, from the shadows, snarling, eyeing my flanks.

Twenty years ago, the beast ran down my oldest sister, Kate. In a shabby hotel room, in a lonely new town, a few weeks shy of forty, she turned on the gas and snuffed the flame. A note poor Katie left on the dresser removed all doubt about her intention. The summit of mortal sin. For the rest of her life, at the mention of Katie's name my mother muttered about the hex or "haint" that stalked her bloodline, a wretched legacy of the Old Country.

"That curs-ed creature knows our scent," she'd whisper.

My father, the village blacksmith—they'd sailed from Ireland together as newlyweds—never had patience for superstitious blather.

"We left all that rubbish behind us, Mary," he'd say whenever she started in. Then he'd stomp out to go belly up to the bar and hoist a few at Blood's.

Where my mother would later dispatch me, which is why I—their youngest of eight—found myself that day, at the appointed hour outside Blood's doors, waiting to walk my old man home to dinner.

Enter—or rather exit—Big Bill.

Cracking open the bottle I've been nursing, I ration out two fingers and take stock, as I'm given to do on gloomy nights, running numbers on my balance sheet.

Twenty-six years a working reporter, the last five overseas—London, Dublin, Berlin. I'd seen plenty, made an honest buck, and earned a respected byline. More than a trade, while covering the big stories of my day—the Great War, the Irish Troubles, the ominous rot in Weimar and Italy—I found an identity, and, through the best and worst of times, something like a calling.

I witnessed those years gut Europe, torch centuries-old empires, toss a last shovel of dirt on the Victorian Age. Until my editor brought me back to Washington—mid roaring twenties—I didn't realize this epoch's end meant the future of Western civilization, by default, had been handed to America. And on my return, seeing my country anew, it seemed we'd reacted to our ascension by plunging into an adolescent spree of easy cash, jazz, sex, and speakeasies. "We the people" may have lost our collective wits but most didn't seem to mind, as long as our go-go economy burned hotter than the forge of Hephaestus.

A platoon of former colleagues, hale and jaunty in boaters and sharp suits, pitched me the hard sell on the hot new game in town: public relations. "It's a science and a business," they preached, "you can't lose, brother. While you're at it, try the stock market, they're practically giving it away!"

I'm still ashamed. That a fever I'd always dodged had grabbed hold of me: fear of missing out on a sure thing. Greed's the word for it, or maybe if you're religiously inclined, the devil. Either way, being of suddenly unsound mind—and no spring chicken—of my own free will, I cast off a lifetime of cautious Catholic ways.

Until the crash of October 29, 1929.

I turned fifty the following spring: By then the blast of Black Friday had cleaned me to the bone. Aside from tossing a few freelance jobs my way, none of my old newsroom pals who'd survived had the bucks to bring me back full-time. To their credit they also had the decency to never say "I told you so."

No need for that—did I mention I'm Irish? Remorse is our mother's milk. The only solace I find in my current straits: At least my parents didn't live to see me like this.

Assets? Ha! Books, clothes, my address book—I cling to the idea all those contacts still hold value—and a few fraying library cards I could fit in a single suitcase.

Liabilities? None, courtesy of a Vermont Yankee's born austerity—pinching pennies comes with the package. Say what you will, but I owe no one a dime. My challenge is survival.

A pencil-pushing government job—a favor two years ago from a pal in FDR's orbit—keeps me afloat. Enough to rent this spare room in a colleague's apartment anyway—hardly a flophouse, but the Ritz it ain't.

Oh and this just happened: Our reactionary Supreme Court, in their wisdom, just ruled that helping folks find union jobs is "unconstitutional." So, in three months my small life raft at the National Recovery Administration is going under.

Pad and pen in hand, I take a pass at the want ad I've been putting off: "Humbled, desperate, middle-aged public servant seeks gainful employment of any sort or . . ."

Except—I'll dispense with fooling myself—mired as I am here in the Depression's deepest gutter, I know if I stay true to my sadder-but-wiser self . . . I'll still hold out for a job that's something like a calling. Don't know what else keeps me in this cold-hearted company town.

My most earnest answer: Because politics matters, and so does a reporter's job of holding that circus to account. But calling it a day and heading home sung like a siren on the rocks. I've got sisters who'd take me in back in Northfield, as safe a place as any to ride out the storm. Which scares the breath out of me.

Because I know damn well I'll never leave Vermont again. The last of my savings will be gone by summer. Inertia, surrender, and the bottle would nail me to the floorboards.

Our black dog would stalk me.

So I buck up: Be gone. I've got persistence and decades of hard work on my side. I'm a unicorn in another good way: a lifelong Vermont Democrat: *Webster*'s Platonic definition of "idealist." Which qualifies me as a shining example of H. L. Mencken's classic American sucker, the sort born every minute.

I hear the phone ring down the hall. Murmurs, footsteps, a soft knock at my door.

"Call for you."

"Thanks—you catch a name?" I ask.

"Says it's Steve Early."

An old pal from Associated Press during the Wilson years. Steve covered the Navy Department during World War I, where we worked the same beat. Never the sort who called to yak about the "good old days," he'd since moved on to better—harder—things.

I pace myself down the hall, pick up the receiver. "To what do I owe the pleasure?"

He sounds like he always does, going three directions at once and a mile a minute. "Bill—good, good—listen, real quick, short notice: What are you doing tomorrow, can you get over here?"

"What time would you like me?"

"First thing, nine sharp, don't be late—"

"Dare I ask?"

"He wants to see you."

"I'll be there at eight forty-five."

He chuckles. "Same old Hassett." Then he hangs up.

I slow walk back to the room as if reining in a team of horses. I stow the bottle. Toss the rest of my drink down the drain. Better safe than sorry. The horses try to pull away from me.

No need to get ahead of yourself now, fella.

Easier said than done.

Steve Early works at the White House. He's President Roosevelt's press secretary.

Friday, March 1, 1935

The rain had moved east, drawing a bitter cold in its wake. I walked a mile and a half down Connecticut Avenue, turned left on Pennsylvania, and checked in at the White House visitors' desk at 8:30.

Steve came down to collect me at 8:45 and we braced ourselves against the biting wind in the colonnade leading to the West Wing.

"How's that job at National Relief working out?" he asked.

"Just happy to make a contribution."

"What do they have you doing?"

"Verifying corporate compliance with Section 7A in the Tidewater District," I said.

"Wow." He shook his head. "Sorry, I dozed off for a second."

"Hey, for all I know I'm the one keeping that whole outfit on its feet."

"Sure you are, pal. But if anyone complains you clocked in late, I'll send you back with a note."

"You can start by reminding them who I am."

We entered the West Wing, and the buzz of a full-throated hive enveloped us.

"By the way, what are they paying you?" he asked.

We're old friends, so I told him.

"Good to know," he said, nodding.

"Why?"

"I'll let him tell you. So you know this didn't come from me—I endorsed it—but he asked for you personally."

Waves of staffers parted as we walked through a series of rooms. A young woman I couldn't quite place waited for us outside the Oval, tall and blond, a dazzling smile.

"Mr. Hassett, so lovely to see you again," she said, shaking my hand. "He's ready for you."

She opened the door, and as we followed her in I realized who she was. I heard his familiar voice before I saw him. A trio of junior aides who looked like college kids scribbling notes stood nearby. He knew we'd come in without looking our way and dispatched his minions with a jaunty wave.

"Off you go, boys and girls, make it snappy. Here he is, come on in, Bill!"

He lit up his sun king smile, and I felt as if I'd seen him last week. We shook hands, his grip still like a wrestler's.

"Hassett, you old so-and-so, haven't changed a lick. You remember Anna, Bill."

I glanced at FDR's only daughter. "Yes, apologies, took me a moment."

"Ha! How long's it been, my friend?"

"October of '19. You were just back from Versailles. Navy Yard cafeteria. Gave me a quote on the Peace Conference, and if memory serves, Mr. President, Anna was with you that day—"

"Oh gosh," said Anna with a laugh. "I'm afraid I pestered you something awful. I just thought reporters were the most fascinating creatures—"

"You had it half right, darling," said FDR. "Told you he'd remember, memory like an elephant!"

"I'll leave you to it, gentlemen," said Anna. "Hope to see you again, Mr. Hassett."

I hoped so too.

"Anna's keeping my appointments for now," said FDR as she

bustled off. "Still wants to give your old racket a try, though. Keeps threatening to run off and join the circus. I have you to thank for that."

I glimpsed the wheelchair behind his desk. Hadn't seen him since he needed one, but you'd never have guessed he couldn't bound to his feet like the vibrant, restless athlete I'd covered for years. Sleeves rolled up, he leaned back, lit a cigarette in his holder.

"Bill, let's not waste a minute of your valuable time. As you know we made out all right in the midterms last fall—"

"Better than all right, I'd say—"

"Better than expected, but won't mean a damn if we don't win a second term in '36, isn't that right, Steve?"

"That's right, Chief."

"I've been telling Steve for months, I'm surrounded by battalions of earnest, well-meaning semiliterates with the life experience of freshman pledges. With our ongoing calamities I need a bat in my dugout who knows our world from Cicero to Calvin Coolidge and can produce square yards of solid prose on deadline. In my voice when needed, for every occasion, from Christmas to the Fourth of July—"

"Like a utility man," I said.

"Exactly right. Not every Yank on Murderer's Row slugged like the Babe—what was the name of that little guy, played infield, Italian—"

"Mike Gazella."

"Mike Gazella, exactly! A spark plug. Never made headlines, but ready on the bench when you needed him. Sort of fella holds a team together 'cause he knows the team comes first."

"Let me save you some time then, Mr. President," I said. "I can start Monday."

"Ha! Knew I could count on you, Bill." He flashed that grin, we shook hands, and then Steve and I were moving toward the door. "Work out the details, Steve, find him a desk nearby. You'll like playing for our team, Bill, you won't have to pretend both sides have a point anymore!"

I must have blanked out a moment. Next thing I remember we were marching the other way along the colonnade. The cold air brought me around.

"The money's not much," Steve was saying. "About what you're getting now. Good news is you're already on government payroll. Do the paperwork, we can transfer you right over. How's assistant secretary sound?"

I must have mumbled something.

"What's that, Bill?"

"Oh. I'm Catholic, you know."

"So I recall."

"I said, some prayers get answered."

I had voted for FDR, uncynically. Yes, I liked him, but I also believed he was the right man in the right job at the right time.

Maybe I could help a little.

Sunday, December 7, 1941

"Have a look at this, Bishop," said FDR. "Just came over from State."

Bishop was the nickname the Boss gave me not long after I joined the staff—he bestowed one on each of us in his inner circle. A way to soften the creeping formality of high office.

Half past one that chilly afternoon, I'd been called to the president's study on the second floor. Remains of lunch sat on a couple of trays. The Boss wore a dark turtleneck and sounded like he was fighting a cold. The weekly packet of new stamps for his collection, from Treasury, lay open on his desk. He bit into an apple and turned to the south window, gazing out at the Ellipse and Washington Monument while I picked up and scanned a typed document from State bearing a "classified" stamp.

"That's page fourteen," said Harry Hopkins. "We intercepted the first thirteen they sent last night. Transmitted in code from Tokyo to their embassy."

Harry reclined on the sofa, arms crossed behind his head. The Boss's closest adviser, Harry the Hop lived down the hall and looked like he hadn't slept for days, even more skeletal and pale than usual in a baggy sweater and slacks.

"They held back that last one deliberately," Harry said, his pale eyes burning. "For over twelve hours. Why do you suppose they'd do that, Bill?"

My job, these days, was more about answering questions, like this one, than asking them.

"Two thoughts," I said. "Either they know we've broken their code—"

"Could be," said FDR. "Hope not."

"—or, in an abundance of caution, they don't want diplomats at their own embassy to know they're terminating negotiations with us."

Harry and FDR exchanged a look. They liked my answer.

"Tokyo gave Ambassador Nomura instructions to deliver all fourteen pages to State in exactly . . ." Harry glanced at his watch. ". . . twenty minutes."

"Here's the thing," said FDR. "Three Japanese convoys escorting multiple carrier groups left their waters three days ago, heading south, destination unknown. On an attack we think they've been planning for weeks—"

"Where?" I asked.

"Malaysia, Philippines, Burma Road, Dutch East Indies," said Harry, waving his hand at the big globe in the room. "Take your pick."

"Maybe all of the above," said FDR. "At once."

I took that in, then reread aloud the key line in Prime Minister Tojo's final page: "'It is the obvious intent of the American Government to conspire with Great Britain to obstruct Japan's efforts to establish peace through the creation of a New Order in Asia.'"

"What's that say to you, Bill?" asked Harry.

"If they're done talking . . . sounds like they want a war."

"Correct," said the Boss, "and they mean to drag us into it."

"We could still hit them first," said Harry, his tone bearing traces of an unfinished argument.

"No, we simply cannot do that, Harry," said the Boss.

"Well, not in twenty minutes we can't—"

"We're a democracy, and a peaceful people; we don't attack anyone preemptively," said the Boss. Annoyed, he was through discussing it and turned back to me. "This morning I had General Marshall put every American commander in the Pacific on high alert—"

A knock on the open door; the president's secretary, Grace Tully. "Navy secretary needs to speak with you."

Harry sat bolt upright. We looked at each other. An electric crackle sparked the room—we both felt it—and it pulled me to my feet. I glanced at the clock to mark the time: 1:47.

"Put him through," said FDR.

The phone rang. The Boss picked up. "Admiral . . ." He listened. "No," he said softly, then listened awhile. "Get back to me the minute you know more."

He hung up.

"They've bombed Pearl Harbor."

Then the phones never stopped ringing.

• • •

FDR called Secretary of State Cordell Hull and asked him to receive Ambassador Nomura in his office as scheduled.

"He'll arrive with a smile and a bow and their perfect formality," he told Hull. "Accept his message without reading it—or tipping your hand we know their treachery's underway—and bow them the hell out."

We soon learned that by the time General Marshall's warning cable reached Hickam Airfield in Hawaii the Japanese had already struck the first blow. Dispatches pouring our way from Pearl grew steadily worse: a second wave of fighters and torpedo bombers, targeting comms and airfields, hitting most of our planes before they could unblock their wheels, battleships trapped in their berths, sitting ducks. Harry couldn't believe it—not only that we'd been caught unawares but, as always, he was looking beyond the moment:

"How can a country that prides itself on being smarter and cleverer than every other on the planet . . . do something this suicidally self-destructive?"

"Don't be naive, Harry." The Boss shot him a hard look. "It's exactly the sort of thing Japan would do and did do in 1904: sneak attack on the Russian fleet at Port Arthur, set off two years of war."

Maintaining steely calm, FDR had called an emergency meet with the joint chiefs as soon as the news hit. As the men gathered, the president dictated two statements to Steve Early and me for the national reporters now swarming the press room.

Harry picked up a call on a secure overseas line. He covered the speaker and said: "It's Gil Winant. He's at Chequers for the weekend."

Chequers is the prime minister's country house. The Boss put Gil on speaker and our British Ambassador came on the line. A poised and elegant Ivy Leaguer, Winant sounded shaky and agitated.

"We'd just sat down for dinner when a valet brought in a radio and we heard the first BBC reports— Here, sir, he wants to speak to you."

He handed off the phone and a startlingly familiar voice broke the scratchy silence: "Mr. President, what's all this about Japan? Is it true?"

"It's entirely true, Winston. We're all in the same boat now."

"They've hit us as well all along the Malay Peninsula. We shall declare war immediately—"

"Bear with me, old boy, one step at a time. I'll go to Congress tomorrow—first, if you please—to ask for a declaration of war against Japan."

A slight, significant pause.

"Following your lead, I'll ask the same from Parliament, within the hour of yours," said Churchill. "Will you declare against Germany as well?"

This was the outcome Churchill had been pushing us toward for two years. I glanced at Harry, who subtly shook his head.

"Just Japan for now, Winston. The little corporal's got his hands full in Moscow. If he's smart he won't stick his nose into this fight, not just yet."

Another hesitation before Churchill responded.

"Remains to be seen. But I'd say this certainly clarifies things. May God be with you, Mr. President."

• • •

The president's council of war wrapped up as daylight faded at 4:30 PM. During the briefing FDR took each incoming update himself, relaying news to his joint chiefs as losses mounted: three of our eight battleships sent to the bottom, a fourth crippled—half our fleet; over a hundred planes burning on the tarmac; service deaths at fifteen hundred and climbing. Harry stepped out to hastily organize two evening briefings with FDR's cabinet and key congressional leaders.

He never flinched, but during a lull after the chiefs left, the Boss fell quiet, ordering his thoughts. I made calls on the far side of the room. As twilight gathered, Mike Reilly, head of FDR's Secret Service unit, came in angry that no one had ramped up security. He wanted to triple his detail and the Boss okayed it. Reilly picked up a phone and barked commands, asking for a company of Marines to deploy on the grounds and that all lights in the White House and the Mall be blacked out so they couldn't be targeted from the air.

"Mike, hold on now," said FDR. "Pearl Harbor's thousands of miles away, they're not about to charge up Pennsylvania Avenue. No military on the grounds, please, sends the wrong message. Your men can handle it for now. And I want every light in this building on and keep 'em burning. People need to know we're here and at work."

FDR wasn't easy to read most days, but I saw cold fury fueling his steadiness. The one still point around which, in this moment, the whole world turned. As Mike left the Boss had me call in Grace Tully with her steno book.

"Have a seat, Grace. I'm going before Congress tomorrow. I'd like to dictate my message. It will be short."

FDR screwed a cigarette into his holder, lit it, took a deep drag, and spoke calmly, his tone not that different from when he routinely answered his mail.

"Yesterday, comma, December seventh, comma, 1941, dash, a day which will live in world history, dash, the United States was simultaneously and deliberately attacked . . ."

Mrs. Roosevelt appeared at the door. She'd been hosting a lunch when the bulletins broke earlier. The Boss looked up and nodded at her. Neither spoke but for a moment he took in her gravity, and she read his. He turned back to Grace. Eleanor's eyes found mine. I knew she'd come for confirmation that what she'd heard was true, then she nodded an acknowledgment to me and walked off without a word.

She'd sized up the whole of it in an instant. It's no exaggeration to say I liked and admired her every bit as much as her husband. The First Lady now had her own role to play. She knew exactly how to respond to this moment and got right about doing it.

Fifteen minutes later, during her weekly radio program, Eleanor became the first Roosevelt to address the country about the war, urging every citizen to listen to her husband's speech to Congress and the nation the next day. The respect and inspiration she'd earned within our borders had never been stronger. With all four of her adult sons already serving in our armed forces, she could speak directly and empathetically to every mother listening whose sons would soon enter the line of fire.

I felt my energy flag and stepped outside for the first time since the news landed to clear my head. Cold and bracing. From the portico balcony I saw a crowd growing outside the gates on Pennsylvania Avenue, in the thousands. Many held lit candles. Before long I heard the First Lady's voice issuing from a radio somewhere inside.

". . . I know that on this night you cannot escape anxiety, you cannot escape a clutch of fear at your heart . . . and yet I hope that the certainty of what we have to meet will make you rise above these fears. . . . Whatever is asked of us, I am sure we can accomplish it."

From the crowd below, a thin wave of voices reached me through the frigid night, singing patriotic songs.

• • •

After a working supper spent refining tomorrow's speech, the Boss asked me to wave members of his cabinet into the Oval at 8:30. He sat writing at his desk until they assembled around him, motionless, then, still holding his pen, broke the heavy silence before he looked up:

"I'm thankful you're all here. This is the most serious meeting held in this room since 1861 after the attack on Fort Sumter."

In plain words, no hint of panic, he laid out the stark facts, a numbing calculus of loss in cold hard numbers. He then read the brief message he would deliver to Congress the next day. He'd changed only one word from the draft I'd heard him dictate earlier.

"December seventh, a day which will live . . . in infamy."

An hour later I escorted in Vice President Henry Wallace and eight congressional leaders. The Boss gave them the updated tally; over two thousand dead, nineteen capital ships hit, seven sunk in the first hour alone. Japanese planes had also struck Clark Field in the Philippines a few hours later, destroying General MacArthur's squadrons before they got in the air. British outposts in Hong Kong, Malaysia, and Singapore had been struck hard in coordinated attacks.

As the politicians filtered in, Harry and I picked up grumbles and sparks of anxiety from both parties. We'd been caught flatfooted, and they'd reacted with a standard pol's instinct to assign blame, laying fault on Naval Intelligence, military brass, cabinet secretaries, and—from the opposition—our commander in chief. When the Boss finally met their eyes he quashed it with his first words:

"Human nature and politics being what they are, on a day like this I expect a lot of finger-pointing. There will be plenty of time for that later, my friends, but not, I hope, tonight."

He waited for that to settle their hash, which it did.

"The only good news I can give you is this: All three of our Pacific Fleet aircraft carrier groups were out at sea on maneuvers. They're all secure for now."

Then he said he'd be happy to take their questions and leaned back like a fighter against the ropes. Giving them their shot, he answered every query with blunt, unvarnished replies—"No, we don't know how it happened," "The systems in place simply didn't hold." He sat unmoving and let their frustrations and anger crash over him, resolute as a breakwater, deflecting nothing, accepting full responsibility.

Once they felt heard—and a lot less worked up—FDR asked the Speaker of the House for permission to address Congress the next day. Before granting it, Sam Rayburn pressed for confirmation he was coming to ask for a declaration of war. To my surprise, the Boss declined.

"These attacks aside, Japan has not yet formally declared war on us," he said. "Without a doubt, that will come, and soon. In the meantime, we have a lot to talk about no matter what they do, and we have a job ahead of us."

In the ensuing silence, an unlikely congressman—a lifelong isolationist who'd never once in twenty years been gung ho about any foreign entanglement—spoke up:

"Damn right, we do. We didn't ask for this fight, but it's high time we roll up our sleeves and go win it."

That spliced some iron in their spines, and the group sounded their agreement. FDR glanced at Harry; I thought I saw him wink. By holding his fire, the Boss had steered this perpetually fractious group to direct their righteous fury where it belonged:

At the enemy who'd forced us into war.

When the last of the now energized politicos made their way out, I hung back and quietly took Harry aside.

"He knows exactly what he's going there to ask them for . . . why keep it from 'em now?"

"What, you think eight politicians can keep a secret?" asked Harry with a grin. "It'd be all over town in five fucking minutes."

• • •

One final meeting, near midnight, closed out the day. The president's oldest son, Jimmy—a major in the Marines, who'd recently handled some discreet diplomatic work for his father—had arrived earlier to sit near him through the last meetings. But Jimmy's primary reason for being on hand had been to locate and deliver our last two guests waiting downstairs.

One was Jimmy's current boss, an old law school mate of FDR's, William "Wild Bill" Donovan. A former Medal of Honor winner and former prosecutor, Donovan had been named five months earlier to a new post as Coordinator of Information. He'd lobbied the Boss to create this position, convincing him that to respond to the rapidly changing world around us our two competing intelligence branches—military and civilian—desperately needed to be centralized and coordinated in one office. Having spent the last two years as an adviser to Great Britain, Donovan modeled this new agency on the Crown's venerable intelligence service, MI6. Within months our version would be known as the Office of Strategic Services.

"Tonight, I'm feeling awfully glad you got me started on this," the Boss told Donovan as he arrived.

An old friend of mine and Harry's entered with Wild Bill: Ed Murrow, the respected CBS radio man who'd covered Hitler's war from London since 1939. Over sandwiches and beer, the president asked Ed to keep what he was about to hear off the record—no need to ask that of the fanatically secretive Donovan. Ed agreed, lighting another in a chain of smokes. For the first time all day, as he talked them through Japan's brutal attack, FDR gave voice to the fury and helplessness he'd kept dammed up since the news broke.

"Our ships defenseless, our planes destroyed on the ground, by God, on the ground!" He banged his fist on the table three times.

He asked Donovan whether any of his sources, either here or in Europe, had reason to believe Germany had played any part in the Japanese assault.

"None, not a word," said Donovan. "In fact, from what we're picking up it seems Tokyo caught Berlin with its pants down as much as it did us."

"Is it likely that Germany, unprovoked, will jump in with them now?" asked the Boss. "Declare war on us too, if we only declare against Japan?"

"Possible," said Donovan. "Fifty-fifty."

FDR paused and studied him. "Could the way in which we respond to Japan, if worded in a particular way . . . encourage Germany to do so?"

Donovan thought a bit longer. Usually poker-faced, he raised a wry eyebrow with a wisp of a smile. "Wouldn't hurt to try."

FDR drained the last of his beer and set it on the Resolute desk. He asked both men how they thought the attack would affect domestic opinion about entering the war against Japan and, as he anticipated we'd soon be forced to do, Germany.

"Will this wake us enough to buck up and bloody our hands, the way the Blitz did England? I want to know our people can stand the strain and sacrifice that winning this is going to take before I ask for it."

Both men assured him, confidently, without reservation, they believed it would, and our people could.

• • •

The next day, when he stood in the well of the House of Representatives, Congress gave the Boss the declaration of war he had asked for against Japan. The lone dissent came from the same pacifist rep from Montana who'd voted against us entering World War I.

FDR didn't mention Germany by name. He knew that in this perilous moment, if he overreached by asking for a declaration against Hitler's Reich as well, die-hard isolationists in the Republican caucus would strangle the motion in the cloakroom. The Boss had already found a more efficient way to work around them.

The next night FDR laid out our predicament for the rest of our country in one of his patented folksy fireside chats, a radio address from the White House, delivered beside an oft-photographed prop fireplace. The Boss had a radical idea once in office: Instead of preaching or pushing a bill of goods to people at home, he talked to them like a friend at their kitchen table. The first politician to grasp the intimacy of this new medium, he mastered it.

On this night, after clarifying that the only enemy America faced—for now—was the one that attacked us, he mixed in a few barbs for an audience of one in Berlin: the unstable monster he referred to in private as "the housepainter" or that "deranged Austrian corporal."

"There is no such thing as security for any nation in a world ruled by the principles of gangsterism. We must face the fact that modern warfare, as conducted in the Nazi manner, is a dirty business. Not only must the shame of Japanese treachery be wiped out, but the sources of international brutality, wherever they exist, must be absolutely and finally broken. Eliminating the danger from Japan will serve us ill if we accomplish that and find the rest of the world dominated by Hitler and Mussolini."

Bill Donovan had sent an update early that morning: Japan, on a high after their coup at Pearl Harbor, had turned up the heat on Germany to add their own declaration of war against America. Seeing our Pacific fleet bloodied and broken, the Nazi military command knew America had our hands full, just as their own spearhead advance was surging toward Moscow.

As a result, Donovan's sources said Hitler's advisers had convinced him to stay silent as far as America was concerned. Once Russia fell, they saw opportunity: England would be alone, vulnerable, and ripe for the taking. Within months Germany could launch a full-on cross-Channel invasion unless London surrendered to Fascism. With their conquest of Europe complete they believed America would back down. Hitler's silence on the war in the Pacific seemed to indicate, for the moment, he'd listened to them.

Until three days later.

During a live radio broadcast from Berlin, we learned the line FDR had baited and cast across the pond had hooked its target. During a ninety-minute rant to his stooges in the Reichstag, the little corporal seemed to have swallowed the Boss's shiny lure down to his shoes.

He accused FDR of aristocratic decadence, damning him as "a slave of the Jews" in his twisted logic that gave him the proof he needed to accuse the Boss of provoking Japan's savaging of Pearl Harbor, an attack we brought on ourselves and richly deserved.

Now I'd heard everything: the lunatic who'd sent storm troopers swarming in every direction, conquering continental Europe in less than two years, blaming President Roosevelt for starting World War II.

I might have otherwise been shocked, but you see, I already knew plenty about the other guy.

The Austrian Corporal

After covering the Irish Rebellion my paper sent me to Berlin and the Weimar Republic in the early '20s. I had caught wind of unsettling developments to the south and sensed a story. I took a train to Bavaria to attend a speech in a Munich beer hall.

I walked into what looked more like a Wagnerian opera house, the air thick with smoke, sweat, and a primitive tribal musk. Towering crimson banners bearing gothic swastikas bracketed the stage and adorned scarlet armbands on the worked-up mob. The corporal had co-opted this mystical sigil for his movement, one that for millennia in the East had served as a symbol of peace. Give the corporal credit: He was already corrupting everything he touched.

Curtains parted and, wearing a crude faux-military tunic, out marched the leader of the National Socialist German Workers' Party. The crowd went nuts. A painter of mediocre landscapes, thirty-four-year-old Adolf Hitler fancied himself an artist. Whatever "artistry" he possessed seemed better suited to the theater; his volcanic delivery verged on cartoonish, but the runty Austrian exuded dank charisma and a con man's flair.

He shamelessly tied his suffering as a soldier in the trenches—grievances that included gassing and a bout of blindness—to all the postwar humiliations imposed on his country by their tormentors. At 1919's Paris Peace Conference the Allies refused them a seat at the table and condemned Germany as the Great War's villain. The resulting Treaty of Versailles exacted a price for the sins of the Hun that even hawks saw as excessive:

Their military was dismantled, and future rearmament banned in perpetuity. Reparations bankrupted an already crippled economy. After forfeiting territory to its injured neighbors, the Treaty also stripped Germany of its colonial possessions, handing them to their hated rivals.

The corporal grabbed his mob by the throat that night. With the fire of "Old Time Religion," his long howl of self-pity sparked a fire for righteous retribution. I left the hall that night fearing Versailles might cost the world a far worse price than the one we'd just paid.

Returning to Berlin, I asked my contacts about him. Learned he'd served in the army's postwar dregs as a military cop. Assigned to infiltrate a right-wing splinter group called the German Workers' Party, he'd wormed his way in only to realize he didn't just share their crackpot conspiracies, he didn't think they went far enough. In less than a year he was their leader. Weimar's elite dismissed him as a raving sideshow bumpkin with a certainty I took no comfort in. I couldn't shake this absurd prophet of doom with the postage-stamp mustache from my mind.

Months later, in November 1923, Hitler led his hardcore believers—a thousand dimwit thugs, most ex-military or police—into Munich's streets. The corporal's demented scheme: to kidnap the commissioner of Bavaria, a move he believed would provoke the fall of the Weimar Republic.

Hitler and his goons surrounded a beer hall where the commissioner was giving a speech and kicked in the doors. After firing a pistol in the air the corporal declared a "revolution." Their putative coup ended in a savage beating at the hands of state police. Men on both sides died violently. Nursing a dislocated shoulder, Hitler hid in a friend's attic like a rat for two days before they collared him. The press called this fiasco the Beer Hall Putsch.

In a public circus of a trial that made Hitler a household name, a Weimar court found him guilty of high treason. He drew a five-year sentence, but a tribunal of sympathetic judges freed him after less than one.

He spent his time behind bars dictating a manifesto called "My Struggle." The work cultivated his theme of victimhood like a hothouse orchid. Vowing to continue his mission, he also promised to be a good boy and play by Germany's democratic rules.

Mein Kampf was published in 1925. Its message, that the German *Volk* had suffered unfairly, reached millions vulnerable to such mendacity. Their self-pity, ripe for exploitation by this monster, turned out to be as packed with nightmares as Pandora's box.

He offered a simple solution: a strong man to redeem your fall from grace. Conveniently I am that man. They believed their problems were his problems but would learn, at their peril, he was about to make his problems theirs.

• • •

The day I was called back to Washington I was in Vienna covering a lecture by a more reputable public figure. Without mentioning the corporal by name, the father of modern psychology, Dr. Freud, laid bare the demagogue's method:

Blame "the other"—Jews, foreigners, Gypsies, fill in the blank—for your pain as a scapegoat to avenge all real or perceived injuries. Accuse your enemy of every evil you're guilty of committing yourself. In this way cults of personality are born, a process Freud called projection.

Twenty-two years later, that shabby madman I'd seen in Munich now posed an existential threat to the world. Hitler condemned FDR's declaration of war as a cynical ploy to mask the "failures of his New Deal." He damned Roosevelt as a "communist" risking the world to save his political hide. All of it so depraved you didn't need a translator: His depravity was the message.

"Germany, Italy, and Japan will now fight this global war together! A war forced upon us by the United States and England!"

The Reichstag responded the way his supine puppets always did: with an operatic standing ovation for their bloodthirsty Übermensch. By the time we switched off Ed Murrow's radio coverage, Germany's ambassador had delivered to the White House the Axis Powers' joint declaration of war against us. FDR gave them his less genteel response; the corporal's messenger boys had twelve hours to clear out and park their rear ends on a flight to Berlin.

Within the hour, we sent Congress the request he already had waiting on his desk: our declaration of war against all the Axis Powers.

This time not even the pacifist from Montana objected.

The Man Himself

So what made FDR tick?

Friends always pressed me on this. Strangers asked whenever they learned I worked for him. Love or hate him—I encountered legions of both—he remained a figure of fascination that only grew the longer he stayed in the job.

I had a stock answer. Presidents are judged in ways few could imagine or endure. I'd met, known, or reported on the last half dozen of them, and studied their predecessors in detail. My conclusion: The Oval acts as a magnifying glass, exposing the occupant's flaws and strengths. Opinions form about our shiny new chief executive. The press can put a thumb on the scale all it likes, but a collective feeling in the body politic coalesces about the "new man" during his first two years—sometimes sooner—like clockwork.

This process is much more intuitive than the balls and strikes of personality or whatever actions they take. You won't see it in a job description, but presidents serve as our proxies for every joy and grievance in the cauldron of the national psyche. How we feel about these individuals reveals just as much about how the country feels about itself. What changes is the name of the man in the chair. The wheel turns, seasons of democratic ritual follow. The current occupant either sticks around for a second dance or is shown the door, making way for the next cockeyed, ambitious party hack who's in over his head.

Does that strike you as cynical? Consider this lineup of twentieth-century immortals: Taft, Harding, Coolidge, Hoover. The last century's bunch, with a few exceptions, didn't raise the bar. The America I had grown up in was a provincial backwater, and this cavalcade of White House Babbitts reflected our small-town chamber of commerce ethos.

I'm a reporter. When I meet a "great man," I can't help but keep an eye out for clay in the lower extremities. And yet, in the Boss's case . . . as objectively as I can put this, FDR differed so completely from his predecessors—even those remembered fondly, a handful at best—he occupied his own taxonomy, sui generis, a category of one. He also reflected a dramatic shift in the country's evolution, more industrial than agrarian; Times Square not town square.

During the Boss's first two terms his try-anything approach to lift us out of a global depression reshaped our identity as a nation—and as a people—for the better.

Near the end of FDR's second term, when those who'd weathered the storms of office were resting on laurels and shopping memoirs, an even deeper darkness appeared on the horizon. But the outgoing chief was expected to politely put himself out to pasture, handing off any looming disaster to the next fella.

Once again FDR broke the mold. He was only fifty-eight, at the peak of political effectiveness, and in abundant good health despite the loss of use of his legs. He saw what was brewing overseas and knew the only training for the trials of his office was doing it. Seeing no able successor in the field, he turned cagey, confiding in no one, allowing the idea of a third term to seep into the political groundwater.

The Boss made no public statements, telling party leaders if they wanted to keep him in harness it had to be their decision. In 1940, they looked into the gathering gloom, sized up the GOP's man—decent, bumbling, and beatable Wendell Willkie—and asked the

Boss to stay. That left it to the voters, and they answered, emphatically, yes.

Thirteen months later Pearl Harbor brought the threat to our door. FDR had already served two years longer than his thirty-three predecessors. The face he showed the world seemed so assured and confident, most never knew the human being behind his hearty image.

I'd grown close enough to him to know the truth was far more complex. FDR had no deep friendships, not in any sense I valued. A strong circle of advisers, yes, but not a single confidant or intimate—Harry came the closest—he would turn to in times of need. The public and private man seemed forever warm and welcoming, with a legendary capacity for charm, but there remained in all his official interactions an aura of the strategic. Which led some of the gifted souls around him to suspect he valued them only for their usefulness.

His affable, graceful manner masked a character more royal than democratic; a benevolent king, but a king nonetheless. My personal view of him made me ask: Was this gulf between inner and outer man a compensation for lack of connection to others? He appeared to the world a joyful, unpretentious patrician, with a zest for living that raised the spirits of family, subordinates, and country. Why, in his center, did he remain so completely alone?

Franklin loved his five children but, except for his daughter, Anna, expressed it in ways more dutiful than devout. His cool, pragmatic relationship with Eleanor seemed almost entirely formal, a partnership of shared responsibility, companionable but hardly sentimental and only occasionally affectionate. His idea of love itself seemed impersonal, more universal in conception than particular to individuals.

Of that inner man, his deepest self, he seldom offered more than a vast trove of well-honed anecdotes to anyone. The grand national monument at Mount Rushmore opened in late 1941, and FDR spoke at its dedication. He appeared most days as remote and unknowable as those immense stone faces, which included his own fifth cousin Teddy.

The closer you got to him the more inscrutable FDR seemed. The press started calling him the Yankee Sphinx, with reason. No one, I tell you with confidence, truly knew who FDR was from knowing him. And I'd "known" him thirty years.

In the early days of 1942, facing a global war vast beyond imagining, I decided that to do my job, and to help him do his, I needed to know not only who FDR truly was but what had made him this way. Looking back through time, perhaps I can help you understand as well.

Eight years earlier the Boss had convinced me to give up standing on the sidelines and take up arms against a sea of troubles. As he'd predicted, I'd found meaning and satisfaction as part of something larger than myself. Perhaps that strikes you as quaint.

I also knew that I was and always would be an outsider looking for answers. That's how life had shaped me. Everything comes at a cost—I lived alone—but this left me with skills to observe the world around me, identify points of interest, track leads, and pursue facts that led me to understanding the previously unknowable.

So I began to try.

The First Alliance

For those in the Oval Office orbit, the war's first month meant frantic, eighteen-hour days of grinding uncertainty. First order of business: FDR and Prime Minister Churchill needed to cement our alliance for all the world to see. As usual, the Boss took his own approach.

The two men had first met four months prior at a secret summit called the Atlantic Conference. FDR had sailed aboard the presidential yacht, *Potomac*, from Virginia to Massachusetts. That night after anchoring offshore, a navy cruiser eased alongside, the Boss transferred to the USS *Augusta*, and headed north. *Potomac* nosed around New England for four days, presidential flags flying and a Secret Service body double tooling the deck in a wheelchair for distant photographers.

While I fed the press daily briefs about how much FDR was enjoying his "brief vacation," the *Augusta* dropped anchor off a barren stretch of Newfoundland. An English battleship came alongside a day later; Churchill on board with Harry Hopkins, who'd been in London working with the prime minister for a week before they crossed.

The Boss had encountered Churchill briefly in 1918, but didn't expect Winston—then Britain's Lord of the Admiralty—to remember. He did not. They worked four days straight. Using his charm to deflect subjects he didn't want to discuss, FDR sidestepped Churchill's attempt to draw us into England's war without hurting his feelings. Hearing what he wanted to hear, Churchill left convinced they were in perfect accord.

Before parting the two men—with Harry's guidance—released the Atlantic Charter describing their agreement. Beyond diplomatic embroidery and paeans to brotherhood, precise details of this "triumph" never made it into print. I saw the real story this way.

FDR sailed off from the Atlantic Conference the winner and both men knew it. Among its few ironclad terms, the charter spelled out as stark as a mortgage how our "cousins" would repay the fortune we'd been sending to Britain—via a legal work-around called lend/lease—to arm and feed them for the last three years.

The Boss and Harry had also pushed Churchill to an even more startling commitment: Every country that joined our alliance, colonial possessions included, would in victory be free to choose their own form of government. The prime minister went home and sold this disaster to his people as a masterwork of statecraft.

Providing England survived, this agreement guaranteed Allied victory would spell the end of two centuries of misery and plunder by British and European colonial imperialism. Second to defeating Fascism, FDR told Harry this was the charter's most important purpose.

FDR had ever so politely picked the prime minister's pocket because England had nowhere else to turn: Churchill agreed because only American money and might could save Britain from annihilation. Winning the war would now also bring the dawn of a new twentieth-century postcolonial world order.

FDR knew now was not the time to rush to Britain's rescue with full military force for one hardnosed reason: Our isolationist heartland wanted no part of shipping soldiers to another damn war across the Atlantic. The Boss would never get the votes that required in Congress.

Once American blood was spilled at Pearl Harbor, FDR and Churchill's second summit came two weeks later. Winston arrived on

December 22, 1941, with his "essential" senior staff; eighty-six of them to be exact. When the minister and his essentials flew to Washington, they found the Boss waiting on the runway behind the wheel of his own car. Harry cut Winston away from his phalanx, and FDR drove Churchill alone, to the White House.

We installed Winston on the second floor down the hall from the Boss and directly across from the Lincoln Bedroom, home to Harry Hopkins, their go-between and confidant. By now Harry knew Churchill like Horowitz knew a piano. Part of FDR's tactical advantage; under the guise of hospitality, he got to arrange the chess pieces.

That night, at a White House dinner welcoming Churchill's entourage, I first laid eyes on the "British lion." Short and stubby in his one-piece air-raid "siren" jumpsuit, he stood maybe five feet seven, pink and cheery as Cupid, sporting a perpetual Cuban cigar and a *Mona Lisa* smile. Sixty-seven years young, his eyes sparkled with vibrant life force.

Once cocktails were in hand, a beaming, radiant Anna, visiting from Seattle, wheeled FDR in. She looked stunning: tall, slender, with a dazzling smile and witty glamour that reminded me of movie icon Katharine Hepburn. With a dash less vinegar at that. Anna could hold her own anywhere, but this room upped the ante.

Introductions took minutes, while all looked for cues from the two great men. I held my breath and watched Anna greet Churchill with high-wattage Roosevelt charm, her father watching with pride. No wonder he wanted her there; Churchill looked disarmed.

World-class raconteurs prefer holding court alone. Putting two in a room usually spells trouble. As we sat for dinner FDR stood from his chair and offered a toast with impeccable tact but clear intent; America held the high ground of our new alliance alone.

When the Boss paused to drink, Churchill popped up at the table's far end and raised his glass to return serve. FDR appeared not to notice, launched into another story, and held the floor without yielding. The prime minister sank into his seat and appeared to pout. As courses and wines flowed Winston's eventual response caught me off guard. Swallowing his pride he graciously accepted the honored-but-subordinate role he'd just been handed. FDR noticed; from then on the two former navy men—an already authentic bond—warmed to each other.

As the two raconteurs swapped stories, waves of relieved laughter from both sides broke enough ice to rescue Shackleton. With equal parts diplomatic theater and blossoming friendship, the men let us know that, all differences aside, England accepted FDR's terms. Time to link arms and face the "tasks of Hercules."

Across the table, Anna and I caught each other wide-eyed: We both knew it couldn't possibly be this easy. I crossed myself. She covered a laugh. I grabbed a moment with her as dinner broke up.

"Thank heavens," she whispered. "Peace among the titans."

"It's a start," I said. "How's the ink-spilling business?"

"Thriving, thanks, Bill. But the war comes first. John wants in. Here to see if Pa has a spot for him."

She and her second husband, John Boettiger, were running Hearst's Seattle newspaper and raising their kids.

"Hope we'll see more of you," I said.

"Hope the weather holds up on Mount Olympus." She smiled and went off to attend to her father.

After midnight, Churchill and his team worked till dawn transforming his White House digs into a working headquarters. A floor below, he commandeered Eleanor's press office, without asking permission, to duplicate his Map Room, after the one in a bunker below 10 Downing Street.

By the time I went down there at nine to exchange cables with the duty officer, every inch of wall held corkboard, maps, charts, troop deployments. Telex and telephone lines linked to Britain's centers of war and empire thrummed round the clock.

Mrs. Roosevelt walked in behind me at that moment. She hadn't been told about Winston's "redecorating." Masking her dismay, she pivoted and left. I walked to the Oval, hoping to give the Boss a heads-up about the earful he was about to get. When I reached the door, I heard Eleanor inside already giving it to him.

"Franklin, this is unacceptable, I need both those rooms as you well know—they're essential to the daily work of my responsibilities."

"Now, the prime minister's only staying a few days, dear. This alliance needs sacrifice from everyone, Babs"—a nickname he used when he wanted something—"and did I mention he'll only be staying a few days?"

She listened, then yielded, grudgingly: "Under those circumstances . . . if you say so, Franklin." She left, and I scooted off before she saw me in the hall.

Naturally, Churchill ended up staying three weeks.

January 6, 1942

Churchill and the Roosevelts spent Christmas Day together. They used the holiday to project a crafted Currier & Ives image of Anglo-Christian unity for our press, who beamed it across America, Great Britain, and the rest of our now fifty-plus global allies, a coalition the Boss had started calling the United Nations.

After accepting an invitation FDR had wrangled for him, the prime minister traveled to Capitol Hill to address a joint session of Congress the next morning. An irony I appreciated: It was Boxing Day, when the English traditionally give alms to the poor.

Some colleagues on staff didn't grasp the significance until I told them Churchill would be the first foreign head of state in our history to ever speak from that podium. And the first English leader to set foot in that building since King George's dragoons burned it to the ground in the War of 1812, the last quarrel with our "cousins."

Alms for the poor indeed, but this time the hat was in the other man's hand.

FDR didn't go with Churchill to Congress. After years of fighting our isolationists, his objective was clear: Let Britain's legendary First Man make his case for our "special relationship" to them alone. The Boss, Harry, and a few others met in the Oval to listen on the radio. I went along to bring them an eyewitness account.

Any anxiety about how Congress would greet Churchill vanished the moment he entered: The assembly rose as one and cheered him all the way to the podium. Moved by their welcome, he seemed modest, vulnerable, a man almost—but not quite—with hat in hand. He paused artfully, waiting for utter silence.

"I feel greatly honored that you have invited me to enter this chamber and address you. The fact that, here I am, an Englishman, welcomed in your midst, makes this experience one of the most moving and thrilling in my life, which is already long . . . and has not been entirely uneventful."

The silence that followed was so profound I could hear people breathing around me.

"I wish only that my mother, whose memory I cherish across the vale of years, could have been here to see it. By the way, I cannot help reflecting that if my father had been American and my mother British, instead of the other way round . . . I might have got here on my own without need of invitation."

Warm laughter followed and he knew he had them. Even our most muleheaded dopes turned out to be pushovers for Churchill's seamless alchemy of humility, self-deprecation, and earnest plea for brotherhood. At the speech's end, they leapt to their feet for an ovation that lasted—I timed it on my pocket watch—for five minutes.

When he marched back into the Oval an hour later, the Boss shook Winston's hand and said: "You did quite well. Now let's get to work."

Winston clearly expected a more effusive response. FDR winked at me as he wheeled away. Winston followed, hat still in hand.

"No point letting him get a swelled head about it," Harry whispered to me as we trailed them.

The real work for the Allies began: setting the plan for when, where, and how we'd prosecute the war. They spent six marathon days in conference with military staffs. Private dinners with Harry followed that went deep into the night. Progress came grudgingly, in fractions exposing vast cultural and political gulfs. Harry worked tirelessly to bridge them but talks ground to a bitter stalemate.

The Boss looked worn out. Winston's volatile temperament, round-the-clock boozing, and nocturnal lifestyle—he barely slept—pushed him past endurance. Both men needed a break from the work and each other. Eleanor and Anna both told Harry only he could get them to middle ground. Before he could try, Churchill left abruptly for a week in Florida. Word filtered back that after straining to open his bedroom window he'd experienced chest pains, perhaps even a minor heart attack that his memoirs years later confirmed. Our security shut tighter than his White House window to keep this from reaching the outside.

Days later FDR delivered his own pitch to Congress. In his rousing State of the Union speech he coated the billions we needed to prepare for war in medicinal patriotism. They would have given him the moon. That evening, he returned to the Oval beaming, and told our crew to join him at midnight for an impromptu trip to Hyde Park.

I stopped on my way to the train station to pick up a notebook at a stationery store. Wartime security required the president to travel under blackout conditions whenever he left Washington; no press allowed, every detail off the record. On what felt like a whim I had decided to keep a diary of these trips, for my own records.

Isn't it funny, the lies we tell ourselves? As the only trained journalist on his team, I felt an obligation, in the interest of history, to make sure someone covered the story. I would keep what I was doing to myself, write only in solitude, and never mention it to a soul. After weighing the ethics, I decided that if I kept my trap shut, and the diary remained a secret, no harm could come from it.

If our world survived, and I someday felt the time was right, maybe future historians might benefit from my notes and observations.

Harmless self-deception, looking back on it. In truth the diary served two purposes: It preserved a daily account of his public and private days during a time of limitless peril. It also became the center of my effort to pierce the lifelong veil of secrecy FDR had drawn around himself.

• • •

The train left Maryland at midnight in a driving rain. We gathered in the parlor of the train car for sandwiches, drinks, and a casual foursome of bridge: The Boss, his witty secretary Grace Tully—she always put me in mind of Myrna Loy; her nickname was the Duchess—Harry, and me.

For the last few years the Boss had insisted, at close of business each day, we set aside an hour to relax and socialize, sipping cocktails he concocted at the bar. During which all official business remained off-limits. To formalize the ritual, the Boss called our gathering the Children's Hour. Because he loved company, and needed diversion, we saw it as an essential part of our jobs to provide both.

Whiskey sours were on order tonight. As Anna dispensed his first round the Boss seemed spry and playful.

"Kids, I do believe we slipped on board without a single soul catching on," he said with delight.

"Just one awfully bewildered switch man," said Grace.

"He looked at us like we'd just landed from Mars," said Anna.

"Not even J. Edgar Hoover has a clue where you are, Chief," said Harry.

"Ha, I love it! Like Dillinger on the lam."

What a treat for the world's most scrutinized man.

"Hate to be the bearer of bad news," I said. "The *Post* called an hour ago. Wanted to know when we were leaving for Hyde Park."

That froze the room but good. "Now, now," I added. "Forgive them their trespasses, kids. Reporters can't help themselves."

A trace of annoyance crossed the Boss's face before he laughed it off. "Of course they can't, poor bastards. This is our shakedown cruise. Have to work out the ballast, trim the lines. Drop an 'ix-nay' in their ear, if you would, Bishop."

"Won't happen again, Boss," I said.

"Same goes for the Dutchess County papers," he said. "Don't want any ink spilled up there that says I'm in Hyde Park either."

"Goddamn Republican papers," said Harry. "They shouldn't need to be reminded."

"It was likely Ham Fish who leaked it," said the Boss. "Leaving the chamber after my speech I spied him hobnobbing with the Neanderthal Caucus."

"That fool just plain hates you, Pa," said Anna.

Republican Hamilton Fish III—or Ham Fish, as he, for whatever reason, preferred to be called—had represented Dutchess County in the House for over twenty years. Although the Boss almost never expressed hatred for his enemies he kept a running tab, and the list was long. He usually welcomed their loathing as a point of honor.

But FDR reserved the right in return to despise Ham Fish, an entitled scoundrel he felt was nothing less than a traitor to our country. A fellow Harvard man, with a family pedigree as storied as the Boss's own, Fish had decades ago decided to make his reputation on how many thorns he could stick in FDR's hide.

"And to this day I've no idea why," said the Boss.

"You took the job Ham assumed was his by birthright," said Harry. "It's envy, Chief, pure and simple."

"He's a creature of ignorance and spite," said Anna.

"Fish is far from ignorant, dear," said the Boss. "That's the puzzle. At one time he was Cousin Ted's champion, and a real war hero in France. I considered him a friend."

"Surely he thought the same of you," I said.

"I'm telling you," said Harry, "that all changed Election Day '32 when you took the job that 'belonged' to him."

"Tall, good-looking, and born rich," I said. "Is it just me or does that automatically stunt moral development?"

"Maybe Ham took too many shots to the noodle playing Harvard football," said Grace.

"Probably couldn't find a helmet big enough for his swelled head," said Anna.

"I can't tell you why," said the Boss. "I'm not convinced the problem's his head. Ham's got cinders where his heart's supposed to be."

"He voted for you over Hoover, didn't he?" I asked.

"He did. Firmly holding his nose."

"That's 'cause Hoover committed a Republican's cardinal sin," said Anna. "Costing him money!"

"So, what was your cardinal sin?" asked Grace.

"Ha! Giving a single penny of it to the poor and needy."

Years before, as the New Deal rebuilt our economy and the Boss's popularity soared, Ham Fish and the GOP's plutocrat wing lurched hard right. As their public face they chose the blandly treacherous celebrity aviator Charles Lindbergh. Welcoming Fascists of every stripe into their tent, Lindbergh's group called itself, absent irony, America First. Many elected officials took cash that prosecutors traced to Hitler's treasury, and they used those funds for the devil's work: Spreading ugly rumors to sow distrust in democratic traditions. Amplifying incendiary white nationalist propaganda. Recruiting battalions of armed militia forces patterned on Hitler's brownshirts. These turncoats wanted to end, by force of arms, the American experiment.

Ham Fish didn't even hide it. He admitted abusing his congressional mailing privilege, sending millions of fundraising flyers that appealed to appalling racial and antisemitic hatred. Fish dodged jailtime for that when one of his staffers took the fall. A year before Pearl Harbor, Fish and a dozen more in the America First caucus were on the brink of receiving federal indictments.

FDR masked his emotions like a blackjack dealer, but the mention of these scoundrels soured his mood. I had an inkling why Fish burrowed so deep under the Boss's skin. His next words confirmed it for me.

"There but for the grace of God go I," he said.

"Ham Fish," I said in the ensuing silence. "Sounds like the worst recipe ever came out of a kosher kitchen."

That prompted a few chuckles. Nearby, the Boss's personal physician, Admiral Ross "Doc" McIntire—not coincidentally, America's surgeon general—saw the Boss smile and guffawed heartily.

"Kosher kitchen," he said, shaking his head.

Doc McIntire never sat with us for cards or cocktails, on the train, at the White House, or Hyde Park. During Children's Hour he planted himself nearby, sipping an ascetic whiskey and rocks—none of the Boss's frothy cocktails for him—while jotting observations about "patient number one" in a tidy notebook. Friendly, yes, but I found his relentless geniality left a patronizing aftertaste.

Harry didn't like how McIntire always lurked but never mingled, so the Boss wouldn't see him as "staff." Harry had earned his role as FDR's most trusted adviser by telling him truths he often didn't want to hear. Why the chief tolerated such a transparent toady baffled him.

Anna's theory was nostalgia: She thought Doc's bedside manner reminded FDR of the folksy country doctors he'd grown up with. I thought his constant presence meant no one could accuse him of not doing his job. After years in the Boss's orbit, I'd seen many lose their compass and drift toward sycophancy. McIntire was far from the first careerist in the bunch, but he had a cunning instinct for never crossing that line.

"Word to the wise, kiddos," said the Boss. "Keep a low profile around town this week. Don't want the locals getting curious about why you're here."

"What if I bump into someone I know?" I asked.

"Tell 'em you came up to see your dentist," said Harry.

"In Poughkeepsie?" asked Grace.

"There must be at least one decent dentist in Poughkeepsie, Pa," said Anna.

"I did see a dentist in Poughkeepsie once," said the Boss, then paused. "Believe he worked mostly on horses."

FDR's timing prompted McIntire to bray his hearty Shriners laugh again.

Hyde Park

I woke before dawn to early morning sun dancing on the Hudson. One glimpse of the valley's sere winter landscape, trees bare and wearing fresh coats of ice, and I knew we were minutes from arriving.

The village of Hyde Park had been home to the Boss's branch of the sprawling Roosevelt family tree for a century. How the line that produced him got here is instructive.

In 1607, Henry Hudson, an English explorer working for the Dutch, came looking for a mythic shortcut to Asia. With hive-like efficiency, Holland had built one of the great trading cultures in history. Their coveted "northwest passage" didn't exist, but Hudson's quest made him the first European to navigate the broad river now bearing his name. He sent word to Amsterdam he'd found "a New Eden," with natural riches ripe for the taking.

Boatloads of Dutch entrepreneurs claimed the region as a colony called New Netherland. They laid out its capital port, New Amsterdam, at the tip of Manhattan and built a trading network upriver to a second city they called Albany.

Four decades later, frigates full of hostile British redcoats seized their Eden with few shots fired. Holland signed over its prized possession, but Dutch wheeler-dealers were used to the Empire's bully-boy tactics. A war with England broke out back home, but these

Manhattan capitalists negotiated a shrewd treaty that left them in charge of the markets. Their freewheeling mercantile skills set the city's "open for business" attitude—the English renamed it New York—that persists today.

Those early immigrant waves included the first Roosevelts from Holland. FDR's great-great-grandfather Isaac had struck gold: Building a refinery to process cane from the Caribbean, he cornered the city's sugar market. Isaac compounded that fortune by funding the First Bank of New York with Alexander Hamilton. Like most Dutch bigwigs he joined the rebellion against King George's oppressive taxation of his "Americans."

The day redcoats routed General Washington's army from Manhattan, Isaac fled north to his in-laws' manor house in Dutchess County. Like future New York tycoons, Isaac ran his downtown business from his upcountry estate. When America won independence, Isaac stayed put. The next three generations of Roosevelts did likewise.

In 1866, FDR's father, James Roosevelt, bought a manse on a square-mile parcel in the hamlet of Hyde Park. He rebuilt it, named it Springwood, and made it the center of a horse-breeding business that became his gentleman's passion. Four years after losing his first wife James courted and married his sixth cousin Sara, daughter of a wealthy import-export man, Warren Delano, who'd made his fortune in China's silk trade. Delano built his estate and raised nine kids just across the Hudson. Three decades James's junior, Sara Delano Roosevelt gave birth to their only child at Springwood two years later.

Franklin Delano Roosevelt grew up a prince of this Hyde Park duchy. After a storybook childhood his parents shipped him to boarding school and then Harvard. The year his father died of heart failure, a fate that dogged the Roosevelts, Franklin earned a law degree. After marrying Eleanor—his fifth cousin—they returned to live at Springwood and raise five children. But not alone; the couple shared their home with Franklin's mother, Sara. A domineering presence until she died in 1941, Sara's unshakable belief in her son's destined greatness steered FDR into politics and away from the law.

Hyde Park was much more to FDR than a weekend retreat. He felt a mystical connection to this exquisite mile of old-growth forest, rolling hills, and streams. Franklin believed those hallowed acres shaped his character and gave sustenance to his soul. Springwood became the "Northern White House," where he played host to commoners and kings. He delighted in social diversions, because FDR was otherwise profoundly alone. Eleanor had moved into Val-Kill Cottage two miles away, and her Greenwich Village apartment twenty years ago. With his sons in uniform and favorite, Anna, in Seattle with her husband and kids, Springwood was the only home he knew. Connecting these dots paints a portrait of a personal life far more complex than I'm describing—I'll come to it—but all by way of saying why, given any opportunity, the Boss took the overnight train from Washington.

Because after returning from Florida, Churchill had decided to travel to Quebec to meet with Canada's prime minister. As Britain's next-largest contributor to her military, Canada wanted a say about where our alliance would fight. Winston needed that card in his hand before sitting down again with the Boss.

• • •

Groggy and chilled to the bone, the staff huddled round the coffee service as we chugged into Hyde Park station. Bracing ourselves, we stepped into the teeth of a vicious January cold snap. The Boss drove on alone and kept to himself that first day. Harry stayed with him in the big house—just down the hall from where FDR entered the world, in the bedroom where Franklin grew up, adorned with school pennants and artifacts of childhood passions. The rest of us settled into familiar lodgings at a snug local inn.

The following day, Harry walked into town to meet me for lunch.

Swimming inside his overcoat, he took me into his confidence over Welsh rarebit and a hearty Irish stew.

"Okay, here's the rub," he said. "All this rosy, hands-across-the-water horseshit aside . . . Now that we're in the damn war, the two of them can't agree on where to fight it."

This was the first I'd heard him sound so alarmed about it, but I gave no voice to mine. Harry worked up enough anxiety for both of us. "What's on the table?"

"Every damn place, name one—I'm not even trying to sound alarmist, Bill. We're still digging out from Pearl, the rest of the world's in deeper shit than we are, and every day—every hour—we keep losing ground to these sons of bitches."

"At least the public's with us."

"Sure, for now—about Japan, anyway. The chief and Winston agree that Germany's the bigger threat . . . but if they can't decide where to go after 'em soon? Arsonists in Parliament and Congress are gonna start setting fires."

Harry hardly touched his lunch. Little more than skin and bones to start with, he'd battled stomach cancer, and serious complications, for the last three years. He'd served as secretary of commerce during FDR's second term, and there'd been hope that Hopkins would head the Democratic ticket in 1940 when the Boss stepped down. Harry's illness scuttled that; he'd operated ever since as "minister without portfolio."

Lack of an official title played to Harry's strengths—improvisation, guile, persuasion, and hard pragmatism—but the strain exacted a heavy toll. Today he looked skeletal, haunted, shining eyes staring out of his skull.

"So what's standing in our way?" I asked.

"Chain of command, who calls the shots. Winston doesn't want to yield, the chief doesn't trust him to run this, and why should he? The Krauts kick the Tommies' ass every time before they land a punch. But . . ."

"But Churchill's the Great Man, soul of the empire—"

"—and best envoy to our European allies, all that. Don't get me wrong, I've spent two years with him, I love the man, but as a military strategist? He's a nightmare. Impulsive, sticks his nose in everywhere, and can't see the forest for the trees. If we let Winnie keep the helm this ends in disaster. We won't last a year."

I took a breath. "So how does the Boss back him down without breaking their bond?"

"The chief knows how to work him—and Winston's no fool, he knows damn well we hold all the cards. What's keeping me awake are the blockheads on our team: He's got to get the plan past the joint chiefs and secretary of war before we can fire a shot."

The Boss had installed Henry Stimson as secretary a year ago. A colonel in the Great War, he'd held cabinet posts for three presidents. The old Republican warhorse had done a solid job rebuilding our armed forces that, by the time the corporal showed his colors, had fallen into shambles. The Boss counted on Stimson to drum up GOP support for the war, and he'd delivered. At seventy-four he was also mulish, inflexible, and an incurable pessimist who saw disaster in every rainbow.

"What's Stimson holding out for?" I asked.

"Stimson and the brass want to go straight at the Krauts, cross the Channel, take a big swing in France, and try to land a knockout."

"Are we anywhere near ready for that?"

"Hell no," said Harry. "That's a year away, maybe two. Our boys aren't ready for that kind of action, we have no air power in place; hell, we don't even have boats to get 'em over there. Churchill knows all that, and he's not shy about saying it to the chief's face."

"What can we do?"

"Not a goddamn clue." Harry pushed his plate away, mopping his forehead. He'd hardly eaten and looked like death warmed over. I signaled for the check.

"You holding up okay?"

"If we can work it out when Winston gets back, and send him home . . . I'll check into Bethesda. Transfusions, injections, leeches, the rack, whatever medieval indignities they want to inflict on me . . ."

"You taking your medications?"

"Pal, there are, literally, not enough hours in a day for that. Coffee, booze, and cigarettes get me through and do just about as much good."

He lit another nail and finished his beer. I kept quiet. Harry was my closest friend in Washington. He'd risen from nowhere to become the second most important man to FDR since he took office. I loved him like a brother, but men didn't say such things to one another in those days.

A boyish lopsided grin crossed Harry's face and he leaned in to whisper: "Hey, did I tell you I met someone?"

"You don't say."

"Get this: She was editor of *Harper's Bazaar* in Paris till the Nazis hit town. Louise Macy. Works in New York now, fashion coordinator for Bergdorf's."

"She sounds swell, Harry."

"Bill, she's a living doll. Gorgeous, glamorous, a blue chipper, old Pasadena money. Chemistry's out of sight. We hit the Copa night before last and closed the place, dancing on air."

"So, I have a question: What's this glamour-puss see in a harness maker's son from Sioux City?"

I was giving him the business. Hard to believe this skinny bag of bones was a born ladies' man, but his Midwestern "aw shucks" sincerity and idealism worked like catnip. I offer this in evidence: Since his wife's death he'd dated two goddesses of the silver screen: Carole Lombard—before Gable, and Paulette Goddard—after Chaplin.

Harry laughed. "Beats the hell out of me. Gotta fall back on the best advice my old man ever gave me: 'Son, never look a gift horse in the mouth.'"

He beamed like a sixteen-year-old hayseed on a date with the head cheerleader. Harry had so little to feel good about outside the job, I'd've felt pitiless to squelch him. So I clinked beer mugs.

"Here's to you and your girl—just stay on your feet, bud. And keep both of 'em on the ground. Boss is counting on you to get Churchill and Stalin into the barn—"

"I know, I know, no sermons, please, Bishop."

I smiled. "Sure thing, Harry. I'll just remind you, nobody else is going to build those bridges. You're the only man alive all three of 'em trust."

Harry stubbed out his smoke and nodded a few times. "I'll get 'em there, Bill. If it kills me, I'll get 'em to a meeting of minds. Just . . ."

"Just what?"

"Don't tell the chief, okay?"

"About your health or *Harper's Bazaar*?"

"Both, obviously." He flashed a sly grin like the old rascal Harry, full of life as he'd been before cancer took his wife and nearly sent him to join her. "Or neither!"

• • •

I spent my hours with the Boss the next morning, sifting through and answering mail while he ate his Hyde Park bacon and eggs. Then he signed the tranche of legislative paperwork that arrived in the overnight pouch. In high spirits, already looking more rested, we listened to news on the radio as we worked.

"I had a word with the local papers," I said. "Won't be seeing headlines about you being home anytime soon."

"Nothing on the radio either, I hope?"

"Spoke to those fellas as well."

"Fine, fine. Run into anyone you know in town, Bill?"

"Only everywhere I go."

"Ha! Find a dentist yet?"

"Funny thing, I actually need one now. New denture's acting up. Made an appointment this afternoon."

"Let me know if you see any horses in the waiting room."

"Will do."

"I'm working on a fix for our privacy next time we're here. Need to keep you all and the Secret Service out of view. By the way, Winston's on the train back from Ottawa, so after dinner we're off to DC."

I checked the temperature before walking back to my room at the inn. Ten below zero. Washington sounded fine to me. Even Vermonters have their limits. It was sixteen below when we boarded the train that night. I handed the Boss my gloves so he could grip the rails of the ramp without freezing his fingers. He asked me to wait, then passed them back down so I wouldn't freeze mine either. If he was really the "tyrant" the opposition always accused him of being, I'd already be shopping for another pair.

At dawn next morning we drove from the station to the White House unnoticed. Having worked out the kinks, the Boss pronounced our shakedown cruise to Hyde Park a success. The template had been set for dozens of trips home and the hundreds of thousands of miles he'd travel for the next four years.

• • •

FDR's last two days with Churchill produced a joint statement extolling "unity and resolve" and that was it. Nothing close to a breakthrough on our impasse, but thanks to internal discipline not a whisper of their fraught standoff reached the press.

I'd reached my own conclusions about Churchill, the leader, by that point and couldn't dispute his greatness. But his chaotic personality was exacting an unreasonable toll on the man I worked for. Churchill, the man, was nocturnal as a bat and he lurched from one outsized passion to the next, by turns lovable, combative, and relentless. He could hold his liquor but I knew a functioning alcoholic when I saw one. Ben Franklin had nailed it about fish and visitors starting to stink after three days. After three weeks, we all volunteered to drive Winston to his train.

The Boss drove him instead. They parted warmly, Harry walked him on board, and both watched the train leave to make sure he was gone. The only person more relieved was Eleanor, who'd reclaimed her offices by the time we got back to the White House.

Later that evening, after the Boss had retired, Harry and I sat deep into the night in the Map Room. Over fingers of Scotch, we faced the sorry state of the world those maps now described.

Grim headlines from every front. Japan's island-hopping conquest of the Pacific toppled one colonial outpost after another. Singapore, the jewel of England's Asian holdings—a fortress Winston thought impregnable—had fallen in a shocking collapse. Newsreels showing thousands of British troops laying down arms without a fight demolished morale in London. By the time Churchill got home scuttlebutt said he could face a recall election in Parliament. At his best under fire, Winston stood the gaff, rallying enough support with honeyed words and fighting spirit to survive. But how much longer he could hold off the appeasement hounds seemed harder to predict.

To the east, Russia's stiff resistance to the Nazi advance toward Moscow gave us hope, but news that Field Marshal Rommel had launched a fierce assault on the Brits in Libya strangled it. Failure there seemed too catastrophic to consider: If more resources in Europe were diverted to help England hold onto North Africa it seemed a sure thing Moscow would fall. And Libya now dangled by a thread.

"You know the last thing the chief said to Churchill before he got on that train?" Harry asked me. "'We will win, but only if we win together.'"

"How'd he take it?"

"Brought Winston to tears. Not the toughest job in the world—he'll cry at card tricks—but the thing is, the chief meant it, Bill."

Harry finished his whiskey and shook his head. If I wanted to know more about the Boss, Harry was the place to start. No one knew him better.

"Where's that sort of confidence come from, Harry?"

"Beats the hell outta me. The abyss is right there in front of us. Can't even pretend we're not on the brink. What do you think?"

"Pretty sure he's not pretending, but I can't tell where it comes from either."

"And the second he makes a decision, life or death? Turns it off like he flipped a switch. No second guesses or looking over his shoulder. Serene as a goddamn Buddha. Plays solitaire, looks at his stamps. Pressure that would drop an average man like a felled ox. He's the damn Yankee Sphinx."

"Hmmm. Maybe it's a class thing. Or a Roosevelt thing. Maybe his mother just drilled it into him."

"Whatever it is," said Harry, lighting a smoke. "All I know is, pal, nobody on the wrong side of Sioux City ever taught it to me."

I thought a moment. "You think Churchill and the Boss like each other?"

"I do. Sincerely. And thank God for that, it's as close as we've got to an insurance policy." He dragged himself to his feet, half disappeared into his overcoat, and put on his hat. Even his head had lost weight. "Now if you'll indulge me, brother Bill . . . I need a lift to the fucking hospital."

He wobbled. I jumped up, caught him by the arm, and steadied him to my car. By the time Harry came out of there—two weeks later, after suffering the standard indignities—they'd put him on eight new medications.

The Boss asked me—and anyone else I could enlist—to help make sure Harry took them.

"Otherwise," said the Boss, with rare candor, "I'll confine him to barracks if he can't take care of himself. The work of that one half-dead man has done more for this country than Congress and the entire State Department."

February 1942

The Japanese had now "spread their fan" across three thousand miles of the South Pacific, islands falling like dominos to their advance. The last major British garrison in the East, Hong Kong, gave up without a fight. American forces in the Philippines, our final stronghold, had to abandon headquarters, and General MacArthur fled to Australia. Outmanned and outgunned, troops left behind were fighting in the jungles of the Bataan Peninsula, but surrender seemed inevitable.

Allied merchant convoys in the Atlantic, carrying our lifeline of food and matériel to Great Britain and Russia, were being stalked and slaughtered by swarms of German U-boats. Often within sight of the coast, our merchant ships were sinking faster at the hands of their wolfpacks than we could build them.

Harry felt that given all this, the blistering Republican yowls about it and the usual Democrat handwringing, the Boss might be feeling the same anguish Lincoln went through in the early days of the Civil War. Lincoln also wrangled with his generals, never finding the right fella to run it till Ulysses S. Grant showed up.

I said I thought FDR would respond with Lincoln's same assurance, with this advantage: He had far more commanders who could prosecute this war than Abe ever did. A deep bench of veteran officers who'd come of age in the Great War who knew how to fight. He wouldn't hesitate to call on them.

The Boss held another ace Lincoln or any other president never had: Eleanor. A tireless, tough-minded partner with acute political instincts. Universally admired, she practically lived on the road, putting in the work that FDR's polio made impossible for him to take on.

For example: In early February, the shock of Pearl still resounding, panic hit the West Coast when a Japanese sub was spotted off the coast of Santa Barbara. The scare paralyzed Los Angeles and most of California. Governor Earl Warren—and many others—stampeded Franklin into maybe the worst decision of his political life.

The Boss signed Executive Order 9066, ordering the internment of 120,000 Japanese-American citizens into "relocation centers," ten hastily constructed camps in our western interior. No evidence surfaced that justified this extremism, and FDR immediately regretted it, as I learned in a conversation I witnessed with the First Lady soon after.

We were in the Oval, going over the wording of a bill. Eleanor came in to say she wouldn't be attending a lunch he'd invited her to because she was leaving the next day.

"Fine, dear," he said. "We'll reschedule. Remind me where you're going."

"Arizona," she said, with an edge he didn't notice.

"And what's in Arizona—"

"Internment camps."

He heard her tone and put his pen down. "That's right. Slipped my mind."

"Unless you have second thoughts about my going."

"I do not."

The air bristled with tension. Used to my presence, neither noticed nor cared I was there. Over the years I'd found a useful way, in such moments, of receding.

"I feel strongly," she said, "that making a mistake should never stop us from doing what we can to help those unfairly affected—"

"We have been over this, dear, I don't see the point of discussing it a third time—"

"Americans, Franklin. These are decent, ordinary people, not some fictional fifth column, being denied their rights as citizens—"

"Given the heat of the moment, with blind terror coming at me from all sides after Pearl Harbor—"

"This is simply, morally wrong—"

"—and it may well have been a mistake, but given the global catastrophes confronting us at this moment there's nothing I can do about it now! And if it was wrong, then or now, it remains far from simple."

He banged his desk to punctuate. Sharp exchanges between them weren't uncommon, but this was exceptional. Sensing that, he moderated his tone.

"All I ask of you, please . . . Say what you like to me, but please keep public statements free of these sentiments."

"Don't I always?"

"You do, yes."

I kept my eyes on the carpet, but noticed Eleanor gathering herself to her full height, which meant she'd ceded as much ground as she was willing to give.

"I also intend to do what I can, Franklin, discreetly, to help these people any way I can, with my own money—"

He gave a resigned, weary sigh, intimate, or as close to that quality as the moment allowed, and spoke softly.

"And the less I know about whatever you may do behind the scenes the better, dear. For both of us . . . Why do you suppose I asked you to go?"

They did fight, yes, that was their way, but usually fought fair. Often both seemed to enjoy it, like a spirited tennis match. Hard feelings seldom lingered.

And with that provisional truce, the First Lady left the room. I stayed motionless. Franklin brooded, picked up his pen, signed off on the bill in front of him, asked for the next, and I handed it to him.

"The stamina of a cape buffalo," he muttered as he signed the next one.

• • •

We left that night for our second blackout trip to Hyde Park. Despite the darkness pressing us from around the world, the Boss seemed buoyant on the train. Sticking to our established ritual, FDR mixed a batch of his favorite Perfect Manhattans and Grace dispensed them.

"Listen, gang, I've sorted out our housing problem," he announced, wheeling up to join us at the bridge table. "To save a buck and keep a lid on security, I've arranged to put a few of you up at the place next door."

We looked at each other warily. The place "next door" was nearly two miles away, and it was an exceedingly particular kind of place.

"You mean the Vanderbilt Mansion?" I said.

He grinned. "I do. Ever been inside, Bill?"

"Haven't had the . . . pleasure."

With Harry still laid up, White House chief of staff General Edwin "Pa" Watson joined us at the bridge table. A burly Alabama-born West Pointer with Silver Stars and a Croix de Guerre from France to show for it. As FDR's appointment secretary and gatekeeper he had the stones to say no to anyone. In private he was a salty, companionable Falstaff, with the most infectious laugh since Foghorn Leghorn. He always put me in mind of the Western actor Chill Wills.

"Can't seem to recall which Vanderbilt knucklehead built that gawd-awful pile," said Pa. "The commodore?"

"The commodore's dough built the place," said FDR, "but it was grandson Freddie's idea."

"Shit on a shingle, I'd forgotten that prize winner," said Pa, chortling. "Freddie the freeloader, titan of industry."

"Rumored on occasion," I said, "to work two days a week."

"Needless to say," said the Boss, "a Yale man."

"You can take a Vanderbilt out of Staten Island," said Grace. "You can't take Staten Island out of a Vanderbilt."

Watson let out a belly laugh. Hearing Pa laugh was all most of us needed to prime the pump, and we all howled. Except Doc McIntire, glowering at Pa from his corner seat. The air always felt frosty between these two army–navy exemplars.

"Of course he hired Stanford White to design the damn thing," said FDR.

"'Course he did!" said Pa. "Most overrated architect of the Gilded Age, and a two-timing degenerate son of a bitch."

We laughed harder.

"Funny thing about White," said the Boss. "As a young Lothario, he tried to elope with my mother."

That cut the laughs short. Without missing a beat, Pa added, "Did I mention his impeccable taste in women?"

Grace nearly fell out of her chair. I doubled over. Even Doc couldn't hide a smile.

"Old man Delano wasn't having it," said the Boss. "He put her on ice in Europe for nine months, and when that didn't cool her off he shipped her to Hong Kong!"

"Just curious . . . was Harry Thaw wrong to murder White for seducing his wife?" asked Grace.

"Not according to Mrs. Thaw!" said the Boss.

Since it was the Boss's line, McIntire laughed louder than the rest of us together.

"Goodness gracious, no, Thaw was justified," said Pa, pausing to sip his cocktail. "His mistake was plugging the bastard in front of the dinner crowd at Madison Square Garden."

We laughed till we ached.

"So that's where you'll be staying on this trip, Bill," he said. "Freddie V's cabin in the woods."

"That joint could make Napoleon blush," said Pa.

"I'll put you in the master, Bishop," said the Boss, dealing out cards. "And Grace, you'll billet in Madame Vanderbilt's boudoir."

"Call me Josephine," she said.

"Oh, you'll feel right at home. Madame V stuck royalist French blue ribbons everywhere; the soup tureens, gravy boats, even the chamber pots."

"In Vermont," I said, "we used to call those a 'convenience.'"

"We called 'em something else in Alabama," said Pa.

That got us going again. The Boss had to wipe tears from his eyes.

"I shouldn't be so hard on the neighbors," he said. "Every old New England clan has skeletons. Early days in Massachusetts an ancestor on Mother's side was accused of 'fornicating with a wench in ye bushes.'"

"Hope the punishment fit the crime," said Pa.

"Whatever it was, Monsieur 'de Lannoy' decided to change his name to Delano and skip town—and he was no common cad; Philippe was the colony's senior surveyor."

"Then perhaps we should be more tolerant of his lapse in ye olde bushes," I said.

"Why's that?" asked Pa, teeing it up for me.

"As a surveyor he had to run his lines wherever the job took him. And, like the Psalmist, he could argue . . . 'the lines had fallen unto him in pleasant places.'"

Pa laughed so hard he kept slapping his knee, which kept everyone going. Wasn't often I could land a capper by quoting scripture, but mission accomplished.

"I love it! Don't you just love it?" said FDR. "Bill, I'll expect a full search of the cabinetry: See if that old 'convenience' outlived the Vanderbilts."

I walked into Springwood's library the next morning to find Pa Watson and the Boss working on his calendar. Not at my best, I bumped into a chair and tripped on the carpet. Opening the mail pouch, I felt them grinning at me.

"We're all ears, Bishop," said the Boss. "How was your first night in the Mausoleum of Halicarnassus?"

I cleared my throat. "Freddie V may have meant to build himself a 'home in the woods.' This is no home. It's a crime against nature."

They tried not to laugh. "Do go on," said Pa.

"Where do I start? Like a Masonic temple without the taste? Color scheme straight out of a brothel? A 'library' twice this size with fewer books than I have next to my bed?"

"Not much of a reader, Freddie," said the Boss.

"Did I mention solid gold plumbing fixtures? Oh, and the windows, dear God, the windows . . ."

The more miserable I got the harder they laughed.

"Loveliest river valley in the world and the windows all face the train tracks. Every half hour I'm about to drift off and a freight roared by."

They loved it. "Any trace of the 'bless-ed convenience'?" asked the Boss.

"There's a cabinet in the master for it but, alas, no chamber pot. Gone with the Vanderbilts." They howled. "Boss, I'm haunted by this: How on earth did that nightmare end up with the Park Service?"

"Freddie left it to a niece in Newport," said the Boss. "Old pal of mine who hated it as much as she hated paying the taxes. I suggested she 'donate' it to Uncle Sam. She couldn't sign it over fast enough."

"But why on earth would you want it?"

"For the trees, Bill! Previous owners planted that parcel for a century with foresight and care. So did my father. I roamed every square foot of it as a boy. A cathedral of American woods."

Now I got it. A passionate botanist, the Boss had tended trees at Springwood for decades, planting and nurturing experimental forests.

"Okay, but why keep the house?"

"Tourist attraction. Cover the cost of keeping the trees. And a cautionary tale along the lines of Midas for those who see it: Greed will turn a heart to stone."

He signed and handed me back a bill I'd given to him without reading it.

"By way of perspective, that's the price tag for rebuilding our navy."

I laid the bill over a chair to let the ink dry and read the bottom line: $26 billion.

Staggering. Like a rube, I whistled softly.

"Turns out replacing our Pacific fleet isn't exactly cheap," said the Boss, already reading the next bill.

• • •

On our next trip to Springwood two weeks later, the Boss and I worked through the mail in his bedroom. He sat in his chair, shaving in a suspended mirror, while scanning the *Times* on a wire hung beside it. Pa Watson knocked and came in, looking gray.

"What's the latest?" asked FDR.

Twelve hours ago, we'd learned a strike force of American, British, Australian, and Dutch warships had engaged a Japanese convoy near the entrance to the Java Sea. The Boss took keen interest.

Pa broke the latest: During the night our fleet had suffered devastating losses. Ten destroyers, including six American ships, sent to the bottom. Worse than Pearl Harbor.

"The Dutch commander of the force was killed," said Pa. "Sir, as an effective fighting force, the Dutch navy no longer exists. The Japanese have complete control of—"

"What used to be the Dutch East Indies," said FDR. He sat silent a moment. "What about the *Houston*?"

"Confirmed: direct torpedo hits. She went down in the Sunda Strait. Six hundred men."

"Survivors?"

"Any survivors, far as we know, were taken prisoner."

"Captain Rooks?"

"Direct hit on the bridge. He didn't make it."

The Boss kept his composure in the face of tragedy day in and day out, but this was a gut punch. In the years before the war he'd taken three long cruises on the *Houston*, sailing everywhere from Pearl Harbor to Newport News. He kept the presidential flag, which was flown whenever he was on board, signed by its officers, framed and mounted in the Oval Office. The Boss knew the *Houston*, its sailors and Captain Rooks, better than any other ship in our navy.

"*Houston* went to the aid of a British ship, HMS *Perth*, after she was hit and lost engines," said Pa. "Cornered by the whole Jap squadron. Houston took 'em on alone, sank one destroyer, crippled three others. Captain Rooks stayed his post. Went down with the ship."

The Boss took a few slow breaths, but his expression never changed. "Bill, please draft a letter to Rooksy's widow. Pa, reach out to his congressman. I'd like him to put Captain Rooks forward for the Medal of Honor."

Pa and I looked at each other and I knew the same thought occurred to us: The burden of command is unthinkable.

June 19, 1942, Hyde Park

Harry and FDR watched from his cobalt-blue Ford convertible, Harry pacing with a smoke while the Boss sat behind the wheel, driver's door open.

A small plane touched down on the grass runway just after noon. Churchill stepped out alone; this time he'd left his entourage in Washington. Harry hurried to greet him warmly and walk him to the car.

"I felt it was my duty to see you alone, Franklin," said Churchill, doffing his hat.

"Glad you did, old boy, hop in," said FDR, patting the passenger seat.

Churchill hesitated. "You're driving."

"Controls are on the steering column. Local mechanic rigged it for me. Safe as houses."

Winston climbed in, Harry closed the door and jumped in back. The Boss lowered the convertible top with a push of a button. He pressed another one on a canvas-covered box beside the wheel, and it served up a lit unfiltered cigarette.

"Same fella worked this out for me," said the Boss as he screwed the smoke into his holder, and gunned the motor.

"Does it dispense cigars as well?" asked Churchill.

"Ha! We'll have to work on that."

FDR sped away at his usual breakneck speed. Winston reached up and white-knuckled the leather grip.

"Taking the long way round!" FDR shouted over the wind and engine. "Thought you'd like a tour of the property!"

Churchill tried twice to launch into policy—their stalemate had only hardened—but with the top down at high speed the Boss cheerfully waved him off. After bouncing along dirt roads through hills and forests for half an hour, they skirted the high cliffs above the Hudson. The Boss finally parked in the heart of a deep wood.

"This is the last stand of old-growth forest on our side of the Hudson," said the Boss.

Harry opened the door for Winston to exit. Winston staggered out, relit his cigar, and stared glumly at the light filtering through the trees.

"Correct me if I'm wrong," he said, "but this came to the Roosevelts by way of a 1697 land grant, did it not . . . from our King William."

"Your King William?" FDR said with a laugh. "William was a Dutchman who waded ashore unopposed, and took England without breaking a teacup."

"Monarchy, old boy, like all hothouse orchids, thrives on the periodic grafting of foreign genes. Even if they're Dutch."

A breeze rustled the leaves. Churchill sipped from a flask.

"Trees give us so much we never stop to consider," said the Boss. "Shade, of course. Their company restores us . . . they purify the air . . . I find they lend us strength . . . and their stillness reminds us how to listen."

Churchill looked amused. "I so enjoy speaking with you, Franklin. Whatever might your trees be trying to tell me?"

"Patience. Think before we act. I believe we, the living, are obliged to leave a better world than the one we found. That makes us guardians of nature as well. Any nation that squanders such a gift destroys itself."

Churchill rocked back and forth. "I quite agree that trees are lovely things. I like to paint them. Forgive me, if in the face of our enemies' monstrous barbarity, I consider the survival of human civilization a more pressing concern."

Harry saw the Boss tense for a fraction, then he answered with an intensity just shy of a rebuke.

"I saw the trenches at the Marne, Winston. We both did. The destruction—the annihilation—of an entire way of life. Horrors that stain the mind. To this day . . . all I have to do is close my eyes. . . ."

Winston flinched. The Boss had reached him. For a moment Churchill couldn't look his way. FDR's next, softer, words went even deeper.

"I told you we will fight and win this war. In the right time and place . . . together or not at all. But not unless you trust me, Winston . . . to the bitter end."

Winston paused, half turned, and tipped his flask.

"May the sun never set on . . . either of our empires."

I watched them arrive at Springwood through the window. Harry walked Winston inside, before he could see FDR's valet lift, carry, and set him in his chair.

After Winston settled in and they had a quick, informal lunch, the two men got down to work. Not in the spacious library but down a long corridor near the kitchen, in a cramped, plain office called the Conference Room. Stuffed with filing cabinets and shelves of binders, it looked like a storage closet. The Boss used it only when he needed absolute privacy. He told Grace to hold all calls and Secret Service manned the door; only Harry sat with them.

The reason, I learned later, concerned a subject Churchill wanted first up on their agenda. The men had corresponded about this often since before Pearl Harbor.

Winston handed FDR a dossier on a research program England had begun in 1940. An innocuous title: the Tube Alloys Program. Churchill launched the project after scientist refugees from Germany told us the Nazis were pursuing a peculiar, nearly occult, line of inquiry. The Brits shared it with us in 1938. Our physicists confirmed this work could lead to a weapon of almost limitless power.

FDR had told Churchill we felt the same urgency and agreed to take this on together, sharing research, costs, and whatever came from it. But Winston had come to say the war's staggering costs meant they couldn't continue. America would have to shoulder the job alone.

What Harry described to me that night chilled me; this annihilated principles that scientists since the fifth century had considered bedrock reality. The atom—the indivisible, elemental building block of creation—could be broken by man, unleashing unimaginable power. Not only did this fiction now live in the realm of the possible, the Nazis were miles ahead of us.

Imagine, said Harry, a bomb that could not only end this war in a single flash but potentially snuff out human existence.

Within days the Boss had authorized the army to set up confidential offices, requiring new levels of security, hidden in the middle of New York City. That's why we called it the Manhattan Project.

• • •

The men made their way to the library. Tea was served and Secret Service cordoned off the wing. Harry sat between them, as referee. A few of us stood by outside, shuffling in and out as needed, while they waded into the agenda's next item: where to fight the war.

Hours ticked by. FDR at his desk, Churchill prowling the room, barking arguments that the Boss deflected. Their stalemate hardened. As night fell, the fondness they began with had broken down completely. Stationed at the door, I heard them shouting at each other. Harry stepped out in a cold sweat. Shook his head, put a finger to his lips, and cracked the door open so I could hear.

"Please don't misunderstand, Franklin! I'm only suggesting your untested troops need seasoning before hurling them at the jaws of the German war machine—"

"You'd be terrified, old top, if you knew how little I care about your opinion of my troops—"

"An indifference, I assure you, not exceeded by mine for your absurd insistence on self-rule for colonial India—"

"Has it not occurred to you, Winston, these 'colonial armies' of yours surrendering left and right are simply sick of dying for the imperialist boot you won't take off their necks?"

"Please, sir, don't say something you'll regret—"

"Our mutual objective, I say it again, is defeating the Axis Powers—"

"We agree: Germany first among them—"

"And we want to fight—Germany first—in the place that offers our best chance of success—"

"Trust me, that place is not where you think it is—"

"My generals and admirals tell me otherwise—"

"I'm telling you, Franklin, we've fought them for years: If your first move is to cross the Channel and assault their strongholds in France it will end in butchery!"

Harry's expression said, "See what I mean?" My eyes felt as big as saucers.

"I cannot and will not accept military advice on blind faith from the architect of Gallipoli and Dunkirk!"

Winston didn't respond, but the Boss wasn't through.

"This is it: If I don't take a swing at Hitler—head-on, somewhere soon—Congress and public opinion will force me to go all out against Japan, and where does that leave England?"

"Alone!" shouted Churchill. "The last hope for Europe! And the world!"

We heard footsteps moving toward us and stepped aside as Winston shoved the door open and stormed by. Spotting Harry from the corner of his eye he muttered:

"I'm late for a call with my staff."

Stabbing the floor with his stick, he hurried on. Two sheepish aides at the base of the stairs fell in behind him and they marched up to his quarters.

Harry slipped into the library, nodding me to follow. Hands behind his head, the Boss leaned back at his desk, composed, almost serene. Studying a large map of Europe and the Mediterranean on an easel nearby. Whistling. We approached cautiously, Harry in the lead.

FDR aimed a wooden pointer at the map. "Winston won't stop going on about North Africa. Operation Gymnast again."

Harry shot me a worried glance. I knew he felt our best bet for an early knockout was in France, but he kept that to himself around both Winston and the Boss. "I'd say, as always, there are pluses and minuses—"

"Winston insists it's our best chance," said the Boss. "Problem is, Rommel's making another charge at the Brits in Tobruk. Maybe he just wants us to bail them out."

"Understandable, Chief, but we can't possibly mobilize and get there in time to relieve Tobruk."

"That's what our brass says too. Winston insists he can hold them off, like last year. What do you think?"

"They did hold him off last year," said Harry. "After six months, Rommel backed away."

FDR eagle-eyed him. "Yes. Last year. What if they can't hold, Harry? They're cornered on three sides and this time U-boats have the sea lanes locked down."

The map, showing deployments on both sides, spelled that out.

"If the Brits lose Tobruk," said the Boss, tapping the map with his pointer, "there's no substantial fighting force left between Rommel's Panzers and their garrison in Cairo. He could blitz right through them to the Red Sea and the Canal."

Harry moved to the map, studying east of the Suez. "They'll seize the oil fields."

"And use the Canal to ship it wherever they need. If Britain loses Egypt, Africa is theirs, and if that happens . . . look. They'll cross the continent to Asia and shake hands with Japan. Every resource in every colony between them—oil, iron, and rubber we need to fight—falls into their hands."

Harry mopped his forehead. "Thing is, Chief . . . and for the love of Pete don't hate me for it . . . I gotta say I don't think Winston's wrong—"

"About North Africa? No, 'course not, Harry, he's completely right. That's why it's been my first choice all along."

Harry and I were struck dumb; first we'd heard of it.

The Boss flashed an Olympian smile.

"Well, for goodness' sake, fellas, I can't let him know that. I need Winston if we're going to win this thing, but only if we run it ourselves."

"But our brass are hell-bent on hitting France first—"

"And it's them I need to convince. Winston's right about this too. Our troops aren't ready to take the corporal head-on. We won't even have the air cover or landing craft for another year—are you with me, Harry?"

"But I thought . . . yes, okay, I get it, I'm with you. . . ." Harry sank in a chair. "Just . . . gimme a second."

"I'm putting Stimson and our brass in a room with Winston, tonight. Fly him back to Washington after supper. Let them go at it. If he softens them up, I'll take another crack at 'em tomorrow."

Harry looked poleaxed. FDR picked up a phone and grinned at him again.

"Don't fret now, Harry. Something's bound to happen. It always does." And then to me: "Have them ready the train tonight, Bill, we'll give Winston a head start," and then into the phone: "Grace, put me through to the Pentagon. Secretary Stimson."

Harry stood and nodded at me to follow him out. As soon as the door closed behind us he said: "What the holy hell am I s'posed to say?"

"Start with: 'Okay, Chief,' and go from there."

• • •

By the time we reached the White House that morning, Churchill had spent the night butting heads with Stimson and the joint chiefs. Neither side budged.

The Boss debriefed Stimson and the chiefs in the Oval. I sat in and took notes. FDR listened to their gripes about Winston's "North Africa hobbyhorse" with a sympathetic ear and opaque neutrality. They filed out believing he was completely on their side.

Minutes later, Winston stalked in, a full snifter in hand, Harry at his side. The prime minister hadn't slept, as usual, and paced, in a damp mode, making quick work of that brandy.

"Our men simply must fight, Franklin. Somewhere. Anywhere. That's the only sentiment on which we agree."

"Not entirely," said the Boss. "We also agree we must start on the offensive. Support the promise we've made Stalin; a second front that takes the heat off Moscow."

Harry let out a low groan, doubling over with stomach pain. He mumbled an excuse and walked out. Winston spun the large globe near the bookshelves, tapping English colonies with his walking stick as it revolved.

"Red . . . red . . . red . . . all red. Because we fought in red, you see. All these places. Red is the story of our empire."

The Boss threw a glance at the globe. "Hmm. Looks more like pink."

"Printer's compromise. If they used our actual shade one wouldn't be able to read the names."

FDR turned to an open folder from his stamp collection on the desk and picked up a magnifying glass. "Cold comfort for the people living in 'em."

Winston bristled, took out a lighter, and tried to light the Cuban that had gone out in his hand. I pulled my own lighter. As he leaned in to take a light he muttered, not really to me:

"Those infernal postage stamps again . . . we invented them, for God's sake."

The Boss heard him and smiled faintly.

A sharp knock at the door: Harry hurried back in with a pink telex slip. FDR and Churchill turned to him; Harry looked agitated but didn't speak. The day we heard about the attack on Pearl, I'd felt an electric charge in the room; I felt the same tingle again. Harry handed Franklin the telex.

"Just came in," he said. "General Marshall."

General George Marshall, the stalwart hand who commanded all our military. When he rushed an order to the Boss, he took it seriously. He read the message twice.

"Confirmed," said Harry under his breath. "It's solid."

Franklin looked up at Churchill, who read his silence as grave. Their eyes locked.

"Winston, listen to me now," said FDR. "I'm very sorry to tell you this . . . Tobruk has fallen."

Churchill shook his head as if he hadn't heard correctly. "What did you say?"

"Your entire British garrison . . . thirty-three thousand men . . . surrendered to Rommel."

The Boss handed the cable to Harry, who carried it to Churchill. He read without looking up. A tremor shook his hands.

"This simply can't . . . can't . . . we held them off six months last year . . . we waved the flag in two days?"

Churchill seemed unsteady on his feet. Harry steadied his arm.

"I can't express how dreadfully sorry I am," said FDR.

I hadn't seen him rise, but he was standing, leaning on his desk.

"Defeat is one thing . . . disgrace is another. . . . I don't know I've . . . ever felt so helpless. Cairo, the oil fields at Abadan, then east to India . . . he'll take it all."

"Tell me right now, Winston," said FDR. "How can we help?"

Churchill looked off guard, hat in hand.

"Help? It may be too late, beyond helping . . . but in a better world, Franklin? Tanks, ammunition, any you can spare."

His eyes alight, FDR looked to Harry.

"Tanks," Harry said. "Our first three hundred Shermans just came off the line. We started training in 'em last week—"

"We'll build more. What about artillery?"

"We've got plenty, and we can build those faster."

FDR turned to Churchill. "You'll have howitzers and tanks fast as we can build and ship them to you."

"But your generals, Secretary Stimson—"

"They have nothing to say about this now. Tobruk makes this decision for us. Send your men into the desert, Winston, fight to survive. Hold on four months and we'll be there in force. We're taking North Africa. Together."

The gratitude lighting Winston's face reminded me of Oliver Twist. He couldn't seem to speak. Harry, equally moved, took his hand.

"As I told you in London," said Harry. "Whither thou goest, I will go, whither thou lodgest, I will lodge. Thy people shall be my people, and thy God my God . . . even to the end."

I saw tears in both their eyes. Churchill moved to Franklin, standing tall at the desk, eyes sharp and clear and dry. They shook hands.

"True friends," said Churchill, "in this tragic world, stand by you in doubtful moments."

"T'were it otherwise, old boy," said FDR, "life would be impossible."

June 28, 1942, Hyde Park

We spent most Sunday mornings catching up on what had arrived in the overnight post. Often he worked in bed over breakfast, but on this day I found the Boss at his desk. I laid out documents while he finished marking up a report stamped "confidential."

"This hits the papers today, Bill," he said. "Have a look, draft a statement under my signature to go with it, please."

He handed it to me. As I read my jaw must have fallen, because he laughed.

"This is true?" I asked. "Eight Nazi saboteurs arrested by the FBI after landing on Long Island and Florida?"

"Oh, it gets worse. Keep reading."

"Foreign agents fluent in English—two of them American citizens—all trained by German commandos to conduct a campaign of terror . . . plans to sabotage the Brooklyn Navy Yard, reservoirs, arms, ammunition plants, and blow up Penn Station—sakes alive, when did this happen?"

"Nazi U-boats put two teams of four ashore two weeks ago."

I kept reading: "In the Hamptons?"

"First team, yes. The second at Ponte Vedra, near Jacksonville, just north of the beachfront hotels."

"When did you find out?"

"Next day. Near Amagansett a Coast Guardsman spotted 'em just after midnight in thick fog. Their clothes were wet. Claimed to be fishermen who'd run aground."

"Did he see a boat?"

"Nope. He tells them they're out after curfew and need to come to the station. One takes him aside, gives the name George Davis, slips him three hundred bucks, and says they're navy intelligence working undercover. While holding a gun in his pocket. Our fella plays dumb, takes the bribe, hurries to his station. Tells his CO they might be spies and shows him the cash. CO calls Secret Service; they trace numbers on the bills to a 1938 shipment we sent Berlin."

"My heavens, Amagansett, of all places—"

"They search the beach. The men are gone but they dig up a cache of weapons, detonators, explosives, and maps they left behind. Mike Reilly brings me the news, we notify every branch of law enforcement, top secret—"

"How'd we find them?"

"Witnesses saw 'em board an early train to the city, but the trail goes cold till 'George Davis' panics. Calls the FBI, says he has intel on Nazi saboteurs. Next day he tries to turn himself in at FBI HQ—"

"Tries to?"

The Boss laughed. "They hear him out and our G-men are about to toss him for a crackpot till he dumps eighty grand on Hoover's desk. Next day we pick up the rest of Davis's team. Pinched the Florida four yesterday in Chicago, all before they had time to blow up a phone booth."

I needed to sit down. "Good grief."

"I've seen their plans. They meant business, Bill."

"Any sign they were coming after you?"

"Wouldn't put it past the corporal. We'll find out when they're tried."

I recalled something from the rules of engagement. "Spies caught out of uniform during war are tried by military tribunal."

"Only you'd remember that. Didn't know it myself. You'll find authorization for it in your mail."

I pawed through my satchel, dug out the form, and gave it to him. "A tribunal of seven sitting generals. Majority vote required for conviction."

"That's right. I'm confident you're also one of the few who knows what happens if they're guilty."

"Hasn't happened since the Civil War, but . . . I believe sentencing falls to the commander in chief?"

"Correct," he said, borrowing my pen to sign it. He handed back both with a searching look. "What should I do with 'em, Bill? Prison or hanged?"

I didn't hold back. "Hanged by all means. Shooting's too honorable: death to traitors during wartime, foreign or domestic—particularly domestic. Make that point to every traitor, or potential one, alive."

My moral certainty seemed to interest him. "What about pictures?"

"Pictures."

"Photographs. In the papers if, as you suggest, these traitors swing. For all to see."

I laid the order on the back of a chair to let the ink dry, giving myself time to think.

"To deter treason in anyone of like kidney? I'd say yes. This comes to mind: Ask anyone who's seen photos of the Lincoln conspirators at the end of their ropes."

"Remember 'em well. Mrs. Surratt and the rest swinging in the hot July sun."

"Everyone in the country saw those pictures. We know it works. Now that the war's reached our shores, do you want to send that message?"

"Think I should?"

I was flattered whenever he asked me for more than information or arcana. I usually made a point of keeping opinions to myself, but not today.

"If they're guilty, yes. By the way, I agreed on those hanging—Booth was dead—except for Mrs. Surratt."

"Really? Thought we had the goods on her."

"I knew folks who lived through it. Some who witnessed the hangings. All thought she was railroaded. They all met and plotted in her house, a few of those mutts even lived there—"

"Her son among them."

"John Surratt was a known Confederate courier and Booth's partner in crime. Original plan was to kidnap Lincoln and ransom him for every Rebel POW we had. Lee's surrender changed everything. Five days later, Booth gave his final 'performance' at Ford's Theatre."

"Sic semper tyrannis."

"That night John Surratt fled to Canada, then England. Ended up at the Vatican, serving in the Pope's Zouaves. His mother should have gone to prison, yes, but she played no role in Booth's last madness."

He thought a moment. "Her son escaped justice. That stuck in the craw: She was his proxy for our vengeance."

"First woman we ever hanged," I said.

"Others were involved, why were they spared?"

"Four more were found guilty, but none were tied to Booth's derringer."

"Including Dr. Mudd?"

"Mudd's a question mark. Facts are damning: slave owner. Met Booth many times, bought him a horse he kept for him. Supplied him on his escape and lied about it after. And he set the ankle Booth broke in his stupid leap."

"So why didn't Mudd swing too?"

"Ducked it by one vote. Life on Dry Tortuga. Four years later, President Johnson pardons him."

"I'd almost forgotten. That no-good son of a bitch."

"So Mudd gets out and has the gall to run for local office in Maryland."

"Is that right? Did he win?"

"Good god, no. Lost by a landslide, but during the campaign an uncle of mine bought him a beer."

"Isn't that something? Seems an age ago!" FDR threw his head back and laughed. "I always forget: You're so much older than I am."

"Eighteen months, but you're gaining on me."

"I'll catch you yet."

"Young folk tend to forget the 'good old days' weren't that long ago."

He turned thoughtful, and more remote.

"It's in the hands of the generals now, Bill. Let's revisit it, you and I, once they render a verdict."

With that the Boss turned to the business of signing billion-dollar checks to keep the war going.

July 30, 1942, the White House

Harry followed Churchill to London. Eleven days later the Boss signed off on our plan for North Africa, code name Operation Torch. Launch date: October 30.

Harry flew home for another mission he had in the works: Three days later, Harry married his new bride, Louise Macy. Harry asked the Boss to officiate, and as commander in chief he had authority to do so. But only on board a US Navy ship. And Harry's bride was prone to seasickness. The White House would have to do.

Guests gathered for the ceremony while I babysat Harry next door. His hands shook so badly I had to attach his boutonniere to the lapel of his best suit.

"Jesus, I'm as jumpy as my first communion, what the hell, Bill? Maybe I don't believe I deserve her?"

"Think you deserved cancer after Barbara died? 'Cause that's what you told me at the time."

He laughed nervously. "Maybe a little. That's nuts, right?"

"Yes. You deserve this, Harry—now hold still."

"Sorry . . . Jesus, shaking like an aspen leaf."

I called on my Catholic training for patience. "Why do you think you're still living here after three years?"

"Case he needs something? Or maybe he feels sorry for me; what other life did I have at that point? You know how he is. If you're not useful he'll just find somebody else—"

"Stop it. Right now. You're the glue holding this alliance together."

"Buddy, we're all expendable, if I drop he'll just tap the next guy."

I put my hands on his shoulders and tried to calm him.

"Listen to me, Hopkins. There's no 'next guy.' The Boss needs you, we all need you. And if you're living on borrowed time, as you seem to think—"

"I don't think, I *know*—"

"Well, if that is the case you deserve happiness. You deserve Louise. And I'm telling you: He will never, ever give up on you. You're indispensable."

He shook my hand with his crooked grin. I walked him in and the ceremony went off without a hitch. FDR served as best man. Harry's boys from his first marriage had flown in: quiet, serious Robert, who we'd soon see again; earnest David on leave from his ship; and young Stephen—known as Hoppy—a freckled high school senior with all his old man's charm. The Boss treated them like nephews and took a particular shine to Hoppy, who was about to enter the Marines. Hoppy beamed. As they tied the knot, Harry looked happy as I'd ever seen him.

I saw one cloud on Harry's horizon. Mrs. Roosevelt attended as well. Louise Macy was a sophisticated socialite, bright and vivacious as a hummingbird. FDR responded to her as every other red-blooded American male I'd seen do: enthusiastically.

Estranged as the First Couple had been for decades, Eleanor's reserved responses to Louise reminded me: There was only room for one First Lady in FDR's White House.

• • •

During a call with Churchill the next morning the Boss gave him an update on the Nazi saboteurs: All testimony had been heard by the tribunal and their fate was in the hands of the generals. Four days later I walked the mail into the Oval. FDR was nose down in a leather-bound tome with a military seal. He didn't need to tell me what it was.

"Guilty as charged?" I asked.

"That's right. You won't be disappointed to hear they recommend hanging. . . ."

I heard something in that pause.

"They came ashore wearing Nazi uniforms, which they took off and buried. Guessing you know what that means."

"Geneva Convention. Means they're POWs. Not spies."

"Nice try, but the tribunal overruled that as a technicality. I agree with them, Bill."

He handed me a page listing the convicted. All born in Germany, their families had emigrated and lived in the States, some for decades. Two became naturalized citizens; one did a stint in our army. All eight had returned to Deutschland after Hitler took power. To enlist.

"These men are traitors, not soldiers," said FDR. "All eight sentenced to hang. It falls to me to affirm or adjust their verdicts."

He signed two legal docs on the desk and handed them to me.

"Two cooperated, one surrendered to the FBI, another helped us nab the Florida squad. I've been thinking about Mary Surratt and Dr. Mudd."

He watched me read his orders. He'd commuted the execution of the one who'd turned himself in, "George Davis." FDR sentenced him to thirty years' hard labor. He also commuted the sentence of the second informant; life at hard labor. A touch of Solomon.

He signed a third page and handed it to me. The remaining six were to be executed by electric chair at the District of Columbia jail.

"Old Sparky," I said. "Not the rope."

"Seems we have no qualified hangmen in uniform. By the time we hang the corporal I'll make sure that position's filled."

I put the orders in my satchel. "Years ago, I covered an execution there. Old Sparky's work isn't . . . quite as tidy."

"No photographs this time either," he said. "Sends the wrong message. I prefer to believe, as a country and people, we've outgrown our appetite for public barbarity. We'll leave that to the jackals."

"Justice, not vengeance."

"That's the whole idea, Bill."

January 9, 1943, North Africa

The Axis Powers were led by three lunatics obsessed with restoring a mythical Golden Age. It was all a ruse.

"Fascism" was a word Italy's prime minister Benito Mussolini coined in 1919. He said the fastest path to power was to promise one's people you can restore past greatness, but only as a strongman with absolute authority. In Italy's case this meant reviving the "Glory of Rome." Their newborn democracy had just crawled out of the cradle when Il Duce drowned it in the bath.

Mussolini's book gave Hitler the blueprint for hijacking Germany's struggling democracy. Once he gained control, Der Führer sent storm troopers into Austria, reclaiming territory once belonging to Frederick the Great. "This is not war," he lied; "we're just taking back what's ours."

The corporal took the rest of Europe in fifteen months. Japan's emperor, selling demented dreams of the medieval shogunate that dominated Asia, started swallowing neighbors and joined the unholy Axis. By 1940, Mussolini's bid to restore the Roman Empire sent his Blackshirts into Yugoslavia, Greece, Tunisia, and Egypt. British forces fell back to Cairo, hanging by a thread. Hitler sent Field Marshal Rommel and battle-hardened tank divisions to finish the job. That fight climaxed with the fall of Tobruk. Four months later, as Rommel closed in on Cairo, America joined the fray.

On November 8, Operation Torch put one hundred thousand soldiers, Marines, paratroopers, and commandos ashore in Morocco and Algeria. Facing token resistance from Fascist Vichy French we took their former colonies in days. I paid attention; one of my favorite nephews went ashore as a lieutenant in First Army's Artillery.

America's knockout came as a shock to the Axis, as stunning as the blitzkriegs that had conquered Europe. Allied codebreakers picked up a tone in Fascist chatter they'd never heard before: panic.

Winston and the Boss needed a face-to-face to decide their next move. Our newest ally, Joseph Stalin, was invited but declined, consumed with defending Moscow against Hitler's armies.

FDR and Churchill decided to meet in North Africa.

• • •

To this day it's unclear to me whether the world ever realized the Boss had lost the use of his legs. The press, in an unspoken arrangement, never published a photo of his wheelchair or him in it. Only two we quashed ever got as far as an editor's desk. We did allow printed references to "infantile paralysis," an illness the president had suffered decades ago but had willed himself to recover from.

We staged photo ops of FDR at podiums, behind the wheel of his car, or standing with an arm across an open door, a foot on the ground, the other on a running board. His jaunty smile and jutting chin sold the illusion.

I felt most Americans sensed the truth, but chose to ignore it. To board a ship at sea, for example, FDR had to be hauled up a ladder over some brute's shoulder like a Persian rug. Secret Service men lugged him up and down fire escapes to reach the backs of venues, or lifted him in his chair by rope and pulley. Dozens of soldiers and civilians saw him in these situations over the years; not one said a peep about it. A Victorian squeamishness about infirm bodies still gripped our psyche: Voters accepted FDR as a father figure and didn't want to see "Dad" as a "pitiable cripple" any more than he wanted to be seen as one.

FDR endured these indignities with patience and humor. To stand or "walk" required forty pounds of crude iron braces encasing him from his hips to his shoes. They cut his trousers long to hide them, but the stirrups were plainly visible. The braces were stiff, hard, and tormenting. Gripping the arm of an escort—often one of his strapping sons—he could simulate walking; pivoting from the hip, swinging one inert, bound leg forward to plant that foot and swing the other around it. A "walk" of fifty feet took over a minute, leaving him drenched in sweat.

So how the hell were we going to get him to Africa?

• • •

On January 11, over Eleanor and Anna's strong objections, the Boss, Harry, Doc McIntire, and Secret Service boarded a clipper ship in Miami. After refueling in Brazil they crossed the Atlantic to Gambia. The last leg of the journey, seven hours in a C-54 transport over trackless desert and snow-capped mountains, brought them to Casablanca, Morocco, on Friday the 15th.

In harm's way throughout, FDR thus became our first president to cross any ocean by air. Harry was convinced the Boss insisted on going because he was sick of people telling him he shouldn't. Meeting Churchill overrode the risks, and he'd have preferred to cross by ship but couldn't spare the time. I believe both things were true: He wanted to raise morale but he also craved adventure. His chair had deprived him of free movement for over twenty years and he hadn't set foot on a plane since 1932. With every takeoff and landing Harry said he cheered like a Boy Scout.

They blacked out the windows and drove the Boss to quarters outside Casablanca, a villa on the gated grounds of a luxury hotel. Churchill had already arrived, and Harry walked him over for a reunion. Joining them there: Lieutenant Colonel Elliott Roosevelt,

Naval Lieutenant Franklin Roosevelt Jr., Captain Randolph Churchill of the SAS commandos, and Sergeant Robert Hopkins. FDR made Robert, a combat photographer, the summit's official shutterbug. They spent every evening with their sons, relief from the hard business at hand. Within four days they'd hammered out a plan for our next objective.

Once they finished the job in Africa, they decided to attack the "soft underbelly of the Fascist crocodile": Italy. Any landings in France would now be delayed until 1944. FDR feigned regret—to placate his sulking generals—but saw the plan clearly. Everything we needed to cross the Mediterranean and strike Italy hard was already in place. A successful landing could knock Mussolini out of the war.

The next day, FDR drove past thousands of jubilant American troops mustered for review, the first clue they had he was there. FDR and Churchill gave a surprise press conference that sent astonished headlines worldwide. News that both had traveled undetected to North Africa boosted morale at home and stunned our enemies.

The Boss improvised a moment before the cameras that became a rallying cry: Invoking General U. S. Grant's nickname, FDR said this war with the Axis would only end in their "unconditional surrender."

That night the flamboyant sultan of Morocco hosted a celebratory feast. Beforehand he presented FDR with a bejeweled gold dagger and a gilded tiara for the First Lady. Trying to imagine that gaudy bauble crowning Eleanor, Harry and the Boss split a gut, deciding it looked more suitable for a gal on a white horse in the circus.

They spent their last evening together at the villa of the American vice-consul. After marveling at the view from the villa's sixty-foot tower, Churchill talked FDR and Harry into joining him up top. Secret Service carried the Boss up six flights of narrow, winding stairs.

They sat silently for half an hour over the tea Winston had arranged, as sunset's glow painted the rugged, snowcapped Atlas Mountains. That view and distant calls to prayer from the mosques of Marrakesh cast a spell. As the air chilled, Churchill draped the

Boss's overcoat on Franklin's shoulders. Harry was touched by his tenderness and the soft affection in Winnie's eyes.

"There exists, I believe, no more lovely spot in all the world," said Winston.

Each man eased into silent contemplation. In this ancient landscape, where kings, caesars, sultans, and pirates had clashed for two thousand years, eternity sweetened the air.

The Boss looked serene, youthful, free of burdens. Harry read Churchill's gesture as a delayed response to FDR's plea in the Hyde Park woods: their obligation as leaders to protect not just humankind, but the natural world.

"I'm grateful you shared this with me," said the Boss.

America's entrance to the war in North Africa had been a triumph. Neither man harbored illusions about the hard road they still faced, but abiding faith was required. Harry felt this interlude in the presence of wonder allowed them to renew that faith and deepen their trust. A bond that might just let them see this task to its completion.

• • •

The Boss headed home by plane the next day, as did Churchill for London. The logistic buildup for advanced operations in North Africa began. General Dwight Eisenhower, a genial former army quartermaster whom FDR had tapped to command the Torch landings, readied plans for Sicily. In October, the Brits' brash field marshal Bernard Montgomery kicked off the next phase of the African campaign, codenamed Husky.

What followed came courtesy of a top-secret British project called Ultra: Their brain trust had just broken Germany's master code. Among a wealth of intel we learned Rommel was short on fuel after we'd bombed his supply lines. The next day two hundred thousand British soldiers charged west from Cairo at Rommel's stalled Afrika Corps. After this decisive win at the Battle of El Alamein, England's first of the war, victory in North Africa looked inevitable.

Until three weeks later, when Rommel flattened the confidence we'd been riding since Torch. It was one thing for us to bullrush half-hearted French Vichy conscripts in Morocco. When thirty thousand of our still-green troops headed east through the Atlas Mountains for our part of Husky, they drove straight into a trap set by Rommel's panzers and bombers in the Kasserine Pass.

Routed in three days. Two hundred tanks destroyed, two hundred field guns lost. The optimism of Torch vaporized and put Eisenhower's leadership of Allied forces in jeopardy. On a short leash because he'd never commanded troops in combat, his strengths were logistics, lines of supply, superb interpersonal skills. Stand-up soldier that he was, Ike offered to fall on his sword for Kasserine. Field Marshal Montgomery, a barking terrier of a man, openly lobbied for his job.

But FDR realized the Kasserine fiasco came not from the top but from poor tactical leadership in the field, one bad decision triggering the next. He learned a hard lesson: Germany's veteran soldiers were far superior to ours. Until our ranks were tested by combat, we had to rely on deception, speed, air power, and daring. FDR believed our boys, once bloodied, would prove far tougher than the enemy expected. To survive until then we needed field generals who could lead, inspire, and drive them.

The Boss gave Eisenhower a second chance. Ike knew his choices would decide his future and with FDR's blessing, he made a key change in command: a thirty-year veteran whose company FDR had enjoyed in North Africa. His staff had handled security in Casablanca and he personally drove FDR during visits with our troops. The Boss admired his gruff, hearty confidence. He was considered America's master of tank warfare and his field leadership during Torch had been exemplary.

I sat in on the meeting when General Marshall set the Boss straight on this soldier's shortcomings. His expertise and battlefield bravado aside, in peacetime the man's raging ego and temper had all but destroyed his path to the top.

But FDR trusted his gut: This moment seemed made for such a

man. So Ike handed a battlefield promotion and command of the US Army's Second Corps to Lieutenant General George Patton.

Our confidence bounced back. FDR showed he had the skill and fortitude to make a superb wartime commander in chief. As summer approached, Allied forces in Africa—led by the one-two punch of General Patton and Field Marshal Montgomery—sent the last Fascist rats scurrying back to Europe.

The curtain came down on act one of our mission in World War II. In act two, another enemy no one saw coming was about to reveal itself.

It would soon pose the greatest danger that ever stood between us and finishing the job.

January 31, 1943, the White House

FDR arrived back in Washington at night and I waited up late to greet him. After weeks away, he looked spent, sick with a severe chest cold. Doc McIntire diagnosed it as a sinus infection aggravated by stress and fatigue. The Boss blamed his method of travel and said he caught it on the plane. A week on a navy ship would have allowed him a week of R & R.

He needed rest but seemed eager to share his adventures with Eleanor. He found on his desk a curt note saying she'd gone to New York on business. I watched his smile die but moments later Anna walked in. She and her kids had arrived days before and this time, she told him, she planned to stay. And thank God for that.

I liked all four Roosevelt sons—decent, loyal, brave young men—but none seemed destined to follow their parents to the heights. Not unusual; the great give both blessings and burdens to their children, but the only thing I saw holding Anna back was the word "female" on her birth certificate. For all her mother's hard work and popularity greater even than her husband's, Eleanor knew voters would never put a woman in FDR's job.

Anna had already paid a price for this legacy in her search for personal happiness. How could she trust the intentions of any suitor on faith? And what prince, poor bastard, to such a princess could stand up to the scrutiny coming from family, palace guard, press, and public? Could anyone pass that test? Perhaps as a result, all the younger Roosevelts had been unlucky in love.

At twenty Anna married a socially prominent New York banker, Curtis Dall. She gave her parents their first two grandkids but they'd seen through Dall early on as an Ivy League peacock, always fanning his feathers. A hopeless mismatch. Anna soon gave her parents another welcome gift: a divorce.

Anna's split would have been the family's first. For propriety's sake, as First Daughter, she delayed it enough to follow brother Elliott's divorce, the first of five—including a Hollywood starlet—in his matrimonial career. I like Elliott's wry sense of fun about their family circus. Often described as a socialite, he embraced his role as the family's black sheep. Coincidence, perhaps, but Elliott was namesake to a more tragic predecessor: Eleanor's father, Ted's kid brother, whose alcoholic self-destruction scarred his daughter for life. Elliott stooped to peddling a scandalous family memoir in his sunset years and all five Roosevelt children divorced eventually. Perhaps we can attribute that as much to rapidly changing times.

Anna and I initially got on because she'd taken such avid interest in my old racket. We'd met again after she left Dall and moved with her kids to the White House during FDR's first term. I taught her shorthand, which helped her manage her father's demands. As Eleanor plunged into countless worthy causes, Anna took on traditional First Lady work that drove her mother mad. Her title was FDR's social secretary. One tinted with bitter irony.

I grew to admire Anna's concern for her father's well-being, because I shared it. No one else in his family or our circle seemed as attuned and attentive to the man behind the Sphinx. His strength, stamina, and self-confidence were legendary. It seemed an affront to even question them.

Anna fell for her second husband while still married to the lamentable Dall. She met John Boettiger, a reporter covering FDR's second White House run, on his campaign train. Keeping their romance under wraps until the election, they married and went west to run a newspaper in Seattle. We didn't see her much for the rest of the decade except holidays.

John and Anna revived the *Seattle Post-Intelligencer*, and Anna evolved from reporter to editor. After Pearl, with her brothers all in uniform, John asked FDR for a diplomatic post to help the war effort. The Boss turned him down cold, insisting he enlist for active duty. John applied for officer training and FDR arranged for his commission as an army captain.

With John in service and her older kids in boarding school, Anna had gone on leave from the paper and moved back to the White House with her youngest boy. When she walked into the Oval the day he returned from Africa, FDR broke into the biggest smile I'd seen in years. But for all their obvious affection, the Boss's relationship with his daughter had been fraught with complexity for decades.

This is as good a time as any to tell you why.

The Other Woman

The story's a familiar one by now; time eroded the vault that had protected it for decades. Chances are you've heard about it, maybe from more than one angle. But not mine.

I was a party to this deception. Guilty as charged. This was the custom then and we judged it a sound one. People who work closely with the powerful are tasked with keeping their secrets. I was one of those so privileged.

I also look back on this as far from my finest hour. Consider this my account, and my penance.

I first saw them in public together in the summer of 1918.

After six years at *Washington Post*'s city desk, in 1913 I drew a plum assignment: covering the Department of the Navy as rumors of war in Europe came to a boil. At that moment our new president, Woodrow Wilson, with a sharp eye for talent, tapped a young state senator from New York to serve as the navy's assistant secretary, second-in-command. With one improbable leap Wilson made that fella this office's youngest occupant ever.

But FDR wasn't some small-potatoes upstart. He was Ted Roosevelt's fifth cousin, his junior by twenty-four years. By giving candidate Wilson an early endorsement that boosted his long-shot chances, Franklin showed keen political instincts. His support, and the family name, earned him Wilson's undying gratitude.

A coincidence? Hardly: Fifteen years earlier the first federal posting in Cousin Ted's meteoric rise came as assistant secretary of the navy. Most days such a ho-hum appointment wouldn't make a ripple, but this one made headlines. Teddy still cast a long shadow, and this bit of "history repeating" was crystal-balled by pundits into a juicy what-if: Could FDR follow his cousin to the highest office of the land?

America, you may have noticed, loves a success story. Especially when history repeats.

In reality the Boss's job seemed like a low rung on a side ladder. His boss, navy secretary Josephus Daniels, a former newspaper man, didn't know his way around rowboats, let alone warships. Daniels stayed focused on his top priority: working Congress for cash. The rest of what he called "bureaucratic busywork" he left to his protégé down the hall.

FDR welcomed the opportunity because he was a navy man, through and through.

As a kid the Boss fell in love with the sea. Sailing endless hours off the Delanos' compound on the coast of Maine, he learned the ropes. Grandfather Warren Delano's romantic tales as a nineteenth-century merchant in the China Sea mesmerized him. Popular seafaring sagas by Stevenson, Melville, and Conrad deepened FDR's obsession. He built so many model ships his collection grew to need its own storage facility.

When FDR took the navy job my colleagues wrote him off as a callow "golden boy," a dilettante coasting on the family name. I saw him differently and found him an invaluable resource. He was approachable, clever and quotable, unpretentious—ambitious, yes, but full of humor and real interest in others.

In unguarded moments that led to friendship, he felt free enough to share private thoughts about life and our world. He possessed a rare curiosity about people and real commitment to the job's mission. He believed the most momentous changes in the history of nations had been shaped or decided by naval power.

"Some folks complain," he told me, "that Cousin Ted governed with the same philosophy. They are correct, I tell them, because both of us are right."

A student of history myself, I realized FDR had even better education and vision enough to see that this infighting between Europe's dying, incestuous dynasties would eventually pull America into their war.

Their tottering empires depended now on resources plundered from their "uncivilized" colonies. Franklin despised Europe's imperialism primarily because it was built on slavery, destroying the lives and cultures of indigenous people to feed our factories. He considered the folly of colonialism the greatest evil of the Industrial Age.

FDR saw the war's outcome and the fates of those colonies as linked. He also thought both could be set right by strategic use of our modern steel-clad battleships, destroyers, and submarines.

As he learned Washington's inner workings, FDR accrued to his office every task Secretary Daniels ignored: modernizing factories and systems, managing our industrial relationships. He soon knew more about how his department worked than anyone in Washington. When the Great War erupted, Franklin pitched to Wilson that the navy was America's best tool to assert our leadership in the world, but it took a stroke of fate to convince them.

In 1915 German U-boat attacks against our cargo ships led to the sinking of the *Lusitania*. Two thousand civilians died, more than the *Titanic*, including 128 Americans. Our provincial disinterest in this obscure war found clarity: Germany became our enemy. President Wilson and Congress had authorized $600 million to rebuild the navy for defense of country and our interests at sea. Six months later we were sending ships and troops across the sea into battle. We had identified the moral might and means that could end this war.

My friendship with FDR grew deeper. I couldn't help but like him personally; few didn't. Long my best off-the-record source, he learned to trust me as a way to accurately get his thoughts in print. I viewed this bargain, standard then between politician and press, as well within my ethical limits.

And although this isn't supposed to matter in my field—but it does—I agreed with him.

• • •

After moving to Washington, the Roosevelts needed time to adapt to the capital's frenetic pace. Bored by the domestic shackles imposed on political wives, Eleanor found the first of countless causes she would champion. She also realized this limited her ability to manage their bustling household.

Anna told me Eleanor had never seen herself as a natural mother. Her own mother, a celebrated beauty, heiress, and narcissist, rejected Eleanor at two as "bucktoothed and plain," mocking her in front of servants, nicknaming her "granny" because she found her "glum and boring."

Six years later her mother and young brother died during a diphtheria outbreak. Her father—Ted's young brother Elliott, a raging alcoholic—jumped to his death in a private sanitarium. Now orphaned, Eleanor became a burden passed between relatives before they shipped her off to an English school for unwanted, unloved rich girls.

The kindness shown her by the school's headmistress gave this "ugly duckling" the confidence to grow into her true self, sharpened more than burdened by her trials. A Victorian success story worth pondering, for those who still believe Dickens wrote only fiction.

When Eleanor began her own family, the upper class still considered child-rearing a task left to nannies in the nursery. Eleanor felt obliged to take it on alone but feared she lacked maternal empathy. After four kids in four years, Eleanor admitted her outside ambitions made raising them impossible without help of her own. Pregnant again in 1914, Eleanor received FDR's blessing to find it.

Eleanor invited a young woman to interview as her social secretary: a comely, soft-spoken, educated twenty-three-year-old Virginian named Lucy Mercer. Born into the same aristocratic class, there was even a family connection: Lucy's father had served under Uncle Ted as an officer in his Rough Riders during the Spanish–American War.

Their fathers had something darker in common: alcoholism. Her father went bust before Lucy turned five. Once a pillar of society, he spiraled down in disgrace, dying broken and alone. Lucy's mother took work as an interior designer to pay for her two daughters' educations. Manners and breeding would stand in for a debutante's customary appeal to upper-crust husbands: a marriageable fortune.

Eleanor and Lucy saw something they lacked in each other. Eleanor had the social standing Lucy had lost; Eleanor was drawn to Lucy's confidence and serenity despite her trials. She hired Lucy Mercer on the spot.

Lucy's warmth and calm had a startling effect on the four "wild Indians" she found running riot in the Roosevelt home. Without Lucy appearing to strain, Eleanor's incorrigibles fell under her spell and into line. Her oldest, Anna, found Lucy a radiant contrast to her harried, distracted mother. Even Franklin began to appreciate her presence. He never told me when he woke to their mutual attraction. I didn't hear about it from Lucy until over three decades later. But from a distance I noticed a change.

The trouble began after Eleanor gave birth to their fifth child. She had stoically put up with the obligations of the marital bed for as long as she could. Once they'd produced as many Roosevelts as Uncle Ted, she let her vital, prime-of-life husband know the subject was closed and moved down the hall.

I've never married myself. Came close once, but realized I was, as one says, married to my work. I'd once considered the priesthood as a career, so a celibate life—one that forbids marriage without prohibiting its physical comforts—was a choice I'd already made. By the time I joined the White House at fifty, I'd long enjoyed a low-key private life never at odds with my professional commitments.

So who was I, or anyone else, to judge? Imperfect creatures, men and husbands and women and wives have needs. When partners find they're no longer having them met within the marriage, eyes wander. Both parties in their marriage eventfully found other havens, but Franklin looked first. No farther than his own front door.

Summer in Washington, DC, is a brutal season. Heat and humidity spreads a blanket of misery across the Potomac Basin for weeks at a time. Before air-conditioning, this practice had become a seasonal tradition: Wives and children of government breadwinners left town for cooler climes.

By 1916, the Roosevelts' summer home was the Delano compound on Campobello Island off the coast of Maine. Franklin's mother, Sara, Eleanor, their children, and staff decamped there from Memorial to Labor Day.

All staff except Lucy Mercer. Eleanor tasked her with running the home in DC for her husband. Franklin promised he'd join them for a month, then a week, then the Fourth of July holiday. He didn't reach Maine until August, a frantic few days spent dawn to dusk with the kids. Sara's overbearing presence created tension that had simmered all summer and now it boiled over.

Eleanor had suffered Sara's domineering since their courtship. The imperious dowager made no secret she felt FDR had married his awkward fifth cousin far too hastily. Traumas from Eleanor's childhood resurfaced the moment Franklin presented his fiancée to the old battle-ax.

Eleanor came from Ted's side of the family, in Oyster Bay, Long Island. They were hardcore, capitalist Republicans who'd looked down on Franklin's father as an idle dilettante with no interest in growing a shabby genteel fortune. Sara's wealth from the Delano empire maintained their standards. And the widow Roosevelt's Springwood, where FDR had brought his bride to raise their kids, remained Sara's castle.

When the Boss earned his law degree and took a city job Sara bought a double brownstone on the Upper East Side. She planned to live on one side and gave the other to FDR and family. Not until the day she moved in did Eleanor learn that Sara had torn out the walls and doors between them on every floor. This was still her mother-in-law's house.

• • •

An unsavory summer tradition had evolved among Washington's elite. In the press we called it, with a wink and nod, "Washington's summer wives." While the cat's away, etc., etc. During my years the practice became shamelessly widespread. Neglecting to mention this in print, in my circle, became an unwritten gentlemen's agreement. We needed men in power to trust and confide in us, on and off the record. Betray that confidence even once and a reporter would end up back home covering bake sales for the local rag. So it came to pass that our subjects' personal lives weren't considered news or any of our business.

It's possible nothing improper occurred during that summer between FDR and his wife's social secretary. When Eleanor and the kids returned in fall, life went on as before. By the time we entered the war the next spring, something had changed in the Roosevelts' home.

Eleanor abruptly fired Lucy Mercer. The war, she explained, meant tightening the belt for all families regardless of class. Later that same week Franklin had Lucy sworn in as an employee of the Navy Department. A real job—she had real skills—but Lucy was now working directly for the assistant secretary.

Weeks later I saw the two of them out for a drive, top down in FDR's roadster on the river road one sunny Sunday afternoon. A familiarity, ease, and fondness on display that could only mean one thing: FDR had found himself a summer wife.

A quarter century later, echoes of these events were about to bring me face-to-face with the worst crisis of conscience my life would ever offer me.

Fall 1943

The Allies' move north against Italy began with Operation Husky, a two-pronged assault on Sicily, led by Patton and Montgomery on the wings. Sicily fell to us in six weeks and Mussolini's support at home teetered. Using Sicily as our base, Operation Avalanche—the invasion of the Italian mainland—began in September. If we knocked Italy's Blackshirts out of the fight the Austrian corporal would be vulnerable to attack from all directions.

During Avalanche's early days, I walked into his Hyde Park bedroom one morning to find the Boss in his chair, head thrown back, writhing in pain. Doc McIntire leaned over him, sticking a silver nitrate stick into FDR's left nostril. I must have gasped.

"At ease, Bill," Doc said with a smile. "The presidential proboscis is acting up again. Sinus infection."

"Mad as a nest of hornets," said FDR.

"Congestion, mild fever," said McIntire. "Nothing to worry about."

McIntire swabbed the stick around aggressively to cauterize the infection. The Boss tensed, white-knuckling the arms of his chair. After ten agonizing seconds, McIntire withdrew it, shoved cotton wadding in the nostril, grabbed both sides of FDR's nose, and pinched hard.

"There," he said. "That should right the ship, sir. Head back now, keep that pressure on for me."

FDR took hold of his nose as McIntire let go, turned, and flashed his keyboard smile at me.

"Steady on, stay the course, calmer seas ahead," he said.

He stripped off his gloves and the president's bib. Tears ran down FDR's face as he gasped for breath. I tried not to notice.

"How's your morning, Bishop?" asked the Boss.

"Better than yours," I said.

"Ha! I had two perfect Hyde Park eggs for breakfast. When I couldn't taste them I called Doc in. . . ."

"That should do the trick nicely, sir, but we'll strike again if needed."

"Have any leeches in there?" I asked, looking in his bag.

The admiral snapped his bag shut, leaned toward me, and chuckled. "Always been curious about this: Why does he call you the Bishop, Bill?"

"My name's Will, actually."

"Really? But he always calls you Bill—"

"That's what my friends call me."

"Ha!" said the Boss. "Mind your p's and q's, Ross, Bishop used to be a hell of a reporter. Covered the navy when I was there."

"Is that a fact?" said McIntire, his smile fading. "What do you know, that's when the chief executive and I met as well."

He leaned in, eased FDR's hand away, jabbed in a pair of tweezers, and yanked out a wad of bloody cotton. "Two young salty dogs on the high seas . . ."

I was about to puncture that whimsy, but as the Boss winced in pain I counted to three and said: "He calls me Bishop because I'm Irish, Catholic, and I can keep a secret."

Wiping tears away, FDR laughed. "It's his mild priestly manner, you see. With a dash of Celtic mesmerism."

"Yes, yes," said the admiral, staring at me. "I see the appeal: the High Anglican country squire and his . . . loyal provincial cleric."

I smiled. "That's one way to look at it."

"Consider yourself warned, Ross," said FDR. "Before you know it you'll be confessing everything."

McIntire's smile overstayed its welcome. "Guess I'll watch my p's and q's then."

"Piece of cake," I said, unable to resist. "For a Presbyterian."

Doc's smile vanished. When the Boss laughed, McIntire grinned and picked up his bag.

"I'll leave you both to it then," he said, then saluted. "Mr. President. Will."

The Boss watched me watch him go. "A bit too much spit in his polish for your taste, hmm?"

"I'd say it's the . . . 'cut of his jib.'"

He laughed, sounding more like himself. "How's the mail this morning?"

Before I could open my satchel, I heard a knock. Anna breezed in, and the Boss lit up.

"Morning— Oh, sorry, Pa, am I interrupting?"

"Anna, no, not a bit, darling, come in!"

"Good to see you, Bill, how's Vermont?"

I laughed. "If I ever make it home, I'll let you know."

Anna perched on the edge of his desk. "Pa, I just saw Doc leaving. What's going on, you feeling alright?"

"Fine, dear," he said. "Sinuses, same old story."

She reached into FDR's cigarette box, took out a smoke, and lit it with a match.

"Well, I just got off the phone with John," she said as she put the cigarette in his holder and handed it to him. "And do I have a story for you."

"We're all ears," said the Boss.

"John's with his unit in Italy, Bill, did he tell you? Full captain now— Don't give me that look, Pa, I didn't say what he's doing, or any other military secret."

He laughed again. "You're among friends, dear."

"So, John's not on the beach more than an hour, all of a sudden this gung ho lieutenant from Connecticut runs up to him in a full lather. 'Action's getting hot, sir, we're in the thick of it but I'm furious at myself.' 'Furious, why?' asks John. "'Cause I haven't killed a Nazi yet!'"

She paused and we laughed in anticipation. "Well, what did John tell him?" asked the Boss.

"John says, 'You go right back up that hill, young man, and shout, "To hell with Hitler." That'll flush one out.' 'Yes, sir,' he says, and he rushes back up the hill. Few minutes later he comes racing back down even more in the twist. John says, 'What the heck's wrong now? Did you yell "To hell with Hitler"'?"

We both laughed again.

"'Yes, sir. And one popped up just like you said he would and shouted, "To hell with President Roosevelt!"'"

Another laugh.

"'What's the problem,' says John, 'didn't you plug the bastard?' The kid says, 'No, sir, I'm so sorry: I just can't bring myself to kill a Republican!'"

We laughed so hard the Boss went into a coughing fit. Anna glanced at me, concerned.

"It's nothing. I'm fine, dear, fine!" He stubbed out his smoke and reached for another one.

Anna closed the lid. "On the level, please. What's going on?"

"I told you, my damn sinuses. Otherwise I'm flush."

"Just now in the hall he said he's doing a full workup on you next week."

"Just routine, darling. Now are we still on for our picnic with Johnny, just the three of us?"

"Already told Mrs. Nesbitt to make sandwiches."

"Ha! Remember how you used to ask her for them?"

"Pwease cut the cwusts off, Mithith Nethbitt," she said, exactly like Baby Snookums, and the Boss howled.

"I love it! Just grand. Now, dear, I've been called back so we'll have to train down after supper. You and Johnny too, of course—"

"He won't sleep a wink."

"—and I've got to jump on a call with Harry, Sis, so why don't you and Bill talk about that thing in Washington we discussed, he can help you with it. Would you mind, Bishop?"

I had no idea what he was referring to. I saw concern on Anna's face.

"Whatever you need," I said.

"Fine. Fifteen minutes, Bill, then back to work," he said, and wheeled out the door.

Anna wouldn't meet my eye a moment, but I tried not to notice. "I guess I need your help with something."

"Anything, of course."

"He wants to invite someone to dinner, the three of us, tomorrow night. At the White House. He thought you could lend a hand?"

"Happy to," I said, hiding my puzzlement. "Just the three of you, then."

"An old friend of ours, I don't believe you know her . . . Mrs. Rutherfurd?"

It took me a moment. "Mrs. Wint Rutherfurd?"

"Yes."

Winthrop Rutherfurd was a wealthy aristocrat and staunch supporter of FDR. Descended from Peter Stuyvesant, and a once-notorious man about town: one of the Four Hundred elite who ruled New York in the Gilded Age. Edith Wharton claimed she'd patterned a few leading men in her novels after Wint. I recalled shaking his hand at a fundraiser or two, but not in years. He'd be in his eighties by now.

"Mr. Rutherfurd is, sadly, in failing health," said Anna. "Pa felt he'd like to support his wife at a difficult time."

"I understand," I said.

But the need for subterfuge seemed out of the ordinary.

"I know her too," said Anna. "Since Mother's away, there are security concerns he thought you can help with."

A bell rang in the back of my mind. Now I saw it on her face.

"We should keep this between us as far as staff and . . . getting her in and out of the building. Pa suggests we call her Mrs. Johnson."

Far from ordinary. "Yes, of course. Whatever I can do."

She pressed my arm. "I really appreciate it. I'll get the details."

With that she left the room. I realized I'd been holding my breath and nearly gasped for one.

Before they'd married, in 1920, Mrs. Rutherfurd was known as Lucy Mercer.

Ten minutes later, FDR returned to start working through the mail.

"Starting with the bad news," I said, handing him a letter. "I'm afraid the DAR's invited you to speak again."

"Say it isn't so," he said, as he popped on his pince-nez and sighed. "And I was so hopeful they'd never forgive me for the last time."

"Oh, you sent those big-bosomed gals with the orchids into a tizzy all right—"

"All I said was that every single American—even I and they—descends from immigrants—"

"There were other remarks they found . . . ambiguous."

"Because I scolded them for refusing to let Marian Anderson sing 'God Bless America' in their damn tabernacle—"

"Yes, and you condemned their fair-haired boy Lindbergh—"

"For trying to stop Jewish children fleeing the Nazis at our border? Damn right I did, I called it a disgrace, what's ambiguous about that?"

"I thought you were perfectly clear."

"Someday I'll tell them what I really think of that simpering Nazi flyboy—"

"Preaching to the choir, Boss. Whenever our local Brownshirts say 'America First' I reach for my hat."

"Lucky you, I usually have to eat mine. You can tell that bunch of nitwits that I decline emphatically. Now I need you to draft a letter. . . ."

I pulled my shorthand pad. "To?"

"Chief Justice Frankfurter, Secretary Hull, and Bill Donovan, to this effect: 'Dear sirs: I'm sending you a young Polish officer I met recently. Jan Karski is an eyewitness to the wanton destruction of the Jewish ghetto in Warsaw. He brings evidence which he claims confirms there is an ongoing German effort for the mass extermination of Jews in Poland and the Reich. . . .'"

A chill ran through me. "Got it."

"'PS, I await your thoughts ASAP to formulate our response, etc.'"

"I'll have it for you within the hour," I said. "Is this . . . true?"

"You've heard the stories, Murrow's reports from London. We know they've built camps. Our worst fears . . . may be true."

I waited. "What can you do?"

He was a mask of inscrutability again. "Confirm them beyond a shadow first. If we do . . . exhaust every effort, financial, diplomatic, public, and private. Military options are off the table until we secure airfields in northern Italy. That's the top of our target list."

"What did you tell him?"

"I told that brave young man he has a friend in this house. We'll do what we can but the best way to help is to win this war and I told him we would."

"I see."

"All I could say. If it is true, we'll find out. Do I believe the corporal's capable of such things? Yes, I do."

I didn't speak. He softened his tone. "Until that time, Bill . . . we must harden our hearts and prepare to face these horrors. Else I fear we may go mad." He pointed at the mail bag, coldly. "What's next?"

I pulled a second letter I'd set aside. "Another invite, of sorts: The Duke of Windsor and his appalling wife have invited themselves to dinner."

He eyed the letter warily: "God forbid America's guests miss a free meal."

"They're about as welcome as a pair of pickpockets."

"Make it lunch. I'm not about to bring up how the fight's going in Italy with that moron, but he's still the king's brother."

"I'm sure they'll find you thoroughly 'ambiguous.'"

"Whatever those freeloaders hear from me will be damn near 'enigmatic.'"

"Boss, sometimes I don't know how you do it."

"If people who want things from me knew what I really thought, they'd've sent me back to Hyde Park in 1936."

"Everyone wants something from you."

"Present company and 'half-man' Harry excepted. I am, I suppose by necessity, a juggler. . . ."

The phone rang, out of his reach. I picked up and listened to Hackie, our switchboard operator.

"Always have been. Sometimes my own right hand doesn't know what the left is up to."

I handed him the receiver. "First Lady."

His tone didn't exactly brighten but sounded more energetic. "Morning, Babs. Just starting the 'laundry' with Bill, dear, how's your day?"

He put her on the speaker, and picked up a new packet of stamps to sort through while he listened.

"Not so terribly busy, Franklin. Breakfast with Cardinal Spellman, a speech with Danny Kaye for the Red Cross, then lunch with Zora Neale Hurston to discuss segregated busing in the military, then selling war bonds on the radio with Mayor La Guardia. . . ."

She stopped. The Boss was looking at a stamp through a magnifying glass.

"And then I'm flying to the moon. . . . Are you listening, Franklin?"

Without taking his eye off the stamp: "'Course I'm listening, dear. When you're back from the moon, we're having lunch with the duke and duchess . . ."

This time she paused until he looked up.

"Of Windsor," he added.

"Last time," she said, "two ashtrays, four teaspoons, and a set of White House towels went missing—"

"It's that enormous handbag the woman always lugs around." He laughed until it turned into a coughing fit.

"Franklin, you're not ill again," she said with more disbelief than sympathy.

"Fine, dear, allergies. Doc says I'm fit as a fiddle."

"Franklin, have your cousin Polly take my place at lunch. With her crowd, royals who flirt with Fascism are all the rage. Send my regards. I'm off to Ohio."

She hung up. He looked at the receiver, then held it out to me, amused. I hung up for him.

"Tell Cousin Polly, please," he said. "Lunch with the lesser Windsors next Tuesday."

• • •

The next night I caught a glimpse of "Mrs. Johnson." I'd arranged her arrival through a side entrance and up back stairs to the White House residence. I hadn't seen her in twenty-four years: Lucy Mercer Rutherfurd looked every inch the elegant upper-class woman she'd become. Otherwise, time hadn't laid a hand on her.

Dinner with Anna and Franklin took place in a private dining room. Only a few Secret Service even knew Lucy was in the building. Away on business, Harry heard nothing of it either, nor did I tell him about it.

Two days later, Anna asked to speak with me alone. During a walk through the Rose Garden, she thanked me for my help and told me about their evening.

"Wasn't sure what I thought about . . . why he wanted this," she said. "But it was nothing like what I feared it would be, not even a little."

I listened closely. An old reporter's trick: Keep your trap shut, you'll learn more.

"Her husband's dying, Bill—he's much older, almost thirty years. Married a vice president's daughter. Immensely wealthy. Wife died young. Father's known Wint most of their lives."

She stopped to smell a white rose. I waited.

"After Lucy left us, a friend introduced her to Wint. He hired her as a governess. Six months later, Father found out they were engaged. At a cocktail party."

"When was this?" I asked.

"February 1920. He'd just run, and lost, as vice president. Year and a half before polio."

She seemed to be considering what I was: Were these things related?

"I just found this out that Father invited Wint to all three inaugurations. And Lucy came with him."

I didn't know that either.

"I was thirteen when she left. We all adored her. I wanted to be her. So calm, sweet, and patient. She was just . . . peachy. Interest in whatever we were doing or feeling. She was . . . this is a dreadful thing to say. . . ."

I waited again.

"She was everything Mother wasn't. It's not that I didn't love Mother but . . . I loved Lucy too. Then one day she was gone. They pretended nothing happened, but we knew. That was the start of it . . . when everything turned rotten. . . ."

"I'm sorry, Anna."

"She was my friend. My dearest friend. At a time in life I really needed one."

I tried not to notice her wiping away a tear.

"These sorts of feelings," I said. "In my experience time doesn't affect them."

She held a yellow rose. "He asked Lucy if she'd like to see me again. She said it was her fondest wish. The moment I saw her, Bill, it all came back, for both of us. We hugged and . . ." She had to gather herself again.

"I understand."

"Wint had a big family, six kids, grandchildren, and they had a daughter of their own, Barbara. Lucy'd like us to meet, I would, too.

She's twenty-three. Pa's known her for years. In a way I couldn't be happier, about all of it. . . ."

She looked solemn and spoke quietly.

"This wasn't the first time she's been here."

"I know." She looked surprised. "I checked the visitor logs. Last three years, 'Mrs. Johnson' listed nine times."

"They go out driving, just the two of them; you know how much Pa loves that car. But that's all, it's not what you think—"

"I don't think anything—"

"They just friends, old dear friends and—"

"—and they're doing what old friends do—"

"Staying in touch, caring about each other, that's right, and that's all it is. Dear friends."

"As you and Lucy were, and are still."

She fought tears. "And what's wrong with that?"

"Nothing. Nothing at all."

I thought what she said next before she said it.

"Except, of course, Mother can't know."

"She mustn't," I said.

"There were others in between, you know, after polio, some I knew about—his secretary Missy, there were no secrets about that. He lived with Missy on a houseboat in Florida, for God's sake. Mother knew all about it. Encouraged them even."

"The rules had changed."

"And you know about Mother's friends. The women she went into business with, Marion and Nancy."

"Yes."

"And that Lorena Hickok woman, for crying out loud, she moved in right down the hall from her. We knew all about that and Pa never said a peep."

"Do not judge lest ye yourself be, and so forth."

"That's what makes no sense to me. Why is this different? Why would knowing about Lucy hurt her so much more?"

I thought a moment. "She was the reason the rules changed in the first place."

"I guess that's fair. I mean, why do you think I got hitched—stupidly, I might add—to the first tall, good-looking stiff who bothered to ask? My motives were hardly pristine. I wanted to get away from them; it all was too much, so I ran away."

I paused. "We're entitled to our mistakes, kiddo."

"You're kind to say so. You never married though?"

I offered my autobiography in a word. "Almost."

"Married to your work?"

"Marry in haste. Repent in leisure."

She laughed. I offered my arm, and we walked back.

"I want to take care of him now. And I want this for him, Bill. He needs a friend. This friend in particular. They need each other. He looked happier last night than I've seen him in years."

I saw the next question in her eyes before she said it.

"Will you help me? I can't trust anyone else."

I told her I would. How could I say no? He was my friend too.

But then, so was Eleanor.

1918–1919

With a million Americans fighting in the Great War, our assistant secretary of the navy crossed the Atlantic for high-level meetings with our English and French allies. He performed with the skill and authority of America's de facto navy secretary, which by this point he'd become.

A US Marines division had recently stopped a desperate German offensive thirty miles from Paris. This secured the Corps' reputation as a world-class fighting force, at a cost of ten thousand casualties. Franklin visited survivors: The grotesque wounds they'd suffered horrified him. He demanded his hosts show him the front lines, as close to the fighting as possible.

He saw countryside reduced to a lifeless hellscape. Bodies rotting in the sepulchral slurry of the trenches. At one point he had to flee a German artillery barrage. FDR's resolve hardened; not just to end this war but prevent any like future catastrophe. He wrote eloquent reports for President Wilson, and dutiful letters to Eleanor, sanitized to spare her from the carnage he'd seen and come close enough to feel.

He poured his more authentic self into dozens of letters to Lucy Mercer. He kept each one she wrote him in response—conveyed via diplomatic pouch—tied with a ribbon among his belongings.

Days after boarding a troopship to return home with a thousand of our seriously wounded, an outbreak of the Spanish flu epidemic swept through the vessel. Hundreds of soldiers died, and nearly half the crew; all buried at sea. Franklin soon fell ill and was confined to quarters. He was diagnosed with double pneumonia. The captain cabled the Navy Department that FDR might not survive the voyage.

When the ship docked in New York, he was taken by stretcher to an ambulance: Eleanor, Sara, and his doctor rushed him home to their Sixty-Fifth Street brownstone.

As Eleanor unpacked his bags, she found the ribboned packet of Lucy's letters. Seeing her name on the envelopes, she opened and read them. In days and nights that followed, stunned by this double betrayal, she reckoned with the confirmation of her worst fears.

The day it became clear that Franklin would live, Eleanor confronted him with the letters. Weak and without the will to lie, he told her they were in love. And when she asked he said yes, he wanted to marry her.

Eleanor calmly told him to be sure this was what he wanted: "I only ask that you think about our children."

No Roosevelt had ever divorced before. At the time it was an act of social self-immolation. Which didn't mean it couldn't or wouldn't happen; days passed, and both dug in their heels, on the brink of the unthinkable.

But neither bothered to tell his mother.

On the first day Franklin felt strong enough to leave his sickbed, Sara asked him into her sitting room. He was surprised to find Eleanor at her side. His wife wouldn't meet his eye but spoke first, saying in a whisper, that if a divorce was what he wanted she would give him one. When Eleanor finished, Sara calmly asked Franklin to respond.

He said he wanted a divorce too.

"Well, now, that's just a shame, isn't it," said Sara dryly. "But if you are both so determined I don't suppose there's anything I can say or do—"

"I'm not changing my mind, Mother—"

"I've heard you both and I'd like you to listen now."

When both began to speak she slammed a hand down on the arm of her chair.

"I said listen, or I will lose my patience!"

They went quiet, staring at the floor. Sara unruffled her feathers and smiled.

"Franklin, I've always tried to teach you to never let emotions overrule our reason. Just to be clear: In spite of all the consequences I'm sure you've carefully considered . . . you insist you love this Mercer girl and wish to marry her."

"Yes—"

"And you're determined to end your marriage to do so."

"You know I do, yes, that's how I feel, and I'm not ashamed of it—"

She held up a hand for silence. "That's your answer then. Fine. Eleanor and I have spoken at some length. She's agreed that she will not stand in your way."

Franklin glanced at Eleanor, surprised. She wouldn't look at him.

"And neither will I," said Sara.

That caught him off guard. "I . . . thank you, I . . . Mother, I'm glad that, well, I suppose I was hoping you'd understand but—"

"Practically speaking, of course, Franklin," said Sara. "You do understand you'll no longer be welcome here in Hyde Park."

"I understand some in the village may feel this way, this—"

"Not the village. I mean Springwood. In this house."

"Wait, what . . . are you saying—"

"Pack your things and go."

"But this is . . . I don't understand, this is my home."

"Is it? Perhaps you don't recall Springwood is in my name, not yours and never has been. Nor will it ever be now after I'm gone: This . . . is my home."

He couldn't speak.

"Let's look at the other things you may have failed to consider: I will disinherit you. That's the end of it. Not . . . one . . . penny."

Even Eleanor appeared stunned. Sara's tone never wavered from matter-of-fact.

"I should hope you also realize divorce means the end of your political career."

She turned to Eleanor.

"Eleanor and I have spoken about this and she's certainly aware of it. Her side of the family's always been more practical. Your father, bless his heart, lived with his head in the clouds too."

Franklin looked at Eleanor, as if expecting her to come to his defense. She kept her eyes on Sara.

"And should you, unwisely, ever decide to seek office of any kind it won't be with the help of my money, or hers. She's from the wealthier Roosevelts, or did that slip your mind too while pursuing this . . . indulgence?"

With that word her mask slipped. He recoiled from the force of her contempt. Then she smiled and continued.

"All your relations, Delanos too, on every side will drop you. Do you think we're going to rally around the family's first divorce? Uncle Ted won't ever speak to you again, if he survives the shock. Do you honestly believe you can still follow him to the White House? President? You couldn't get elected as an alderman."

In the silence, her ticking grandfather clock sounded like a blacksmith's hammer.

"I know this woman's family. The Mercers were New York society, but flawed; a rot took hold. Her grandfather lost most of it and her father squandered the rest. He joined the military, served with Ted, married well. For love, I'm told. Her mother was a stunning beauty. I knew her too, the fairest of them all."

She looked at Eleanor.

"But the rot had set in: He drank. Like your father, Eleanor. Weak, pitiful. Hardly a man at all. Threw his life away, died last year. Lucky they buried him at Arlington, or he'd have gone in a pauper's grave. Did you know all this, Franklin? Or perhaps she hasn't shared it with you."

"She told me," said Franklin in a whisper.

"You'll need a paying job now. As a lawyer, I suppose, that's your only other trade. I know you find it—what was that word you used—'grubby'? Rooting around in 'business,' or people's personal lives. But even after this scandal, the family name will help. Maybe a Harvard chum can hire you, one of those new-money Wall Street men. You'll most likely be able to afford a rented apartment with this woman."

Franklin felt unsteady on his feet. His hand sought the arm of a chair beside him.

"You'll see the children once a month or so— Oh, were you unaware that's how these things sort out? Never on holidays, sadly. But thank heavens you and this Mercer girl will always have . . . your 'love.'"

Franklin sank into the chair. Sara turned to Eleanor and smiled.

"I suppose I should first ask you this, Eleanor: If by some miracle—if Franklin somehow regains his senses . . . would you even consider staying married to my son?"

Eleanor swallowed and blinked repeatedly.

"Oh, I'll keep this from the press. No one will hear anything but idle gossip. The disgrace you're feeling now will pass. Papered over. The whole sordid business forgotten. Never mentioned again."

Sara saw possibility dawn in Eleanor's mind, and sensed hesitation.

"There's a practical side for you to think about too: You'd no longer be his 'wife,' not in any way you'll find burdensome. A partner, for appearances' sake, in a going concern. By that I mean his future, or shall we call it the family business?"

Their eyes met, as the implied took form.

"You'd be free in private to live wherever, however—and with whomever you choose."

Eleanor's cheeks flushed and she looked away.

"I'll take the children, give them the support they need till they're grown. They'll hardly care; I'm practically their mother anyway. And I do hope, from now on, dear, that's how you'll think of me as well. What do you say to that?"

Eleanor looked up, only at Sara.

"Just one thing," said Eleanor. "He must never see . . . that woman. Ever again."

Sara smiled. "I'm so pleased. Not so hard as all that after all, is it?"

She turned back to her son, frozen in the chair. He hadn't moved an inch.

"I tried to raise you to a higher calling, dear. I did my best. But if you've truly had a change of heart about the destiny you once saw for yourself, that choice remains entirely yours. . . ."

The clock ticked. Sara kept smiling.

"And whatever you decide, as I do hope I've made clear . . . I won't stand in your way."

November 1943

Our advance toward Rome against a demoralized Italian army trudged north. Mussolini begged the corporal to rescue him and when he refused, Italy turned on the father of Fascism. The king ordered his arrest; Il Duce was taken into custody. His successor disbanded the Fascist Party, but assured the corporal that Italy remained his strongest ally. The man then used back channels to sue for peace with the Allies.

When General Eisenhower announced our Italian Armistice to the world Hitler heard it first on BBC radio. We promised Italy we'd push to capture and protect Rome from a vengeful response that wasn't long in coming.

Hitler sent crack divisions he'd stationed in the region swarming toward Rome. The rest of Italy's conquests, from the Balkans to Greece, fell to the Nazis in days. Any Italians who turned to fight and were captured they slaughtered wholesale. As Rommel approached, the royal family and Italy's new leaders fled south into our protection in Naples.

Hitler abandoned the country's southern half and his hardened troops dug in. Our drive to Rome would now be fought against elite Nazi divisions in the rugged mountains of central Italy.

In winter.

• • •

The fortunes of war had turned with astonishing speed. In less than four years, America's industrial might—what FDR called "the arsenal of democracy"—had put eight million Americans in uniform around the world.

In the Pacific, a year before Sicily, we answered December 7 by smashing the Japanese navy at the Battle of Midway. Our first offensive against the Empire of the Rising Sun followed; an enormous island-hopping campaign to recapture bases, ports, and airfields lost in the wake of Pearl. Seven months later, the Stars and Stripes went up over the island of Guadalcanal.

In Europe, FDR's greatest challenge came in deciphering the poker-faced character of our strongest ally. We'd repeatedly warned Joseph Stalin the corporal would betray their nonaggression pact from 1939. Stalin dismissed such self-destruction as an absurdity only a madman would consider.

In summer 1941 four million Axis soldiers stormed the Russian frontier and in weeks drove within two hundred miles of Moscow. Stalin frantically turned to Britain for help and Churchill delivered. After Pearl we inherited England's unlikely alliance with Stalin.

FDR left all personal dealings with Stalin to Churchill, who'd known him a decade, but sent Harry to Moscow to open a back channel. Mastering Soviet doublespeak, Harry persuaded Stalin to give FDR his provisional trust. The Boss thus paved the way to partnership with Russia six months before Pearl.

Stalin's enormous army slowed the Nazi advance. The corporal had promised his generals defeating Russia would take three months; it turned into a stalemate recalling the horrors of the Great War. As a fierce Russian winter descended, Hitler hurled one elite division after another into the furnace of the Eastern Front. Unlike Napoleon, who captured Moscow and still lost his precious empire, the corporal's army had been stopped fifteen miles short.

With Stalin begging us to open a second front in France, FDR decided it was time to play cards with Uncle Joe. With the wolf at his door, Stalin insisted it take place at the Russian Embassy in nearby Soviet-occupied Iran. We began organizing the first Big Three Conference.

Before they sat down at the table, Roosevelt and Churchill decided to first meet in Cairo and coordinate their approach to the Soviet strongman.

• • •

On the day Anna learned about the summit she pleaded to go along and look after her father, as she was in Washington. The Boss said no. She pitched husband John, working in Italy as the army's coordinator of civil services, to go in her place. The Boss relented and gave the go-ahead for Captain Boettiger to head to Cairo.

Anna had insisted Doc McIntire give FDR a thorough exam before he left and requested a meeting to hear his findings. Anna asked me to join them. As I arrived—before McIntire—Eleanor, Anna, and Harry were already in discussion.

"No, dear," said Eleanor, "I'm curious to know what he's said about his health that would make you worry?"

"Nothing specific—morning, Bill—but you know how he is, Mother. It's always his sinuses or bronchitis, but I've been watching—"

"So he hasn't said to you he doesn't feel well enough to make this trip?"

"Not in so many words—"

"Well, if your father's not feeling up to something, he never hesitates to let me know about it."

"It's nothing I can put my finger on, just a feeling something's off."

Eleanor sighed, then smiled patiently.

"Dear, I've nursed him through pneumonia, typhoid fever, appendectomy, influenza, and paralysis. Does this rise to that level of concern?"

"Of course not."

Eleanor turned to Harry and me: "Do either of you share Anna's feelings about this?"

Harry shot me a "how did we get into this one" look.

"The pressure," I said, "it goes without saying, never lets up—"

"For Pete's sake," said Harry. "He spent eight years saving us, now he's supposed to rescue the rest of the world? You couldn't get Atlas to swap places with him."

"That may be so, Harry," said Eleanor. "Should that prevent him—or us—from doing our jobs to the best of our ability?" She paused for a breath. "No, it should not. Good health is more a matter of will than physiology. But since Franklin requested this exam let's hear what Ross has to say, shall we? After all these years, I trust him to give us the full picture—"

Doc McIntire knocked and bustled in wearing his full admiral's kit. "Morning, Mrs. Roosevelt, Miss Anna, all. Straight to the point: The picture, thankfully, is all blue skies." He glanced at notes without reading them. "With the exception of his chronic sinus condition, which we continue to treat, the chief executive is as healthy as a horse."

Eleanor smiled, but asked for details. Now McIntire did read from his notes, a bit louder than necessary.

"Blood panel sound, kidney and liver normal, cardiovascular functions all on solid footing—"

"How's his blood pressure?" asked Anna.

"Well within normal standards for a man his age."

"So do you believe Franklin is fit to travel?" asked Eleanor.

"Affirmative, ma'am, and I'll be on board. Keeping watch on how the chief executive tackles his orange juice and eggs. Looking for that jaunty tilt of the chin."

I could feel Harry's rising annoyance but resisted the urge to look at him. I glanced down the hall and saw the Boss wheeling toward us.

"Many thanks, Ross," said Eleanor. "Greatly appreciated and quite reassuring."

"Mother, you know all my brothers have gone with Father on at least one of these trips and—"

"This just isn't a convenient time, dear," said Eleanor, a bit frosty. "He wouldn't let me go either."

"Word has it," said McIntire, "Eye-ranians take quite a dim view of women in any position of authority—"

Just as the Boss rolled in behind him. "That's why Anna asked if my son-in-law could join us," he said.

"John's already in Italy," said Anna, pointing to FDR's globe. "Which, as you know, is on the way to Iran."

McIntire bristled. The Boss winked at Anna and said: "That is unless you take a 'dim view' of an army officer on board ship, Ross?"

"Goodness no, haha, Lieutenant Boettiger's—"

"Captain," said Anna.

"Captain Boettiger is welcome anytime, ma'am."

"John, yes, this is good," said Eleanor. "I'm pleased to hear this, Franklin. If you'll excuse me all, I've a plane to catch myself. Ross, a question, if you'd walk me down?"

She strode out, the admiral hurried after her.

"Don't worry, Chief," said Harry. "I'll be on board too. 'Case Doc needs a second opinion on how you . . . 'tackle your eggs.'"

"Ha! Maybe John can take daily measurements . . ." He stuck in his cigarette holder and grinned, raising it to the iconic angle. ". . . of my 'tilt.'"

That got us all going.

• • •

The night before FDR departed, Anna pressed him on why he was taking such enormous personal risk. He told her visiting troops in war zones—and whatever peril that might bring—had always been a president's solemn duty.

"And if we're going to win this war, Sis," he said, "I need to lay eyes on our wily Cossack."

Putting his life on the line was part of his obligation to the job. As the mother of a young child and his grandchildren, he simply couldn't justify his daughter taking the same risk.

• • •

The next day FDR, Harry, General Pa Watson, and crew sailed from Virginia on board the USS *Iowa*, the new flagship of our fleet. Three destroyers formed their escort.

The Boss wasn't wrong about the risks. The day after leaving Norfolk, during defensive drills a mistakenly armed torpedo was fired by one of the escorts, headed directly at the *Iowa*. With only three minutes to impact the *Iowa* took evasive maneuvers. When the Boss heard this he insisted on going topside; Harry tore out what was left of his hair. Like fans at a football game, FDR led the crew in cheers as the torpedo sailed by astern and detonated in a distant wave.

The crew rallied around the Boss. Outraged senior brass put the destroyer's captain and the torpedo man responsible for this near disaster under arrest. FDR immediately and cheerfully exercised his prerogative, pardoning both men from a stretch in the brig at hard labor.

During a stop in Tunisia the Boss spent a day with General Eisenhower to discuss the Italian campaign. He was also sizing up Ike for an even bigger job one year away: command of the invasion of France. General Marshall remained the front-runner, but "Unflappable Ike" from Kansas was gaining on him.

The Cairo conference with Churchill went without a hitch. John Boettiger made it in time to join them for a full-on American Thanksgiving, served within sight of the pyramids at Giza. John's cable about it reached the White House just before our own Thanksgiving feast. Anna read it to us at table, John deftly describing how the president had charmed everyone with this toast:

"How appropriate that our dear friend Winston's first Thanksgiving, our most festive gathering, should come in a year when America and Britain have formed a family more united than ever before. May it long continue!"

Churchill rose to answer, John added, "in his usual masterful and inspiring manner."

This set me thinking about something Harry'd confided before they left: Once they reached Tehran, in order to forge his own bond with Stalin—without warning Winston ahead of time—the Boss told Harry he needed to cut our "friend" off at the knees.

I noticed Anna looked troubled. When I politely asked she hesitated—Eleanor was holding court at the far end of the table—then leaned in:

"Bill, I just have the most terrible feeling."

"About the summit?"

She shook her head and whispered in my ear: "About Pa's health."

December 24, 1943

On his first morning back in Hyde Park, Christmas Eve, the Boss asked me to join him just after dawn outside the library. A deep chill, fog on the river. I found him with a blanket in his lap, using his birding glasses. I'd brought mine as well. A bird call sounded, and we scanned the forest.

"What do you think?" he asked.

"Sounds like a hawk," I said.

"Good ears, Bishop . . . close; American kestrel. Female."

Then I found her, perched on the limb of a bare beech tree.

"A real beauty," I said. "Part of a setting pair?"

"Seems likely," he said.

He lowered his glasses, drifting into what seemed a thoughtful reverie. I was slightly behind him, to one side. Seeing him only in profile, something felt off.

"Boss? . . . Franklin?"

He shook off whatever had drifted over him.

"Is Harry here too?" he asked.

"He stayed in town this trip."

He thought a beat. "Christmas with his family. Moved into their townhouse in Georgetown the other day."

"I dropped off a bottle of cheer. He was grinning ear to ear."

I heard a flutter of wings. FDR tracked our kestrel as she flew off.

"His boy Robert was with us in Tehran. On Ike's detail, you know. Brother David's on the *Essex* out west, close to Harry's youngest . . ." He stumbled on the name.

"Stephen," I said. "Yes, Harry told me—"

"Hoppy, we call him Hoppy, delightful lad. His first deployment, Marines in the Solomons." He took off his pince-nez and rubbed his eyes. "Going to miss having Harry down the hall. Like part of the furniture. Sorry, didn't get much shut-eye. Usually sleep like the dead on the train. Tossed and turned all night."

"Still on Middle Eastern time?"

"No, a week on the *Iowa* did the trick. Not sure what it is."

He'd arrived in Washington a week ago, plowing through sixteen-hour days after a month away. This was the first time we'd been alone outside the office. He looked strong and tan from his days at sea, but fatigue shadowed his eyes.

"Heard about your first meeting with Stalin," I said. "Alone."

"Needed to take my own measure of Papa Joe. Winston always has his own agenda and . . ." He trailed off mid-sentence. I waited, then prompted him.

"First impression?"

"You expect a slab of granite but he's small, squat as a fireplug. Huge hands. Make a hell of a linebacker."

"Harry describes him as 'implacable.'"

"Ha! Broke the ice by offering him a Camel and we complained about doctors telling us to cut down. There's a lot going on behind that cat's eyes. Could only get so far. He expected Winston and I to gang up on him, you see, but we had a plan for that. . . ."

I remembered what Harry had told me.

"Harry thought the best way to soften up Joe was to make fun of Winston. He'd caught a cold and he gets fussy when he's ill, so I teased him, about his tea, his chronic 'Englishness.' Mild stuff, but he went red as a scalded babe . . . voilà, the little Cossack smiled. When Winston kept going on about doctors trying to kill all his fun, Joe and I burst out laughing. From then on? Comrades in arms."

"Do you trust him?"

"For a cold-blooded sociopath he's surprisingly practical. Then I brought up what he really came to hear, our plans for Overlord. . . ."

Code name for the invasion of France, set for the following summer.

"In jumps Winston with his usual hobbyhorses—take Rome first, bring Turkey into it—any excuse to avoid crossing the Channel. Stalin brushed him aside while doodling on a napkin; Russia has no interest in sideshows. Winston clammed up like he'd stuck a cork in him."

"Did you mend the fence?"

"As we parted that night, Uncle Joe took Winston's hands in both of his and said—in English, mind you, I heard it—'You were right about Italy, my friend.' Winston nearly wept."

I paused. "If God's on our side, where does that leave your 'godless' new friend?"

He paused too. "After dinner Harry reminded me of a Balkan proverb: In times of danger, one is permitted to walk with the devil till you've crossed the bridge."

"The enemy of our enemy remains our friend."

"As long as our interests align. Uncle Joe may even be nice to his mother but he probably murdered his wife. Having met him my money's on 'of course he did.' But we can win this war with him. Without him, I'm not so sure."

"What about after the war?"

"Two global powers will be left standing: America and Russia. Winston doesn't see it coming. My fondness for him aside, the Age of Empires is over. High time. And as a man of that age . . . so is he."

The wind stirred. He took a deep, unburdening breath, looking out over a crescent of the Hudson.

"Needed so badly to be home for Christmas. Feel that breeze off the river . . . smell of cut pine in the air . . . first Christmas here since 1932, Bill."

He wasn't often in a reflective mood. I held my tongue.

"All I've ever done comes from here. The more I see of the world I realize none of it belongs to us. We're stewards, that's it. Flew over the pyramids coming into Cairo. Good God, man's desire to be remembered is staggering. Truth is we're just . . . passing through."

I sensed opportunity but waited.

"We've known each other, what, thirty years, Bill?"

"That's right."

"In that time, how many letters, columns, speeches you suppose you've written?"

"In your voice? Well over a hundred thousand? Maybe twice that."

"You know my voice."

"Fair to say."

He kept his eyes on the river. "Do you feel as if you know me?"

I decided to answer plainly. "Not as well as I might have liked."

He paused. Drifted a bit. "Hardly knew myself back then: in such a dreadful hurry. My future all laid out, Navy Department, governor, straight to the White House. Ted's footsteps, you see, laid out like paving stones. All I had to do was keep going. For the family. Like I was just along for the ride."

I didn't move.

"We don't use a 'box' like your tribe. Outdoors will do . . . would the Bishop take my confession?"

I said nothing. Just moved to take a seat on the bench beside him. Maybe I nodded. He waited awhile.

"You've met Mrs. Johnson now . . . you met her back in the day, as I recall."

"When she worked for you."

"Lucy woke me up, you see. Showed me . . . what life could be, on my terms. I was ready to toss it all away, one foot out the door. Leaving politics, I could live with . . . but I couldn't live without my children."

He cradled his forehead in his hands.

"I told Lucy . . . Eleanor wouldn't give me a divorce. I lied to her and I broke her heart . . . the love of my life. . . ."

I closed my eyes. Heard the wind in the trees.

"They put me on the ticket—that is, my name—the next year for vice president. Like Ted, twenty years before. I ran hard. We got slaughtered—Warren Harding, of all people—but I kept running . . . until I couldn't anymore. I believed God had reason to punish me. . . ."

The following summer, polio did. FDR disappeared from public life.

"Five years, Bill . . . chasing a cure that didn't exist, a bum. Half a man. Living on a secondhand houseboat—and checks from Mother—while I 'wintered in Florida.' Glad you didn't see me then."

I shook my head. He took a deep breath.

"Tried everything. Considered Lourdes. Stumbled onto a rundown resort, hot mineral pools, middle of nowhere. Still hoping, selfishly, they could fix me."

Warm Springs, Georgia. The Little White House.

"There is no cure. But the people . . . farmers, shop owners, tradesmen, most of them indigent. Kids we swam with in those pools who'd never walk again. None gave a good goddamn who I was, or thought I was. Not one of them felt sorry for themselves, not for a second. Washed the high and mighty right off me."

His hands were over his eyes, staring at the ground.

"They had nothing . . . and I'd wasted every gift life handed me. 'Wasn't my legs needed healing. The shame I felt . . . didn't know how, but I said I'd find a way . . . to help all of 'em. That was my cure."

A line from scripture came to me. "And rivers of healing water will flow from within, and everything will live where the river goes."

That seemed to help. He was a man of faith, raised to believe grace was a private matter, but this was the center of him I'd been looking for.

"This job . . . you'd think things would feel more in my control. It's worse than that. It's folly. Few days ago a storm blew one of our transports off course from Sicily to Greece. Lost contact.

Two doctors and thirteen American nurses on board. Got word last night Brit commandos found it in a field in Albania. Intact but empty."

"Alive?"

"We have reason to hope partisans may be leading them to the coast. That sector's swarming with SS."

"No wonder you couldn't sleep."

"Sent a destroyer and an airborne brigade nearby. All we can do is wait."

He took out a cigarette, hands trembling.

"I keep thinking . . . 1918, just before I left for France: My cousin Quentin's plane went down."

Ted's youngest son. I remembered.

"It finished Ted. Six months, put him in his grave. So much for the glory of war. There is no such thing. Harry and I talked about it on the ship. His three boys in the fight. All four of mine. In the action. They wouldn't have it any other way. Neither would we. But it's a hell of a thing."

I offered a light, steadying his hands with mine.

"That Polish officer who came to see me, Bill," he said quietly. "We've confirmed . . . there's a network of camps, all linked by rail. Half a dozen in Poland. They're killing them systematically."

He blew out a plume of smoke.

"We have to win. Any cost. We simply have to."

• • •

That evening FDR hosted his first Christmas Eve party at Springwood in twelve years. The sight of the old house, decked in holiday finest and full of life, was a balm for the soul. A towering fresh-cut pine brightened the halls, while a military choir on the porch sang carols. Before joining them, the Boss filmed a holiday message for newsreels and posed for photos in the room we used for press.

"In this tender season, our prayers and good wishes go out to all brave Americans serving far from home this Christmas, defending the very values we celebrate this time of year."

I slipped out while he finished, stepped to the library, and set the book I'd wrapped for the Boss on his desk.

"Merry Christmas, Bill," said Anna, entering behind me. "Is Pa done yet? We're about to take photos with the kids."

"Shouldn't be long."

The choir broke into a new holiday favorite, "I'll Be Home for Christmas." Gave me chills, and it touched Anna as well, watching the happy crowd in the main rooms.

"Just like the old days," she said. "Think half the county's here. I'm guessing we spiked the eggnog."

"Some traditions are worth preserving," I said.

She paused. "Bill, may I ask you something?"

"Of course."

She lowered her voice. "I got off the phone with John earlier. He's back in Italy."

"The Boss said John was indispensable—"

"Bill, he agrees with me that Father isn't well." She had my attention. "Reporters, like us, we tend to notice things."

"Not a habit you lose."

"I know you keep yourself in a corner, like an old shoe . . . but you notice everything. Please . . . your honest opinion. Off the record."

I hesitated. "I believe John is right."

"What he saw at the summit doesn't sound like a sinus infection or flu. Dizzy spells. Gaps in memory. Twice he found Dad slack-jawed, blank, glassy-eyed. One night he and Harry rushed him straight to bed from dinner, his whole body drenched and trembling. Harry thought he'd been poisoned. Have you ever seen him like this?"

"This morning, something like it, yes."

"Of course the admiral brushed it off as fatigue or travel sickness. Why would he say that if it's so obvious to us?"

"The admiral's out of his depth or protecting his position. Maybe the latter because of the former."

"I haven't told my brothers or even Mother—you know how she is—but I did tell Lucy. She's seen it too—"

We heard a commotion outside, and the Boss wheeled in, full of life, his beloved Scottie Fala in his lap, Doc McIntire behind the chair.

"Anna, here you are, darling, round up the brood; let's get these photos done before Mother throws a shoe—"

He handed Fala to Anna.

"—and tell that photographer I want Fala in every shot, please, his poll numbers are better than mine: That's my good boy."

Anna managed a smile, gave me a glance, and waved McIntire to follow as she headed out with Fala.

"Doc, I need a hand, please," she said.

"Bill, I need my copy of *A Christmas Carol*, please, and my reading glasses— Oh, Anna! Eggnog for me, dear, and invite the choir in for a glass, too, it's freezing outside."

Anna, Fala, and Doc left the room. I gave the Boss his book and glasses when he spotted my present on the desk.

"Now what's this, for me, Bill? You're too kind." He picked up my gift and shook it playfully.

"Marbles again," I said.

He laughed, reached in his pocket, and gave me a small, perfectly wrapped box.

"And for my Boswell," he said.

I shook it playfully.

"It's a bicycle," he said. "Go ahead, open it."

I did: an exquisite—and not cheap—fountain pen.

"Long as you don't mind me borrowing it from time to time," he said.

I didn't know what to say. The phone rang and saved me. I answered, heard urgency from our operator, and covered the mouthpiece.

"A General Collins for you."

FDR flushed red, wheeled over, and grabbed the receiver just as Anna walked back in.

"Pa, we've got the kids wrangled—"

"Collins, this is Franklin Roosevelt—Where the fuck are my American nurses? It's been over a week, didn't I make it clear I want them safe by Christmas? If one so much as skins a knee I'll have your head on a pike!"

He slammed it down, looked up smiling, and waved to Anna.

"Pardon my French, dear, won't be a moment!"

Anna gave me a wide-eyed look and left. FDR picked up my wrapped gift and opened it: an original edition of *A Christmas Carol*. He shook my hand warmly.

"Merry Christmas to you, my friend."

"Merry Christmas, Boss."

With the book in his lap he wheeled up the ramp, called out a greeting, and a cheer erupted next door.

"And a Merry Christmas to all!"

Winter 1944

Days into the New Year, the Boss held an impromptu conference with the White House press. He described himself as "Doctor New Deal" looking after a once gravely ill patient: us. No sooner had we made a robust recovery than World War II hit us as we walked out of the hospital.

The summit in Tehran exacted a toll on everyone save iron-man Stalin. Brought low with pneumonia, Churchill was still convalescing. Harry took ill New Year's Eve. His doctors reached a dire conclusion; his stomach cancer had returned, requiring surgery, but not until he had weeks of bed rest.

I watched the Boss during his presser. Dark circles his fading tan couldn't hide. A rattling cough that grew worse by the day. Although he hid it, his hands tremored now. His bold signature grew increasingly thin and feeble.

Doc McIntire insisted he had the flu and a chronic sinus infection and just needed ten hours of sleep. After a week he showed no improvement. Our work pushed later into the morning. At least once a day he nodded off while we worked. I'd never seen that before.

We returned to the White House. Doc suggested the Boss lighten his work hours and that his rest must be strictly enforced. But by whom? Eleanor was away on the country's business. Anna was about to fly back to Seattle and put her two older children into new schools.

Before she left she told me John had put in for a transfer from Italy to the Pentagon so he'd be closer to home. I promised to let her know if I saw any change while she was gone.

I had to call her in less than a week.

• • •

On February 2, Harry sent a letter to his youngest boy, Stephen. Hoppy was aboard a transport, his Marine division on their way to the Marshall Islands, where Harry knew an offensive against the entrenched Japanese was about to begin.

Dear Hoppy,

You can imagine how much my thoughts have been with you during the last few days and I hope all has gone well. The Japs will never be able to withstand what we're throwing at them in the Marshalls.

I've been laid up awhile and I'm going to take a real rest in Miami Beach for another month. Nothing serious, but I having a bit of trouble bouncing back. Do write when you get a minute, but I presume you'll be pretty busy the next few weeks, so I do not expect to hear from you. At any rate you know that I wish you the best of luck.

Love, Dad

Ten days later, I got an early morning telegram for the president marked "urgent." I took it in immediately. Propped up in bed, weary, scanning the morning papers. When I showed FDR the telegram, he asked me to read it to him.

I did. He sat still and listened. Put a hand to his head, lowered his eyes, and took a breath.

"Should I call him?" he asked.

"Think he knows?"

He shook his head. "Send this first. I'll call after."

I took out my steno pad and pen.

"Dear Harry, I am terribly distressed to tell you I've just learned that two days ago . . . your son Stephen was killed during his first action in the Marshalls. We have no details yet but I'm confident that, when we do, we will all be even prouder of him than ever. I am thinking of you, now and always. F.D.R."

I sent the cable. I later learned a nurse gave it to Harry at a whistlestop near Jacksonville.

Harry and the Boss spoke by phone a few days later. By then, FDR had learned enough to tell him that Stephen had been running ammunition under heavy fire to a forward machine-gun emplacement on Kwajalein Atoll. He was digging in for cover when a Japanese sniper took him out. He died later that day on an offshore US hospital ship. Eighteen-year-old Hoppy was buried at sea with honors.

Stephen's death made worldwide headlines. Condolences poured in, dozens from avowed political enemies. None offered him more comfort, he told me, than a passage from Shakespeare, sent by a friend in England:

Your son, my lord, has paid a soldier's debt;
He only liv'd but till he was a man;
The which no sooner had his prowess confirm'd
In the unshrinking station where he fought,
But like a man he died.

To Harry Hopkins from Winston S. Churchill.

Days later, the letter Harry had sent Stephen two weeks earlier was returned unopened.

Harry underwent surgery at Mayo Clinic in late March. We were grateful to learn his cancer had not returned, but his surgeon used the occasion to try to mend Harry's benighted digestive tract. His bride, Louise, worked as a nurse's aide as Harry made a slow recovery, complicated by jaundice that had set in after surgery.

Once Harry was strong enough General Marshall arranged military transport to fly Harry, Louise, and their daughter to a golf resort in West Virginia, now serving as a convalescent center for our wounded.

We wouldn't see Harry until August. By then the world had once again tilted sharply on its axis.

March 4, 1944, the White House

On a busy Saturday, FDR felt good enough to take part in what had become a tradition in the East Room: a simple religious ceremony to commemorate the anniversary of FDR's first inauguration, eleven years ago.

I was pleased to invite my nephew Warren to join me—only son of my favorite niece. All of eighteen, in dress whites, a chief petty officer on a day pass from Newport, where his destroyer escort was days away from its first deployment. Frosty, as we called him, was greeted at the door by Admiral Leahy, chief of the American Navy. That made an impression. I then sat Frosty next to Supreme Court Justice Hugo Black, a man I greatly admired. I was even prouder to introduce him to the president and Mrs. Roosevelt after the service. They went out of their way to make this handsome young navy man feel welcome.

Needless to say, Frosty was walking on air. Due back on board by six, after lunch I walked him out to say goodbye. My eyes welled up as I watched his taxi leave. I knew where he was going, you see. The USS *Borum* was headed across the pond for Operation Overlord. A few months later we called it D-Day.

Afterwards I rushed to the annual White House Correspondents' Association dinner at the Statler Hilton. Enjoyed seeing the crowd and the Boss get such a kick out of emcee Bob Hope's wisecracks—often offered, gently, at FDR's expense. He offered a good-natured tip of his hat in return to end the evening.

Got home too damned late, of course, after rounds of cocktails and gatherings afterwards. Not too late to offer a bedside prayer for my nephews, Hoppy, and every other mother's son and what awaited them across the English Channel.

March 25, 1944, Hyde Park

On March 19, Lucy's husband, Winthrop Rutherfurd, passed away at eighty-two. Lucy broke the news to Anna, who relayed it to the Boss. He spoke by phone to Lucy that day, offering sympathies and apologizing—for many reasons, some more obvious than others—why he wouldn't be able to attend Wint's funeral.

Anna had returned from Seattle. The First Daughter, John, and their five-year-old, Johnny, settled into the Lincoln Suite down the hall from the Boss, the rooms vacated by Harry and family before Christmas.

We boarded the train for Hyde Park the next night. After FDR retired, I had my first chance to catch up with Anna. We turned the lamps down, put classical on the radio, and started with a refresher on stenography.

"I cleared it with Mother first," she said. "Before moving us back in. You know how she is about 'rivals.'"

"Sara Roosevelt casts a long shadow," I said.

"You have no idea," she said with a laugh. "Granny spoiled us something awful, but we were terrified of her. She was an absolute gorgon."

We both laughed.

"But Mother seemed pleased. Before she left for wherever she's off to this time—"

"Visiting troops, South America," I said. "Yes, she's more than pleased."

"Do you really think so?"

"You lift her spirits; you lift everyone's spirits, it's who you are. They both feel life's more manageable when you're around."

She smiled wistfully. "The good old days we never actually had."

"I know."

"Always wanted to help him after he got sick. Just never got the chance. We scattered to the winds."

"You're making up for it now."

She closed her steno book and patted the cover. "Thanks again for this. There's so much to keep track of and you know how he talks a mile a minute."

"He seemed better tonight."

"He's excited about his houseguest."

"And when does the widow Johnson arrive?"

"Sunday morning. He'll pick her up at the station and drive her all over. Can't wait to show her Hyde Park."

"I'm giving them a tour of the library."

FDR's library had been built to house papers and effects from his first terms. Built with locally quarried stone, wood from his forest, and dedicated in 1940. I was one of the trustees for what became the first presidential archive in history.

"Don't know why I feel guilty about Lucy coming. Pa feels lousy, Lucy's grieving, they need a boost. But God forbid Mother finds out he's with the widow Rutherfurd."

I held her eye. "How's he seem to you?"

"He rallies when folks are around, but that's all for show. What's he say to you?"

"Says he feels 'rotten.' 'Like hell.'"

"Bill, I've decided . . . if he's not on the mend after Lucy's visit . . . I'm going to do something."

Lucy did lift his spirits. They spent their day alone, or with Anna, exploring the grounds; a crisp, sunny spring afternoon. I took them through the library. They shared this elegant curation of his life with graceful ease and affection. Don't think I ever saw him happier.

After supper, FDR and Anna drove Lucy to the train. They came home and he went straight to bed, chilled, with a fever of 104. By the time we boarded the morning train, the fever had broken, but he never left his berth. At the White House he stayed in and took dinner with Anna, not a word to anyone.

As I left that night, Anna asked me to meet her early the next day. I didn't ask, but I had an idea why.

• • •

Admiral McIntire arrived at Anna's door at nine in full dress. Maybe he had reason for the uniform but I suspected he was propping up his authority; he came in sharp-eyed and annoyed.

"I appreciate you coming, Admiral," said Anna. "I promise not to keep you long."

"Of course, Miss Anna. Only too happy. How may I help?"

"Let's talk about Father's health."

He scowled his eyes toward me. "Wouldn't you prefer to speak privately?"

Anna smiled. "No."

I leaned back against a desk and folded my arms.

"This can't wait," she said. "Something is seriously wrong, I believe, and that's not my opinion alone."

She glanced my way, and I backed her up.

"Well, speaking medically, he's been fighting influenza and bronchitis all winter and I—"

"You didn't let me finish, Ross."

He recoiled. "All he needs is rest, a week in the sun."

Anna smiled. "This has gone on long enough. Goodness, Ross, you've known him almost as long as I have."

Her friendliness seemed to baffle him.

"The truth is he became ill in Tehran and he's grown worse ever since," she said, firmer. "You're going to arrange a comprehensive examination at Bethesda for him this afternoon."

Doc stepped back as if she'd pushed him.

"I want top specialists in every discipline to deliver and report directly to me a complete and reliable diagnosis."

He spat out the words: "The chief executive's health . . . is his own . . . private . . . business."

Anna glanced over and I gave her a nod: Spring the trap. She stood toe-to-toe with him.

"I know you're an admiral, the surgeon general, and his longtime physician and friend—"

"What, what does Mrs. Roosevelt say about this?"

"Mother's out of the country, returning tonight, at which point I'll speak with her . . . but let me remind you: I'm a Roosevelt, too. And you may assume I'm speaking on behalf of my father, my family, and our country."

McIntire went pale, his lips a tight, thin line.

"Because if you don't cooperate, I'll take this across the hall to him right now. I haven't been around so I'll remind you of this as well: I'm the only one he listens to. We've canceled his day. I'm driving him to Bethesda at noon, with or without you. Nor will you tell him I suggested this: I'm sure you agree it's best he believes this his doctor's idea. Have I made myself clear?"

He took two deep breaths before the smile returned, half curdled.

"As you wish."

He gathered his dignity, put on his hat, snapped a salute sharp enough to wound, and left.

Anna turned to me, eyes wide. "Too much?"

"No, yeah, you know what? Pardon my newsroom French, but fuck that guy."

We were both almost giddy.

"By the way, I don't believe your mother's back till tomorrow."

"The Admiral doesn't need to know that."

• • •

On arrival, FDR insisted on wheeling himself through Bethesda, spreading cheer to staff and wounded veterans. After preliminary tests and blood draws we took him into a private suite. Nurses helped him into a robe and onto an exam chair, his wasted legs dangling.

Minutes later a sturdy, youthful doctor joined us. "Mr. President? Dr. Howard Bruenn, an honor to meet you, sir."

"Pleased to know you," said FDR, with obvious reserve. "Where's Doc McIntire? Haven't seen him yet."

"The surgeon general's asked me to run a few tests. How are you feeling?"

"Like a boiled owl. Your people have been poking and prodding me for hours . . . what sort of doctor are you?"

"I'm head of the Electrocardiograph Department here."

The Boss eyes him closely. Bruenn glanced at his clipboard, concealing the nerves he later confessed he felt, sweat trickling down his back.

"And I am here because . . . ?" asked FDR.

"You've had a long bout of the flu, we want to take a closer look."

"I see." The president paused again. "Well, go ahead then."

Bruenn warmed his stethoscope. "Take a few deep breaths for me if you would, please."

Moving his stethoscope around his chest, front and back, Bruenn listened to a series of labored, wheezy breaths.

"Breathe normally now," said Bruenn. "Are you still swimming every day?"

As they spoke, Bruenn slipped on a blood pressure cuff and pumped it full.

"Doc asked me to stop when the flu bug bit. Save my strength. Take it you're a navy man."

"Yes, sir. Lieutenant commander. Enlisted."

"That so? Where'd you go to school?"

Bruenn watched the mercury in the gauge and took his reading. He took a bit longer to answer.

"Columbia and Johns Hopkins, sir. Could you lie back a moment, please? I'll like a reclining reading as well."

Bruenn lowered the rear of the table and eased FDR onto his back. Even this slight effort left him short of breath. Bruenn pumped the cuff monitor again and took a second reading.

"I'm a Columbia man too, you know," said the Boss.

"So I'm given to understand," said Bruenn.

"How old are you? You don't mind my asking."

"Thirty-nine, sir."

"Thirty-nine. And you're already head of your department."

"Correct," said Bruenn, jotting down his findings.

"You're what they call a cardiologist."

"Yes. This is a relatively new field—"

"Guess they send you all the officers with ticker problems."

Bruenn raised the table again and helped FDR sit up, noting his shortness of breath again.

"When they're up for promotion, yes, I see my share. May I have a look at your hands, please?"

Bruenn examined his hands, paying attention to the nail beds. "By the way, Mr. President, do you happen to know where your medical records are? I've asked the admiral but haven't received them yet."

"Imagine those might be helpful to you."

Bruenn smiled. "Standard procedure."

"I'll mention it to him. Doctor, I have a tremendous amount to do. Don't have time for much more of this."

A soft knock at the door: A nurse came in to hand a slender file folder to Bruenn. He thanked her, she left.

"Those my charts?" asked the Boss.

"Yes, sir," said Bruenn, glancing inside. "Won't keep you much longer: I'll have them take you for a couple X-rays and you'll be all set."

"Chronic sinus infection and acute bronchitis then," the Boss asked him. "That about the size of it?"

"I'd prefer to wait till I have all your results. I'll share them and my recommendations with the admiral."

Nurses came in and transferred FDR back to his chair.

"Sure he'll be eager to hear the good news," said the Boss. "Feel free to discuss it with my daughter as well."

Bruenn walked us to radiology, the president greeting everyone we encountered with a grin and a wave.

We returned to the White House. The Boss insisted on holding his weekly presser, giving the White House gaggle his standard bonhomie. One asked about his health. FDR said tests at Bethesda had gone well; his bronchitis was under control, and he had full confidence in his doctors. In other words he lied, and so did the stories they printed.

The next day Dr. Bruenn asked for a meeting at Bethesda and shared his report with Admiral McIntire. Doc's face flushed red as he finished and slammed the file on the desk.

"Unacceptable. You cannot be goddamn serious—"

"I'm one hundred percent confident of my diagnosis, sir—"

"You're talking about the goddamn president!"

Bruenn stood eye to eye with him and didn't flinch. "That's why I'm convening a full review by our department heads here at the hospital—"

"That's fucking outrageous—"

"—to approve my treatment plan and I'm confident they will. After I first share with them the president's complete medical file."

Bruenn held up the thin folder he'd received the day before. "Am I to tell them this is the full extent of your observations about your patient's health for the last four years?"

About to bust a vein, McIntire held his tongue, unlocked a cabinet drawer, took out a thick three-ring binder, and slammed it on the desk.

"Push me and I'll have you up on charges, you hear me? I'll ruin you. Make no public statements about this. That's a direct order, you understand?"

Bruenn picked up the binder. "Loud and clear. That's your department."

• • •

Returning to the White House, Eleanor's account of her whirlwind South American trip took up most of supper with FDR and Anna. Anna mentioned he'd had a few tests done and Eleanor felt confident all was well. The Boss turned in early. Weary from her travels, Eleanor retired not long after.

Anna caught me on my way out and asked me to follow her to an empty office. She pointed at an extension for me to pick up, grabbed a phone on the desk, and said:

"Dr. Bruenn? Bill is on the line. Could you repeat what you just told me, please."

"Of course," I heard Bruenn say. "Admiral McIntire is correct about this much: Your father is suffering from chronic bronchitis and an acute sinus infection . . . but these are secondary and the least of our concerns."

I heard a page turn. Felt my heart pounding in my chest.

"His skin is pale and discolored, his nail beds as well. That's from lack of oxygen—"

"Because?" I asked.

"Because his heart is dangerously enlarged, particularly around the left ventricle."

I glanced at Anna. Trying to keep alarm from my voice, I asked: "What's causing this?"

"High blood pressure. When the heart can't function it adds mass to compensate. X-rays confirmed. I took two pressure readings, seated and reclined: 186 over 108 and . . . 212 over 136. . . ."

"Good God."

"What's worse? Near as I can tell from his file or what little I've been allowed to see of it? That's the first time his pressure's been checked or recorded . . . since 1941."

I didn't know what to say. Anna had already heard this. She was ahead of me.

"How is that even possible?" I asked.

"I can't speculate. The admiral's had a long, distinguished career—"

"Yes," said Anna. "As an ear, nose, and throat man."

"I'll give you a 'fer instance,'" I said. "When Harry thought he had stomach cancer, McIntire insisted it was indigestion and prescribed bicarbonate of soda."

"Repeat your diagnosis please, Doctor," asked Anna.

"The president is suffering from hypertension and advanced congestive heart failure."

A heavy beat.

"And your treatment plan," said Anna.

"Digitalis to lower edema, that's number one. I want him on a low-sodium diet and codeine for his cough. He needs twelve hours of sleep a night. Cut way down on cigarettes and alcohol. And complete rest."

"So," said Anna, looking to me. "You're caught up."

"How long will he need to follow this?" I asked.

"Start with a month. If I see improvement in symptoms he could begin light exercise—"

"A month," I said, struggling.

"At a minimum. During that time, under no circumstances can he work more than four hours a day."

"Is that even possible, Bill?" Anna asked.

"It had better be," said Bruenn before I could answer. "If you want him to live."

Anna asked what I couldn't bring myself to say. "How long do you think he has?"

"If he follows this protocol to the letter and responds favorably? Maybe two years."

I couldn't even look at Anna.

"Dr. Bruenn," she said. "Are you obliged to share any of this with my father?"

"Only if he asks," he said.

"And my mother?"

"The same."

"I'll speak to her first, please. May we assume you've already shared with Admiral McIntire?"

"Yes. I can't say he was . . . overly receptive."

"What's the next step?" I asked.

"Present this to a senior review board at Bethesda. I need their say-so, and I believe they'll give it to me. At which point we can start medications immediately."

"Will McIntire abide by their decision?" I asked.

"He damn well better," said Anna.

"He may oppose it at the hearing," said Bruenn. "But the facts are what they are, and I think they'll prevail."

Anna thanked him and ended the call. We looked at each other. She spoke first.

"Can we get Harry on the phone?" she said.

I asked the switchboard to put us through to his rehab facility in West Virginia. It took minutes, but we got Harry on the line. He sounded better than I had hoped, but like the Boss, he was masterful at putting up a good front. He took the news, which Anna delivered straight, better than I expected; he'd handled more than his share lately.

"Okay," he said. "So it is what it is. At least we know . . . it's better to know than not know, right?"

"That's right, Harry," I said.

"Do you trust this Dr. Bruenn?" he asked.

"I do," said Anna.

"We both do."

"Has Pa said anything to either of you about running again this year?"

"Not to me," said Harry. "But I've been out of the loop."

"He's just said this, and only once," I said. "'If the people want me, let them decide—now let's get on with winning the war.' That's it."

We fell silent.

"Anna," said Harry, "I don't think for a second he'll step down or aside. Not till the war's over."

I agreed.

"So we keep it quiet," she said. "I'll share this with Mother and my brothers, no one else."

"The country's shut its eyes and pretended he can walk for twenty years," said Harry. "We can manage this too."

"What other choice do we have?" I asked.

"None," said Anna. "If his plan's approved, Dr. Bruenn wants a complete break, now, from everything. See if the treatment works and he gets some strength back."

"For how long?" asked Harry.

"A month," she said.

I could hear Harry calculating before he spoke: "What about Bernard Baruch's country place? Hobcaw, South Carolina. He's been pestering the chief to visit for years."

"I've been there," said Anna. "It's huge, isolated, thousands of acres on the water, fenced and gated."

"Security's doable," said Harry. "Easy to keep press away. And Baruch will keep his trap shut."

"Call it a fishing trip," I said. "A working vacation."

Anna looked at me. "Hobcaw's not far from Mrs. Johnson's estate near Aiken."

"He'll go for it then," I said.

"I agree," said Anna.

"Uh . . ." said Harry. "Pretty sure you need to tell me who Mrs. Johnson is?"

We looked at each other. Anna nodded.

"Lucy Mercer Rutherfurd," I said.

"Oh," said Harry, then after a pause, "Ohhh . . ." Then another pause. "Oh, shit . . ."

"I'll read you in if you like," said Anna.

"Yes, please."

She did, in detail. Harry took it matter-of-factly, as he'd always been able to do, and moved on to solutions.

"Talk to Mrs. Johnson, then," he said. "If Bruenn prevails with the board, and you do with the chief, I'll make this happen with Baruch. Hell, he'll turn cartwheels."

We said goodbye to Harry and ended the call.

"Does your father want to hear his diagnosis?" I asked.

"Not for a second," she said.

I agreed.

• • •

Bruenn needed three meetings with the board at Bethesda. McIntire opposed him aggressively, telling them this "young man" was overreaching and exaggerating his findings. Bruenn relied on his evidence; no point accusing McIntire of misconduct or negligence. Nor did the board bring it up.

Given the urgency of his symptoms, they met again the next day. McIntire called in two senior doctors to back him up, including the president of the American Medical Association. Still the only man in the room with training or experience in cardiology, Bruenn presented his diagnosis even more forcefully.

McIntire's experts asked for a visit to examine FDR at the White House the next morning. I ushered them in and waited with Anna. When the board reconvened that afternoon, both "experts" decided their observations supported Bruenn's findings. One admitted cardiology was outside his area of expertise. When McIntire tried one last time to discredit him, Dr. Bruenn stood his ground.

"Respectfully, sirs, I appreciate that you accept my diagnosis," he said. "But if you're unwilling to follow this treatment plan, I'll step aside and resign my commission. I stake my career on what I believe he needs."

After the board voted and announced their decision, McIntire and Bruenn paid a visit that evening to the White House. I escorted them into a foyer outside FDR's bedroom. Anna came out to lead them inside. McIntire, wearing his surgeon general's uniform, turned to Bruenn.

"If you don't mind waiting, Howard," said the admiral, "I'll speak to the chief and First Lady and—"

"He'll see you together, Ross," said Anna.

McIntire's smile froze, and they followed her into the president's quarters. Eleanor and Franklin—in pajamas and robe, out of bed and in his chair for the first time that day—were waiting for them.

"Here's the fella I told you about, Babs, a Columbia man." He turned to McIntire: "I'm quite bullish on your Dr. Bruenn. We should get on with what he recommends, don't you agree, Ross?"

"Uh, yes, yes, Mr. President," said McIntire, fumbling open the folder he'd brought along. "First, so I, uh . . . well, we have some . . . preliminary findings to share—"

"I know, sinus infections, bronchitis, so on and so forth," said FDR. "We've been over all that. Let's hear how Dr. Bruenn wants to move forward."

Before McIntire could interrupt, Anna said: "He's gone over the plan with me, Pa, simple things really, I can fill you in. I just wanted Mother to meet him."

"Well, that's just fine then. Thank you both so much for coming." He shook McIntire's hand, and then Bruenn's: "You're going to make a fine addition to the team, Doctor."

"Sorry?" asked McIntire.

"Please arrange to have Dr. Bruenn attend me personally, Ross. And kudos to you, my friend. You've always had a marvelous eye for talent."

FDR grinned at McIntire, the full-on Sphinx. McIntire looked flummoxed.

"In fact, as long as Dr. Bruenn's here, why don't we get started, and we'll let you get on with your evening," said the Boss. "Thanks again for coming, Ross."

"I'll walk you out," said Eleanor, taking her cue.

"Right, yes, if you'll excuse me, Mr. President."

Eleanor took McIntire's arm and steered him out. He cast a dark glance back at Bruenn, who wasn't looking at him.

"Ross, I'm headed out to hike Yosemite next week," she said. "Having some trouble with this trick knee of mine. Is there someone you trust out west to take a look?"

She walked the admiral past me into the hall. McIntire stumbled slightly on the carpet.

"Yes, that can be arranged," he said.

I entered the bedroom. The Boss was laughing. "Remember the last time Babs hiked Yosemite? Ran the park rangers ragged!"

"Didn't they name a trail after her?" I asked.

"That's right," said Anna. "It's called Abandon All Hope Ye Who Enter Here."

We all laughed; even Bruenn cracked a smile. FDR reached for a Camel from his cigarette case. Anna took it before he could put it in his holder.

"Now, Pa," said Anna. "Dr. Bruenn does have new marching orders for you."

"Really? About my smoking?"

"Among other things," said Bruenn, opening his bag. "I'd like you to stop altogether if possible, but no more than six a day."

Anna held out her hand. "And he's put me in charge, so . . . hand 'em over, bub."

The Boss handed over his cigarette case. "Well, you're no fun."

"Drinking, too," said Bruenn. "A glass of wine with dinner is fine, but let's lay off the hard stuff." He handed Anna a vial of pills. "Three of these a day: morning, noon, and night."

"Got it," said Anna.

The Boss read the label, eyeing the little green pills. "What's digoxin supposed to do?"

"It's a distillation of foxglove, digitalis," said Bruenn. "Reduces fluids and the congestion you're feeling. Should make you feel a lot better."

He handed Anna a second vial, codeine, for the president's cough, pointing out the dosage.

"Most important: Catch up on your sleep, sir," said Bruenn. "Ten hours a night, if you can, and a couple of naps during the day."

"Have you told him yet?" FDR asked Anna slyly.

"Haven't had the chance," she lied.

"I'm taking the train down to South Carolina tomorrow," said the Boss. "To do exactly that. A vacation, if you can believe it. And you're coming with us, Doc."

"Am I?"

"Head home, pack a bag, and my thanks to the Mrs. for loaning you to us awhile, Lieutenant."

"I'll take it from here, Doctor," said Anna.

Bruenn looked full of emotion and seemed at a loss for words. He straightened and offered a crisp—and, to me, quite moving—salute.

"It's an honor, sir," he said and left us.

"So, tell me," the Boss asked, eyeing us, "how many other ways am I no longer allowed to enjoy myself?"

"We'll have a nice long talk about that, you and I."

"Oh, we will, will we?"

Eleanor returned from seeing McIntire out.

"Now that you're both here," said Anna, "I've talked this over with Mother, Pa. John has put in for a transfer to the Pentagon. He hopes to be here by the time you're back from South Carolina."

"Why's that?" he asked.

"John, myself, Johnny, we're all going to stay."

"For how long?"

"For as long as you need."

For the only time I can remember I saw tears well in his eyes. His voice went husky.

"What about your job?"

"I got a better offer."

"I agree it's a good idea," said Eleanor. "Anna's up to the task, and we both feel it's for the best. Until you're better."

FDR's control came as close to cracking as I'd seen. "As long as it's not an inconvenience. . . ."

Anna kissed his hand, holding it a moment. He looked away first.

"I'll get started on my rest, then."

He turned and wheeled into his room, where his valet waited to help him into bed. I made my way out. In the corner of my eye, I saw Anna hug her mother as the door closed behind me.

South Carolina, April 1944

Our entourage reached Hobcaw Plantation on Easter Sunday. A wealthy and powerful wizard of Wall Street and one of FDR's trusted advisers, seventy-four-year-old Bernard Baruch proved a splendid host. He'd attended to every detail for FDR within the confines of his "island barony," miles from the eyes of the world. Ramps and rails installed everywhere made the estate navigable.

Both doctors traveled with us, Bruenn actually in charge, McIntire along to maintain the impression he was. Bruenn's presence and area of expertise we kept strictly off the record. We stashed our traveling press pool at a quaint inn eight miles away. As sequestered as the Boss, they filed softball stories on local color while running up their bar tab. I joined them every few days to make sure their curiosity about why we were here remained back of mind.

"Surely the chief's banked enough vacation days to enjoy an extended holiday," I said.

Timing couldn't have been better: News from the war remained positive. National papers picked up the fluff our pool fed the wire, and major dailies cut the Boss some slack. Only the lowest yellow press, who whined and hollered about every move he made, complained he wasn't doing all those things they despised from behind his desk.

Twelve hours of sleep a night, days in the sun, and the Boss's new medication paid dividends. After a week his lungs were almost clear of edema, and the enlargement of his heart had begun to recede. The Boss went from dropping a bobber off a dock on day one to trolling for game fish from a Coast Guard cutter by our second week.

As the president improved, Doc McIntire delivered his patented glowing updates to our press. Once Doc learned FDR had never asked Bruenn about his condition, he insisted we keep it that way. The admiral's act wasn't fooling the Boss: The Sphinx's power lies in keeping its own secrets.

Bruenn confirmed a pattern I'd seen in people new to FDR's circle time and again: The staunch, lifelong Republican quickly came under his spell.

FDR was an ideal patient, Bruenn said, following instructions faithfully without complaint. Within a week he felt good enough to resume his role as master of revels during cocktails. By the third week, people joined us for dinner almost every night. I took this as his most hopeful sign of improvement: Holding court with smart, convivial people was more than FDR's favorite diversion. It was how he kept the darkness at bay.

I'd taken a liking to Dr. Bruenn, not only because he'd saved the Boss from the brink, although that colored my affection. Bruenn also realized, astutely for having known him only weeks, that anyone expecting personal intimacy from the Boss would leave disappointed. Bruenn didn't take it personally, as many do, but FDR's impenetrable self-containment puzzled him.

I told him he'd just been raised this way, a custom of his privileged class. His office also demanded caution and restraint, particularly in wartime. Bruenn agreed with both points.

But by now I suspected the roots of FDR's isolation ran deeper, to some undiscovered reason for his distance from those in his life. I recalled how I'd been affected by my introduction to mortality, courtesy of Big Bill Blood.

This gave me a new line of inquiry. But how to dig discreetly into the past of such a private man—the most famous man alive—presented difficulties.

Start with his heart, I decided. And keep it to yourself.

• • •

During our third week, the Boss received the only person with whom he'd ever shared his private self. Anna and I had arranged for Lucy to call for a day and night, driving down from her South Carolina estate with members of her family.

I told the staff of the Boss's long social friendship with Lucy and her late husband. This made it unnecessary—within Baruch's domain—to maintain the fiction of Mrs. Johnson. Dr. Bruenn knew nothing of their story, but the night before Lucy arrived he found the Boss in high spirits, working on a diagram to arrange seating for our meals. He placed Lucy to his right hand for both lunch and dinner.

After our lunch the next day, on the quiet verandah, Franklin and Lucy spent an hour together. From a distance Bruenn took note of their chemistry, and asked me how they'd grown so close. He didn't add "with another man's wife," but I sensed he was thinking it. I told him that before her marriage Lucy had worked for the Roosevelts, so the Boss felt no need to put on a show for her.

This was truer than I knew. Lucy told me later this was the hour she became—before anyone else in his life—the first to learn FDR knew perfectly well he was much more seriously ill than anyone had dared to tell him.

He didn't blame them for keeping him in the dark. He knew they sincerely believed the stress of his knowing might weaken or discourage him. He had his own reason: If his loved ones knew that he knew that they knew, he thought life would be too difficult for them. Although he remained grateful for Bruenn's intervention, FDR told her that living or dying no longer mattered. That was in the hands of his maker.

His only concern, Franklin told Lucy, was to finish the job he'd started: winning the war.

Late May, Early June 1944

Churchill pressed the Boss to join him in England in early June: The curtain was about to go up on the Main Event, a moment he wanted them to share. FDR's health had markedly improved by the time we returned to the White House; brown as a berry, looking as fit and relaxed as I'd seen him since Christmas.

As days passed I realized that beneath this veneer his legendary drive had not. Including our morning work the Boss stuck to Bruenn's limited schedule: Four hours a day maximum, and he was spent by the end of them. He sent regrets to Winston; the job demanded he stay home.

Anna became her father's guardian and defender, and enlisted me to protect him from any impulse to push. This put us at odds with Eleanor, who believed no one should yield to frailty when urgent work remained undone. She made those demands most ruthlessly on herself, which often kept her away from the White House.

But Eleanor pushed Franklin hard whenever she felt there was more he could do, and she always felt that way. She was used to ignoring anyone who stood between her and her husband, but through this difficult spring, Anna held her at bay and kept the peace.

We continued to arrange stolen hours for the Boss and Lucy. His calendar in May included two weeks in Hyde Park, a visit to Warm

Springs, and a weekend at Shangri-La, the Maryland retreat later known as Camp David. Lucy joined him at all three.

Among his limited appearances in Washington, FDR endured a visit with our most vexing ally: General Charles de Gaulle, the imperious, petulant, self-anointed leader of the Free French. A hero of the Great War, he'd fled to London when Hitler took Paris. From exile, de Gaulle had become an inspiration for La Résistance, the courageous men and women fighting undercover in France.

As far as the Boss was concerned, he thought "the grand asparagus"—a nickname de Gaulle had earned in military school—was a nut. He'd made himself a huge pain in the neck during our liberation of North Africa's French colonies. Now La Grande Asperge complained no one had asked him to approve our plans for the Main Event. He told anyone who'd listen that our refusal to let him lead the first Allied troops across the Channel—à la Washington crossing the Delaware—was a grievous affront to his dignity, which usually preceded his imposing nose into a room by a good ten seconds.

"De Gaulle's problem," the Boss told me, "is he seems to believe he's the reincarnation of Jeanne d'Arc."

But when we finally granted him a White House visit in May, even the Big Asparagus came to heel before FDR's charm. He still moaned to the press that we'd refused to recognize him as "president of France in exile"—a job he'd never held or run for—but he settled for what FDR gave him: de facto authority over all liberated French territory. There was precious little of that to date, but de Gaulle left the White House preening.

"His role will be, when the time is right, for the French people to decide," said FDR once he was gone. "And to them I say, God speed."

The most nettlesome issue that cropped up during our weeks at Hyde Park was a kerfuffle involving the navy and local fishermen whose livelihood depended on working a fertile stretch of the Hudson around Springwood.

Our pescadores were up in arms because a PT patrol boat had snagged a shad net in its propeller and dragged it upriver. Once the

Boss intervened on behalf of the workingmen, the Coast Guard retrieved and repaired the damaged net. FDR told the fishermen to confine their work to the waters south of Springwood.

Solomon ruled and once again all was right with the world in Hyde Park. Now he gathered his strength for the night the curtain went up on act three.

June 6, 1944

In late May the battle for Italy broke our way. After a fierce four-month siege the Nazi stronghold, an ancient abbey atop Monte Cassino, finally fell on May 18. The road to Rome turned into an open highway.

Our bombers and fighters exacted a fearsome toll on their retreat north along the peninsula. The twisted maze of burning trucks and tanks they left behind became the last obstacle slowing our advance. On June 4 American forces entered Rome, greeted as joyful liberators. The first of three world capitals that had fallen to the Fascists again belonged to its people.

Mussolini wasn't around to see it. After his arrest the previous fall, Hitler sent commandos on a daring airborne raid to rescue Il Duce from a mountain compound held by Italian loyalists. Instead of letting him flee into exile, Germany propped him up as leader of a fictional Italian Social Republic in a remote resort town. "Fascism's Poppa" was, in fact, under house arrest by German storm troopers, and under threat from all directions.

"I am little more than a walking corpse," he wrote.

• • •

During a fireside chat on the evening of June 5, FDR announced to the world that Rome had been freed from twenty-five years of Fascist rule. He gave all credit to our soldiers and praised Italy's contributions to Western civilization down the ages. We had spared Rome from destruction; Italy's Republic now rejoined the family of free nations who would share the burden of her repair. He closed by making it clear this fight—at seventy thousand casualties, our costliest yet—was only a prelude for greater challenges to come.

Our circle sat with him as the Boss delivered these powerful fifteen minutes. I noticed Anna and John holding hands; both had made key contributions to FDR's speech.

John had served with distinction as director of Civil Services for liberated Italian cities. His confidence had blossomed and he'd been promoted to lieutenant colonel. Although he seemed a hardy soul, John suffered from crippling self-doubt. I'd known him since before he'd met Anna; his fragility compounded the strain he felt as the only man who'd married a Roosevelt. Any son-in-law alive would've struggled under those pressures. Separation had been hard on the young couple, and I hoped his new Pentagon job proved rewarding. This night seemed as fine a moment as he might have experienced in their marriage, if not his life.

Given the great news he'd delivered, FDR seemed subdued afterwards. I gave him the short whiskey he had asked for and noticed his hands shaking. Anna wheeled him up to bed shortly after the broadcast. What the Boss knew, I had learned in the previous hour.

Victory in Italy marked the end of the war's second act. Many leagues from Rome, on the western edge of Europe in the middle of the night, the curtain was already rising on act three.

• • •

The invasion had been set for June 5, but after consulting with meteorologists General Eisenhower delayed the launch because of a passing storm. We wanted calm conditions to cross the tempestuous Channel by air and sea; the next day's forecast offered a window of hope. We'd gone to bed deferring our dread for another day. Unlike millions of American, British, and Canadian families who remained in the dark, the next night sleep would be harder to come by.

When he retired FDR told Eleanor the news. She asked the switchboard to call her first so FDR might rest a few more minutes. She lay awake all night until the call came at 3 AM. She went to Franklin's room, woke him, and put General Marshall on the phone. The Boss sat up, put on glasses and a sweater, and the Longest Day began.

At four operators woke the rest of us on staff. I'd spent the night on my office couch tossing and turning. I switched on the radio as I dressed and heard the news as it broke to the world; bewildering, almost surreal, as if I was dreaming. Newsmen knew only that the show was underway. I knew more; grim, awful news lay ahead.

I knew, for instance, that my nephew Warren aboard the USS *Borum* had days ago learned their role had changed. Destroyer escorts had been built as submarine killers. When they formed up for the invasion, the navy was short two minesweepers to clear lanes through offshore German minefields.

On June 6, the *Borum* and a sister ship sailed toward Normandy three hours ahead of the fleet along with four sweepers. Escorts relied on sonar to spot mines lurking below the surface, but many had been magnetized and sent to the bottom, where they could be triggered by any metal hull passing overhead. A sweeping cable strung between our ships carried an electrified wire that could disable those magnetized mines. In theory.

The men on board would have heard passing overhead an endless phalanx of twelve thousand fighters, bombers, and gliders headed for France. They baffled engines, inching forward in darkness and near silence, enemy guns on shore so close they had to whisper. If successful, they would ease back out of range to wait for the invasion.

When skies lightened on June 6, Frosty saw no enemy ships in front of them. Looking aft, the largest armada in human history, seven thousand combat ships, steamed toward them. On the day he turned twenty. Once the armada came within range of the Normandy coast its big guns opened fire on Nazi positions shooting at them from cliffs above a stretch of beach code-named Omaha. The rest of the day would be a riot of constant thunder.

I had a second nephew on a landing craft headed for Omaha. This rectangular flat-bottomed boat could glide up and drop soldiers at the water line. Each carried a thirty-six-man platoon, or jeeps with a full command squad, even small tanks. Captain Bill McNamara, First Army—who'd fought with distinction at Kasserine Pass—was now an artillery officer in charge of reconnaissance. He and his squad were going in with the first wave, to spot positions so our guns that followed them ashore could shell Nazi positions miles inland by midday. In theory.

Four miles of broad beach on Omaha led to the base of six-hundred-foot cliffs, where the Nazis were dug in and waiting. My nephews and their families in Vermont—my closest living relations—were much on my mind as I joined the president in the Oval that morning at 5 AM.

• • •

Over coffee the Boss briefed those of us who'd gathered. Since General Marshall's call he'd been in constant touch with the Pentagon. He outlined the size of Overlord, and we heard these startling numbers: over three million soldiers taking part on six beaches across a sixty-mile front. Thirty-nine divisions of soldiers, sailors, paratroopers, and airmen; twenty American, fourteen British, three Canadian, one Polish, and one Free French naval group . . . sans General de Gaulle.

I went to work distributing the president's first official statement. He followed that up with a recitation of facts on the radio: The entire country and free world spent D-Day glued to their radios. Places of worship filled in every city, town, or village for prayer. Millions went to work as if it were any other Tuesday, but few did more than focus on the unfolding story. Papers issued fresh editions every few hours, snapped up by tens of thousands who left work to gather in the streets.

As morning dragged on, hard news remained limited, creating a mix of hope and dread with little to relieve or confirm our fears. Only our ships offshore kept steady radio contact with Allied headquarters in England.

Eleanor came in midmorning. She mentioned she'd just heard a frontline sweeper had gone down after hitting a mine. I felt the blood drain from my face and she noticed my response; I said my nephew, whom she'd met at the White House in April, was on one of those ships.

During these agonizing hours there was little more to do than wait. FDR briefed congressional leaders and our top military men. He seemed calm, focused, and on top of his game. We learned that of Normandy's five beaches—Sword, Juno, Gold, Omaha, and Utah—the resistance we'd encountered was by far the worst on Omaha, the one being attacked almost exclusively by American divisions.

Near noon a reliable report reached us that British infantry had established a foothold on the easternmost beach—Sword—nine miles from the central hub of Normandy's capital, Caen.

Soon after we learned that on the next beach—Juno—crack Canadian divisions, over twenty thousand men, were driving Nazis back in door-to-door, hand-to-hand combat through a string of fishing villages.

But still no good news from Omaha. Its steep cliffs were the highest ground on the peninsula and its most defensible real estate. Ships shelling those ridgelines remained under intense attack from German guns and strafing runs from Luftwaffe fighters. Rough seas had created a fouled tangle of boats, most of which reached the beach nowhere near their designated landing spots. Densely laid defenses of posts, gates, and steel beams forced many others to lower their gates so far from shore men who stepped off with hundred-pound packs sank like stones. The sea claimed as many lives as that hailstorm of bullets raining down from the cliffs.

When not on the phone, I spent the morning at FDR's side. Mrs. Roosevelt came back in before noon, saw me in the mix, and came over, God bless her, to tell me the name of the sweeper that had gone down: not the *Borum*, but one of her sister ships. Seeing my relief she took my hands in hers. I had trouble finding words—this did nothing to change the loss of the other ship's crew—because I knew she would have been prepared to comfort me had it gone the other way.

I heard FDR plead with General Marshall on the phone to tell him the moment we'd heard from any soldier who made it onto Omaha alive. When he hung up on impulse I told him my nephew Captain McNamara had been headed for Omaha. Given my faith in Charlie as a soldier—he'd won the Silver Star in North Africa—I felt his chances were as good as any man's that day. And given his assignment, I knew his squad would have a radioman.

The Boss jotted a note and handed it to me. "Call this number, say it comes from me: 'Make all efforts to contact Captain McNamara, First Army, and reply ASAP.'"

The Boss went to take his only break of the day, a brief lunch alone with Anna under the magnolias outside the Oval. I hustled to a phone and called the number he'd given me. An officer in General Marshall's HQ answered and I conveyed the president's order, adding that it should be shared with General Marshall immediately.

Two hours later, near twilight in Normandy, after our emotions had been buffeted and battered all day by the fortunes of war—which leaned, absent news from Omaha, toward hopeful—a colleague called me to a phone.

"General Marshall's office," he said.

I took the receiver and have no memory of what I said but I wrote what the soldier told me as he gave it in shorthand.

As words took shape on the page an eerie feeling I had no name for swept up my spine to the base of my skull. I thanked the officer, hung up, and saw the president at his desk and on the phone. I walked to him, notepad in hand.

He registered my expression and said, "I'll call you back." He hung up the phone and gave me his attention.

"They got through to Captain McNamara," I said.

About to hand him the message I remembered it was in shorthand, so I read it to him.

"'Action heavy here. Casualties high. Pockets of men gathered behind dunes below the cliffs. German defenses and fire overwhelming. Awaiting engineers to breech. Two miles to our right Rangers scaled Pointe du Hoc. They're flanking the guns above us. Position secured. Believe worst is over.'"

The president slapped his hand on the desk and called out the news to the room. A cheer went up. His cigarette tilted skyward, and he shook my hand heartily. He noticed something lingering in my expression.

"What is it, Bill?"

"Radioman must have told him our request came from the White House. He added something, meant for you."

"Tell me."

I didn't need my notes. "Captain McNamara's closest friend is a captain in the same unit. They went through basic together and survived Kasserine Pass. He was best man at Bill's wedding, which is where I met him. They came ashore in separate boats but found each other on the beach."

"Isn't that something?" said the Boss.

"Sir . . . that man is your cousin Quentin . . . Quentin Roosevelt the Second."

I saw a dawning wonder cross his face akin to what I'd been feeling since the message reached me. The Boss put a hand on my arm; neither of us could speak for a moment.

Quentin was the son of General Ted Roosevelt the Third, Uncle Ted's oldest. Born sixteen months after Ted's boy Quentin died in France in 1918. This Quentin was his namesake. Wounded by enemy fire at Kasserine Pass, he'd worked his way back to take part on D-Day.

"The Lord works in mysterious ways," I said quietly.

The president slowly nodded, then a rush of people reacting to the good news from Omaha converged around him. I stepped back, saving a cherished place in my memory for this stunning coincidence.

The explanation I later settled on to define my feeling was a concept from antiquity: fate.

The Greeks would have said that with the offering of this sign at that moment on a day when we most dearly needed it, fate had decided to grant us fortune's favor.

• • •

I watched from the back of the room as FDR held his only press conference on D-Day late that afternoon. He told the entire press corps to squeeze in around the Resolute desk, many huddled on the floor. The Boss's confidence calmed this famously fractious bunch. When he finished his statement, I heard something from the White House press corps I'd never experienced: dead silence. It occurred to me my former brethren might be sensing the presence of what I'd felt earlier. We had entered a crossroads that might change the course of history.

The president handled their questions with humor and candor. Fulsome in praise for our soldiers in the line of fire, asking for or assuming no credit for himself. We'd made a good beginning on this day, but he discouraged any overconfidence in our soldiers or citizens. The twelve hundred miles between Normandy and Berlin could only be won with equal measures of the persistence, courage, and sacrifice we'd given in abundance on June 6.

The answers he gave their last two questions lodged firmly in my mind. When asked his hope for the future on this momentous day, he said:

"Well, you know what it is, it's win the war and win it a hundred percent."

"Last question, Mr. President. How are you feeling?"

"I'm feeling fine," said the Boss with a final grin. "I'm a little sleepy."

With that he left them laughing.

• • •

The last words FDR offered the world on the night of our Longest Day came at ten o'clock that night. Without a trace of triumphalism or gloating, nothing that could serve as a rallying cry for our enemies. Words solemn and grave, and entirely his own. He'd shared them only with Anna and John and showed the page to me before the broadcast. I handed it back with nothing in my throat but a lump.

He'd nicknamed me Bishop as an assessment of my character, but I'd long suspected it also came from a trait we shared: a cleric's call to be of service. FDR always put his peerless oratory to finest use in moments that required a believer's faith, not by arousing fear, anger, or zealotry but by inviting us to believe in and embrace Lincoln's better angels of our nature. I didn't know a clergyman or pastor alive who could have given comfort to us as sincerely and skillfully as he did that night.

In doing so, FDR united more members of our human race, over a hundred million listening around the world, than had ever been engaged, before or since, in a shared act of prayer:

"Almighty God: Our sons, pride of our Nation, this day have set upon a mighty endeavor, a struggle to preserve our Republic, our religion, and our civilization, and to set free a suffering humanity. . . .

"They will need Thy blessings. Their road will be long and hard. For the enemy is strong. He may hurl back our forces. Success may not come with rushing speed . . . but we know that by Thy grace, and the righteousness of our cause, our sons will triumph.

"They will be sore tried, by night and by day, without rest until victory is won. . . . The darkness will be rent by noise and flame. Men's souls will be shaken with the violences of war. . . .

"For these men are lately drawn from the ways of peace. They fight not for the lust of conquest; they fight to end conquest. They fight to let justice arise, for tolerance and goodwill among all Thy people. They yearn but for the end of battle, for their return to the haven of home.

"Some will never return. Embrace these, Father, and receive them, Thy heroic servants into Thy kingdom. . . . And for us at home . . . whose thoughts and prayers are ever with them, help us, Almighty God, to rededicate ourselves in renewed faith in Thee in this hour of great sacrifice. . . .

"With Thy blessing, we shall prevail over the unholy forces of our enemy. Help us to conquer the apostles of greed and racial arrogancies. Lead us to the saving of our country, and with our sister Nations into a world unity that will spell a sure peace, a peace invulnerable to the schemings of unworthy men. And a peace that will let all people live in freedom, reaping the just rewards of their honest toll.

"Thy will be done, Almighty God. Amen."

I haven't included all of them here, but later committed them to memory. Five hundred and twenty-five words. Twice the length of the Gettysburg Address, but I know of no other presidential speech delivered, in my lifetime, that deserves mention in the same breath.

• • •

The bitter facts of any war are culled and rendered down to bloodless numbers on paper of incalculable pain and sorrow. The cost of our first day at Normandy came to this:

British forces at Sword Beach, Gold Beach, and elsewhere: four thousand killed, wounded, or missing.

Canadian divisions at Juno Beach: 946 casualties, including 335 dead.

US Fourth Infantry at Utah Beach: only 197 killed or wounded out of 21,000 deployed.

The US First Army on Omaha Beach: 1,465 killed, 1,928 missing, and 6,603 wounded.

German casualties on June 6, never exactly accounted, were believed to roughly match ours. By the time the fight for the Normandy Peninsula ended with the capture of Caen six weeks later, over twenty-two thousand German soldiers were in their graves and over two hundred thousand had surrendered.

In those six weeks over a million Allied soldiers followed the first wave to the shores and ports of Normandy.

The battle hinged on Omaha, and Omaha turned on the bravery of 225 men of the Second Ranger Battalion. By rope, hook, and ladder they scaled the cliffs at Pointe du Hoc under withering fire to silence German artillery and bunkers along the ridge above Omaha. Thirty gave their lives, which allowed the five-hundred-plus Rangers who followed to redeem their sacrifice and those who'd paid in blood on the beaches below.

• • •

The Boss retired not long after his radio address. A double shot of whiskey calmed the nerves. Before retiring Eleanor told me, after Anna took him up, how pleased she was that her husband seemed himself again.

I placed a last call that night before returning home. Near midnight I got through to the day's forgotten man, who'd led the effort to rebuild our armed forces since 1939.

"Did no one think to call you earlier?" I asked, after hearing mine was the first he'd gotten from HQ.

Harry Hopkins had spent the day reading every paper he could find, listening to the radio of his hospital room in West Virginia.

"Other fish to fry, pal, no hard feelings. I've been on the bench too long."

"Sorry it took me till now—you're back on your feet, right? Still on the mend."

"Sure, sure. Early July, that's what they say, if the chief has any use for me—"

"Stop that, now, you know he does—"

"I know, I know, don't worry, rotten joke. Last thing anybody needs is a mope. . . . The old man really came through, didn't he, Bill?"

I couldn't speak for a moment. "As only he can."

"Least he won't have to hear any more bitching from the Brass that we should'a done this two years ago."

"Water under the bridge."

"Never hear any complaints that William the Conqueror waited to cross the other way till 1066, do you?"

I laughed. Who else but Harry would've seen it that way?

"It's all in the hands of history now," he said.

June and July 1944

The mood after D-Day remained buoyant. We spent the following week with FDR in Hyde Park, along with an assortment of displaced European royals, frequent guests during the war. Eleanor, Anna, and her kids came along for a full-on *Swiss Family Robinson* summer vacation.

A small development that pleased me to no end: The First Lady began using the bedroom of her late mother-in-law, Sara—gone to her reward three years now—as her office. About time Eleanor had her own place in the old house.

Combat reports poured in from every front. Our push inland after D-Day had been slowed by German counterattacks amid dense, impenetrable hedgerows in the boggy Norman countryside. Slowed but not stopped. Elsewhere east and west the fight turned in our favor.

With thousands of our new P-51 Mustang fighters operating from liberated French airfields, our control of the skies over Europe became absolute. In the Pacific, we clawed back the Mariana Islands and Guam; airfields there would allow our bombers to reach Japan. The same week we busted into the countryside beyond Normandy's hedgerows, British and Canadian forces captured Caen. General Patton took command of the Third Army on August 1 and set his sights on Paris.

Our ships that had taken part in the landings cleared the seas off

Western Europe. My nephew Frosty on board the *Borum* regaled me with stories of rescuing downed Allied fliers from the North Sea, and assaulting the last Nazi strongholds on the Isle of Jersey.

I got word that my nephew Captain McNamara had been awarded a second Silver Star for his actions on D-Day. Bill had crossed back and forth from cliffs to the waterline five times under heavy fire, leading survivors to safety. (He'd had to threaten at one point to shoot them if they didn't move, which, Bill wrote, "did wonders to clarify their situation.") He'd also picked up a Bronze Star for his heroics at Kasserine Pass that, at the time, he'd been too modest to mention.

This good news put the Boss in the "pink." Dr. Bruenn seemed to be humming the same tune as the unsinkable Admiral McIntire. Two days after returning to Washington, a prize piece of legislation finally reached the Boss's desk. He'd proposed it as the solution to a dilemma that had dogged every civilization since the fall of Rome: finding a way to reward soldiers who'd risked their lives to defend us after their service.

The Servicemen's Readjustment Act of 1944—known ever since as the GI Bill—addressed our veterans' needs in ways as radical as the New Deal. Continuing education that would have remained out of reach for most returning soldiers was offered for anyone who'd spent ninety days in uniform. To cover the steep cost of reentering private life: a full year of unemployment benefits. And low-interest loans were made available for housing, or starting a business or farm. Eight million veterans benefited over the next thirteen years, easing the way for a decade of postwar prosperity with few equals in history.

FDR borrowed my pen. I felt prouder to watch him sign this bill than any other I had set in front of him.

• • •

Harry made it back to Washington after the Fourth of July, but wasn't ready for the daily grind. He had the energy to put in a few hours from home, but that was it. As I feared, Harry felt demoralized when the Boss didn't immediately turn to him on everything as he had for years. I stopped by his place in Georgetown to reassure him at least once a week.

"Your job now is getting yourself strong enough to stand the gaff," I said. "The Boss wants you back, but he needs you healthy—"

"I told you this would happen, I predicted it, you heard me, this is what he's like—"

"What was he supposed to do, Harry, sit by the phone waiting for you while the world's on fire?"

He paced, clothes hanging off him, brittle and vexed. "Look, I need to talk to him; if he's gonna run again the convention's in three weeks. There's no way he can keep Wallace on the ticket now, he'll get clobbered; somebody's gotta tell him that. Harry Truman's the man he should be looking at."

He was right about Vice President Henry Wallace, as it turned out. Truman too, for that matter. He'd known and trusted the junior senator from Missouri since 1933, but the Hop was in no shape to lobby for him yet. I left more worried about him than when I got there. When he gave in to darkness his demons took over, and that might be the end of him.

I turned to mutual friend General Marshall, who made a house call and gave Harry a booster shot of discipline; a version of the message he dispensed to wounded veterans once a week:

"If you wish to be of further use to our country, your first job is getting your health back in order."

Harry took Marshall's "order" to heart and cooled his heels at home a few more weeks.

But the point Harry had made about the Boss's pragmatism stayed with me. Their friendship would last, come what may, but I wasn't sure if Harry would be able to give the Boss the help he needed again. At this point, that was the only thing keeping Harry alive.

• • •

Turned out FDR agreed with Harry about his vice president. Like his predecessors, FDR selected his VPs solely for their strategic political value. He otherwise considered the ceremonial duties of the job itself "about as useful as a bucket of warm piss."

Sensing a conservative shift in the nation's mood, he worried that Henry Wallace's soft spot for Socialism was about to become a liability. Weeks before the convention, the Boss had me write the Democratic National Committee, letting them know he had no intention of running again, but if the Party saw fit to offer him the nomination he would accept "like a good soldier." And if chosen by the people again he would serve. That was all he'd say on the record.

FDR faced no opposition for the nomination before or during the Democratic Convention in Chicago. Focused on the job at hand, he didn't even make an appearance, accepting the nod by radio from his train in San Diego. He was about to depart for Hawaii for crucial meetings on the war in the Pacific.

The one question remained: Who would run as his vice president? The Boss's instincts about his VP, who'd been a capable secretary of agriculture and loyal New Dealer, were correct: The Party now dismissed Wallace as a Russian-speaking intellectual gadfly, infatuated with the Soviet Union's ideology.

With the end of the war in sight, any clear-eyed strategist knew that in its aftermath democracy would be arm-wrestling Communism for leadership of a new world order. Given concerns about FDR's health, if the unthinkable occurred during a fourth term and this VP took over, Wallace looked far too pink to play hardball with the Reds.

A day after FDR's nomination, the Convention voted for vice president. The Boss did not identify his preference. Instead he floated four names—including Wallace—and privately told all four they were his pick. The odds changed every hour right up to the gavel on the first ballot.

Wallace won the first round but fell far short of the number needed to confirm. When also-rans and favorite sons dropped out, the Party started throwing its weight around, but their favored dark-horse candidate—the junior senator from Missouri—told them he didn't want to be seen coveting another man's job and refused their overture.

The Boss leaned in with a bit of gamesmanship: He told Party leaders to bring the man into a meeting in their Chicago hotel suite. All of a sudden a "surprise" call came in from FDR. They put him on speaker so he could ask:

"So what's the holdup? Do you have that other fella lined up yet?"

Without saying he was there, they told him this fella—standing there, gobsmacked—was still refusing to take the job.

FDR blew his top: "Goddamn it, Bob, then you tell him from me that if he wants to wreck the Democratic Party in the middle of a damn war that's his responsibility!"

He slammed the phone. The junior senator paced the room, trying to compose himself. They waited for him to speak—but put yourself in his shoes for a second and see what you come up with.

The chairman called the hall and ordered the second ballot to proceed. Twenty minutes later Henry Wallace was replaced by a man whose chance to join the ticket five days earlier had polled at less than 2 percent. A fella with no national profile, a reliable centrist, and Harry the Hop's first choice: a former haberdasher named Harry Truman.

After monitoring these shenanigans from my office, I reached the Boss on board the navy cruiser *Baltimore*. He was scheduled to set sail under blackout conditions just after midnight, FDR's tip of the cap to the old navy superstition against starting any voyage on a Friday.

The Boss said he'd just broken the news to Wallace about "the Party's decision." FDR let him down easy: If reelected, he promised to appoint Wallace to any cabinet position he wanted. Wallace asked for secretary of commerce, and the deal was done.

I asked the Boss how he felt about Truman. His answer was quick and practical.

"I hardly know the man," said FDR. "But if it keeps our Southern senators in line, he'll cost us fewer votes."

Harry did have a point about FDR: His pragmatism often had a chill of the Arctic about it. Before I could answer he asked me to draft a response to breaking news of an assassination attempt against Hitler:

A bomb hidden in a briefcase had exploded during a meeting in the corporal's Eastern Front bunker. Officers responsible—a cabal of military Prussian aristocrats—felt the Fascist madman leading Germany to its doom finally had to go. All it took was twelve years of worldwide slaughter, but aristocrats tend to be slow on the uptake.

The blast tore his fancy uniform right off the corporal's back, causing minor flesh wounds, but profound ones to his invincible pride. He would live to fight another day, and the coconspirators were summarily rounded up and shot.

"Had the corporal died," the Boss told me, "I would've canceled this trip and flown home, Bill. It would have led in short order to the end of the war."

I believe he was right. I also believe that if the corporal had died that day FDR would have declined to run a fourth time. Had the war ended before November he knew he would probably lose that election.

I asked instead: "Where did they go wrong?"

"Some damn fool moved the briefcase without knowing what was in it, damn the luck. But I'd rather get the bastard ourselves anyway."

• • •

Five days later, the *Baltimore* delivered the president to Pearl Harbor on Oahu to meet with his commanders, General Douglas MacArthur and Admiral Chester Nimitz. Two and a half years on, Pearl Harbor was once again home to our fleet; the Boss said the trip was worth it just to see how splendidly it had recovered. As he arrived news came in that after their latest defeat in the Pacific, Japan's

Prime Minister Tojo, the man who'd ordered the attack on Pearl, had resigned in disgrace.

From Hawaii the Boss's return would take him to the Aleutian Islands—just recaptured from the Japanese—and then Alaska. He wouldn't reach the mainland again until August 17. Republicans had just chosen a new standard-bearer to run that fall, a former prosecutor and first-term governor of New York, Thomas Dewey. In his first comments the dapper Dewey ripped the Boss sideways for taking what they called this "Hawaiian vacation in the middle of the war."

It was, I shouldn't need to tell you, no damn vacation. Momentous strategic decisions were hashed out while he was in Pearl. None of this made the papers because the army and navy were seriously at odds about how to proceed.

The fix came down to managing the monstrous self-regard of General MacArthur. Flattery was enough to get you anywhere with that titanic egoist, but the Boss agreed with MacArthur about our next move. Nimitz and the navy wanted to attack the Japanese stronghold on Saipan; MacArthur insisted on retaking his beloved Philippines. Unable to agree, they'd decided to split their forces and take on both at once. The Boss patiently nudged these two hardheads to compromise: Philippines first, then all hands against Saipan.

He did something more notable the next day that I heard about from Dr. Bruenn. Staging FDR's appearances to hide his disability had been job one since the day he took office. While visiting a military hospital in Oahu, FDR asked to be rolled in his chair through the ward treating vets who'd lost limbs. He stopped at every bed, offering a smile, a handshake, a word about home. His withered legs, for the first and only time ever, on full public display. He thanked each man for their sacrifice, but his more lasting message was left unsaid:

If I can do it, have faith that you can too.

As they left the hospital, Dr. Bruenn told me he saw tears in the Boss's eyes. If you think Thomas Dewey would've done the same, there's a bridge in Brooklyn I'd like to sell you.

After departing Hawaii, the *Baltimore* headed for our shared border with the Soviet Union, a key location from which to assess our postwar future. After visiting troops on our northern frontier, he sailed south to Puget Sound. The Boss was scheduled to give a radio address before coming ashore, where Anna and his train awaited.

I didn't learn until they reached Washington five days later of two serious incidents FDR had suffered on board. His health was nowhere near as robust as he appeared in the newsreels.

August 18, 1944

The day after returning, FDR invited Harry Truman to lunch for their first proper sit-down. Trailed by his new Secret Service detail, who struggled to keep up with him, Truman walked briskly from his modest apartment and arrived early. After small talk in the Oval, the men moved outside to the Boss's favorite table: under the canopy of the twin magnolia trees flanking the South Portico. The Boss favored this spot; those majestic trees had lived through much of our country's history, allegedly grown from acorns Andrew Jackson brought from Tennessee after his inauguration, to honor his wife who'd died suddenly days after his election.

The Boss also knew, because I'd briefed him, that Andrew Jackson was Harry Truman's political hero. And the story reliably charmed him.

FDR had a rare talent for making visitors feel welcome. Knowing Truman was the proud father of an only child—twenty-year-old Margaret—he asked Anna to join them. She graciously offered to reach out to Margaret and help her make the difficult adjustment to life in the White House bubble, a gesture Truman greatly appreciated.

Just before escorting press in to take photos of them together—another reason for staging lunch—I stopped by to ask the Boss a question.

They were discussing cars. Both were avid motorists, which I'd also briefed the Boss about. FDR told me he'd just learned the senator serviced and maintained every car he'd owned back to his first roadster. I liked Harry Truman up close. He was sixty but seemed a decade younger, trim, energetic, and fit. An artillery officer in the Great War, he was still a colonel in the National Guard. Truman had a nattiness about him that didn't seem fussy; he favored bow ties, which I frequently sport myself. Affable and unassuming, his reputation as a straight shooter of sound character seemed on the mark. When I left them, I found out almost exactly eight months later that their conversation had then turned to me.

The Boss liked keeping ceremonial get-togethers breezy. They didn't speak about politics, and hardly touched on the war. As I walked him out after they said their goodbyes, Truman seemed happy, but a touch nonplussed. He confided he'd been hoping for a clearer idea of what important role FDR had in mind for him. No so fast, Harry. He left instead with a single rose the Boss had me pluck from the Rose Garden, to give to his wife, Bess.

I found out later Truman told Bess all he'd heard from FDR that day was "a bunch of hooey." He said their lunch of sardines on toast and thin coffee was ghastly. The infamous Mrs. Nesbitt had again lived up to her reputation as the worst cook in town. Truman also told her he hadn't seen FDR in person since January's state of the union and frankly thought "he looked like hell."

So Truman had no idea about what the president wanted or expected of him if they won. The only advice FDR gave as they parted: He should officially accept the nomination from his home in Missouri, and he'd soon be in touch about the fall campaign.

Other than that he should stay out of airplanes till the election because FDR had told him, "I'm not a well man."

There's a confidence builder for you.

• • •

After their lunch I took a stroll in the Rose Garden with Anna, first chance I'd had since they'd returned the day before. FDR had come home with a deep shipboard tan, looking a bit leaner, and he'd seemed sharp as ever in Truman's company.

Anna told me she'd arrived in Seattle in time to meet the Boss on board for his radio speech. The circumstances had been badly vetted and the result was lamentable; the ship was lurching side to side in heavy rolling swells. Standing in his iron braces for the first time in months, he gripped the lectern for dear life to stay upright, holding its edges so hard he couldn't turn his pages. The result: He'd improvised his most rambling, lackluster speech in years. Worse, throughout those thirty-five minutes, the Boss endured agonizing chest pain. Dr. Bruenn took an EKG afterwards, and determined he'd suffered a bout of angina so severe it was a wonder he got through it. The national press ripped his speech to pieces, and Republicans gleefully pounced on him.

That wasn't all. A press pool photo taken while FDR spoke to the convention by radio on his train in San Diego had been published across the country. The president's open mouth, caught between words while leaning toward the microphone, made him look aged and haggard. We'd limited initial damage from it by playing up his effectiveness in Hawaii, but his bad hour in Seattle had brought the hoo-ha about infirmity back in play. During their train ride home to DC another development made it worse.

Anna showed me a copy of the latest *Look* magazine: An uncropped version of the same photo revealed that among those seated near the Boss that night was an unidentified Dr. Bruenn. An unwitting friend of Bruenn's at Mayo Clinic had called the magazine and named him. Bruenn's name then appeared for the first time in print as a "prominent cardiologist and a recent fixture in FDR's entourage."

The ammunition Republicans needed to make FDR's faltering health their argument in the election had just fallen into their lap. During August his poll numbers faltered. More disheartening from my vantage point, after returning, the Boss's energy sank with them. Our work slowed to a crawl.

The only sign of his usual good humor came the week before

Labor Day. At the end of that day he handed me a wrapped gift. Having reached an age where such joys are best unnoticed, I'd forgotten it was my birthday. He'd never failed to remember it.

Inside was a beautiful Florentine leather portfolio monogrammed with my initials.

"Make use of it, Bishop," he said. "High time a man like you start on his memoirs. That can hold your manuscript."

"Maybe I will," I said. "And maybe it will."

Which made me wonder if he'd somehow learned about my diary. Or perhaps he was suggesting—or giving me permission—to start one? But why?

Other than that, during the Labor Day weekend we spent in Hyde Park FDR seemed for all the world what Dewey and the GOP accused him of being:

An exhausted, unwell, listless old man.

The Final Campaign

Presidential campaigns traditionally began after Labor Day. The Boss gave Truman his marching orders and, ever the good soldier, he followed them, but the running mates never appeared together. The next words Truman heard from FDR wouldn't come until election night. The senator was game and able, but was starting to realize that, as far as the Boss was concerned, his job was the constitutional equivalent of a human appendix; functional, maybe, but no one could tell you what it actually did. He'd been, at best, the Boss's fourth choice. FDR, I could have told him—and later did—was a hard man who preferred making solitary choices.

As time often revealed, sometimes even when he wasn't even trying, he somehow made the right one.

• • •

The Boss had no time to campaign during the first weeks of September. First came a conference with Churchill in Quebec. Spirits ran high during their meetings; the Allies had driven the Nazis from Paris in late August. Their agenda focused on how to finish off the corporal before turning our full attention to Japan.

I joined them after a side trip in Vermont and a visit to our old family home, which I planned to restore and inhabit after my retirement. The

First Lady went along on this trip as did Winston's wife, Clementine. My first task was to escort them on a shopping trip, photographed for the benefit of both nations' Women's Sections. They got along splendidly, but it was clear Eleanor resented putting her vital agenda on hold for a public relations stunt.

The Churchills then traveled south with us to spend two days in Hyde Park. Eleanor was expected to play hostess to a swarm of visitors who descended—including the ever-ghoulish duke and duchess of Windsor—on the house she didn't consider home. She delegated many of these tasks to Anna, who handled the assignment flawlessly.

Harry Hopkins joined us for lunch that first day. I watched Churchill struggle to hide his dismay at Harry's deteriorating health. It also worried him that Harry job's as FDR's essential man seemed diminished as well. Harry tried to reassure Winston he was on the rebound, and would soon be back in his usual saddle. Harry seemed to be trying just as hard to reassure himself. From what I saw, Churchill appeared unconvinced.

On their last night, the president updated the prime minister on the Manhattan Project: A version of the bomb might be ready to test as early as next summer. With the Third Reich collapsing, both men agreed that if the test went well it could play a part in ending the war for good.

The Churchills left the next afternoon for New York and the voyage home. It was a melancholy parting; the Boss looked spent, and Winston couldn't hide his sorrow. FDR retired when they left and spent the next day in bed before we took the overnight train to the White House.

Harry Hopkins called me as I packed to go. A bit of the pot describing the kettle, he shared his anxiety about how weak and listless the Boss seemed.

"When's he going to campaign, Bill? For Pete's sake, that prick Dewey calling him a tired old man, how does the chief answer the little bridegroom on that?"

Harry pinned that nickname on Dewey after Uncle Ted's notorious blabbermouth daughter Alice Longworth said he reminded her of a "bridegroom on a wedding cake." Never failed to make everyone who knew Dewey laugh.

I couldn't disagree with Harry about FDR's exhaustion, or his lassitude about the election. The only reassurance I could offer was what the Boss had said to me about Dewey; he wasn't worried about a man he considered an opportunistic political lightweight.

"Dewey plays the part of heroic racket-buster like he's in one of those old gangster pictures," FDR had said, laughing. "Buster the All-American Boy talks to voters as if they were the jury and I'm a villain on trial for my life."

But Harry wasn't the only one in our circle worried now. General "Pa" Watson, who spent more time with him than I did, told me FDR "didn't seem to give a damn about things." In the following days Dewey continued landing shots about the Boss's age and fitness for office and so far they'd gone unanswered; FDR's sagging polls became a trend.

Until in one of those broadsides "Buster" Dewey made the biggest mistake of his political life. Bear with me.

When FDR first heard this whopper I saw a spark in his eye for the first time in months. He turned cagey and later that day asked me to accept an invite to address the annual meeting of the Teamsters Union in Washington. He also told me to have the Party quietly buy radio time on all three major networks: FDR's speech to the Teamsters would now be broadcast coast to coast.

Dewey had shaken the Boss awake and the country was about to hear his reply: He wrote this one word for word. My only suggestion: I thought it would play best after dinner, by which time the open bar would have them ready for the dessert he planned to serve. Full disclosure: I enjoyed a few tipples myself that night, but as a professional I stand by my reporting.

Family and friends took a table close to the dais, where FDR centered a panel of union grandees. I sat between Harry and Anna. As FDR was introduced, Anna nervously asked if we thought he was up to putting this across. He'd decided to speak from his chair, which he'd never done before, and this troubled her. I told her Dewey was about to be more thoroughly cooked than our rubber chicken.

His intro ended and FDR wheeled himself close to the microphones, waved and smiled and waited for their lusty greeting to subside.

"Well, here we are together again—after four years—and what years they've been! I'm actually four years older myself—which seems to annoy some people."

You could feel the room warming already.

"In fact, millions of us are eleven years older than when we started to clear up the mess that was dumped in our laps in 1933."

They cheered.

"So much for the 'tired old man,'" Harry leaned in to say.

Sensing he was in classic form, the crowd was ready to go wherever the Boss wanted to lead. He asked if they'd noticed, as he had, an odd change in our opponents: Republicans had developed a peculiar habit of trying to discourage more people each year—that is to say the "right" people—from exercising their right to vote.

"This time, of all the folks they could go after, Republicans are trying to stop our men in uniform overseas from casting ballots: They're trying to pass a law to do it! In the middle of a war in which these men are laying down their lives. One that, thank God, we're winning decisively. Guess they're afraid our boys might be feeling a tad too fond of their commander in chief—imagine that!"

They roared.

"They're also doing everything they can to hurt the working man. You know how it works: Then six months before every election they magically turn pro labor!"

A union leader stood and banged a silver serving tray with a ladle to lead that ovation.

"They've developed a nasty habit of offering you folks a steady diet of whoppers like this one: Buster the All-American Boy and his pals claim that in the 1920s, when they held the White House and majorities in Congress, they'd had nothing to do with the stock market crash or the Depression. It was all the Democrats' fault!" He paused. "I should call Herbert Hoover to tell him he's off the hook!"

Now they stood and cheered.

"As you know, the GOP also holds me personally responsible for failing to prepare our military for war. The same men who fought tooth and nail to keep us out of it now accuse me of failing to use my crystal ball to predict Japan's dastardly attack on Pearl Harbor!"

The cheers continued. Now came the haymaker. I put a hand on Harry's and Ann's arms.

Here it was: Tom Dewey had tried to exploit a ludicrous, unfounded rumor about the Boss's trip to Alaska. Heaven knows what lunacy dwelt in the mind who'd thought this canard would fly.

Americans, like our president, loved dogs. Two of the biggest stars of the day were Lassie and Rin Tin Tin, and the most popular member of the Roosevelt family was FDR's little black Scottie, Fala. His charm, intelligence, and impish humor were a perfect match to his master's. Fala had traveled the world with FDR more than any other family member, including FDR's recent trips to Hawaii and Alaska.

FDR gestured for quiet, and the room hushed.

"Now it seems these Republicans are no longer content to make personal attacks on me, my wife, or my family . . . they now include my little dog Fala. Now I expect attacks, and my family and I don't resent them . . . but Fala does resent them."

He glanced at our table and winked.

"You know, Fala is Scots, and being a frugal Scottie, when he learned that Republican fiction writers had concocted a story that I'd left him behind on some frozen Aleutian island and sent a destroyer back to retrieve him—at a cost to taxpayers of two or three or eight or twenty million dollars—his Scotch soul was furious. He's not been the same dog since!"

He waited for the laugh to crest and then topped it.

"Ladies and gentlemen, I'm accustomed to hearing malicious

falsehoods about myself . . . but I think I have a right to object to libelous statements about my dog!"

In the midst of the standing ovation that followed, Harry leaned over and shouted so Anna and I could hear him:

"After tonight, this election is Dewey versus Fala!"

As usual, Harry had it right. Anna embraced us as we stood with the crowd, not the only one with tears in her eyes.

FDR the Great Campaigner, just in the nick of time, had returned to the fray.

October 1944

After the Boss's triumph with the Teamsters, many of us thought he should send Fala out to campaign by his handsome little self. FDR himself waited two more weeks.

He sent me and two others to represent him at a funeral for his predecessor as governor of New York, Al Smith. The man the Boss had dubbed "the Happy Warrior" had died at seventy, after losing his wife of forty-four years.

As I sat in the pew during the governor's memorial service at St. Patrick's I offered my own thanks to Smith, who had resurrected FDR's political career.

A few years after finding Warm Springs, Al Smith asked FDR to put Smith's name in nomination for president at the Democratic Convention in Madison Square Garden. Making his first public appearance since he'd been stricken, wearing his braces and using crutches, FDR "walked" slowly and dramatically across the stage to the rostrum. The crowd went wild.

The dazzling speech he delivered benefited from a helping of "Roosevelt luck": This was the first political convention ever carried on national radio. Smith won the nomination but FDR's stunning return to public life won the night. The Boss had bought and expanded Warm Springs with a substantial portion of his inheritance; colleagues were calling him Dr. Roosevelt. At the same moment he was about to dedicate his life to that mission, the myth of FDR the Chosen One rose from the ashes.

But in order to head the 1928 Democratic ticket Smith had to leave his seat as New York's governor. FDR now emerged as the favorite to replace him. Smith assured the Boss he could govern from Georgia in absentia; they'd give him a seasoned lieutenant governor who'd do the real work.

Eleanor hated the idea, but his mother, Sara, swooned over it. When Democratic donors began writing serious checks to "Dr. Roosevelt's" noble enterprise, FDR said yes out of obligation to the Party.

I'd made it back to the States by then, abandoned my vow of poverty, and in my wisdom thrown every penny I had into a public relations company. But when I heard my old friend was back in the game, I paid close attention.

That election night, it quickly became clear Al Smith was on the wrong end of a landslide. He lost his own state to Republican Herbert Hoover by one hundred thousand votes. Predictions of a national Republican massacre sent FDR home early, prepared to begin his new life as director of the Warm Springs Rehabilitation Center.

At four that morning Sara Roosevelt woke her son to tell him he was the new governor of New York. Outperforming almost every other Democrat in the country, "the Chosen One" landed in the governor's mansion in Albany, where three previous presidents—including Cousin Ted—had served.

I wrote FDR a note of congratulations. He sent me back a warm and friendly response. I wouldn't hear from him again until Steve Early called me to the White House that morning in 1935.

President Herbert Hoover took office on March 4, 1929. Bruised by defeat, Al Smith expected FDR to perform as his figurehead while Smith continued running the Empire State.

FDR said, "Sorry, pal, those are the breaks." Smith turned on him for this, viciously, later even switching parties to campaign against him.

Which is why three of us from FDR's staff were in St. Patrick's Cathedral for Smith's funeral that day, and not the Boss.

Any debt he owed Al Smith had already been settled in full.

• • •

Now the fire was lit. FDR hadn't lost an election since his first run for vice president in 1920. He wasn't about to lose his last one either.

"People need to see me, Bill," he said. "They need to see for themselves I'm not at death's door."

To put those rumors to rest, the Boss started with a bang where voters knew him best. Two days later we took the overnight train from Hyde Park, key political reporters in tow.

We reached the Brooklyn Navy Yard at dawn on October 21. Eleanor joined Franklin in the first car of our motorcade; he in his thick navy cape, she wrapped in fur. With the top down and Secret Service on the running boards, we set out in a heavy mist that turned into a pelting, steady rain, the tail end of a late-season hurricane. I rode two cars behind the Boss in a closed car with Doc McIntire, who pitched a fit at the Boss riding in this downpour, and doggone it, this time he was putting his foot down. I smiled like the Cheshire cat.

His route had been heavily publicized, and crowds lining the streets grew larger and louder by the mile. When we reached Ebbets Field fifteen thousand were waiting in the foul weather, singing along—wise-guy style—as the Dodgers' organist played a hit from the Broadway smash *Oklahoma*: "Oh, What a Beautiful Mornin'."

During a stop under the grandstands to change into dry clothes, the Boss confessed to me—as a lifelong Yankees fan—this was his first visit to the home of the Dodgers. He planned to say he often rooted for them. I said all is fair in baseball and politics. Moments later, he drove through a gate across the outfield and up a ramp to a platform built over second base with a waiting bank of microphones.

FDR shrugged off his cape and hat, leaned forward from the back seat, and gave his good-natured confession to Brooklyn about their beloved Bums. When he finished his brief remarks a steady chant of "We want Roosevelt" followed us all the way out of the park.

The rain sluiced down for three more hours as we toured through five stops and fifty-one miles of the city. From the Bronx to the Battery, as word spread crowds surged every time we turned a corner, weather be damned. Ticker tape cascaded down from office buildings as we made our way down Fifth Avenue.

We stopped downtown so the Boss could put on his tux in Eleanor's Greenwich Village apartment, the first time he'd ever been there. After a rest and a shot of bourbon, they drove off to finish the marathon, a speech to a thousand more voters—old, white, mostly Republican—in the ballroom of the Waldorf Astoria Hotel on Park Avenue.

Feeling soggy and bedraggled in that black-tie affair, Grace Tully and I edged into the ballroom. I spotted more ossified remnants of Mrs. Astor's original Four Hundred—living ruins of the city's Gilded Age aristocracy—than you could shake a stick at. For a moment I worried that the Boss had picked the wrong crowd.

In the bar I met the city's police commissioner, Lou Valentine, who took me aside, wide-eyed, to tell me an estimated three million people had seen FDR that day. I slipped backstage, where the Boss awaited his introduction, to share the news. He was not displeased.

Neither was I. It didn't even bother me to reach my table and find Doc McIntire sitting to my left. In his surgeon general getup, looking oh so Gilbert and Sullivan, I found Doc describing to a dazed matron his humble role in maintaining FDR's exemplary health. To my right sat a pleasant, middle-aged Republican socialite. As we tucked into our salad she leaned in to share that she'd never seen FDR in person before and was terribly excited.

"Have you ever seen him?" she asked me.

"Once or twice," I said.

The woman actually sighed as FDR made his entrance to polite but dutiful applause. She thought he looked "splendid," bless her heart. The Boss proceeded to gently draw this uptown crowd into a kind of trance, using simple and plainly reasonable words about the price required of free countries to preserve the miracle of democracy.

I watched in wonder as he willed that ballroom full of gimlet-eyed upper-crust swells into his embrace. He surgically peeled the patriotic masks worn by native isolationists off their well-fed faces. I was pleased to see he had left a few of the more vile quislings present disarmed and squirming. And I had never heard him deliver a more serious speech greeted by such genuine enthusiasm.

Just a day earlier General Douglas MacArthur had repaid the Boss's confidence at their Hawaii conference. His forces had retaken the key island of Leyte. In typical Hollywood style, with cameras rolling, footage soon flashed around the world of MacArthur wading ashore and portentously announcing: "People of the Philippines, I have returned!"

A coincidence that only hit me eight years later, when General MacArthur made a swanky apartment upstairs in the Waldorf Astoria his permanent home.

In the throng making their way out after the speech, I rescued Grace in the foyer outside the ladies' room, cornered by a gaggle of grandes dames. A strapping Secret Service agent rescued us both. As we fell into step behind this bruiser, he carved through the crowd like a Notre Dame pulling guard to the hotel's private elevators.

We descended to a location I'd heard of, but always thought was mythical: a private rail line installed during the hotel's construction for use by tycoons who didn't want to rub shoulders in the lobby with the hoi polloi.

The elevator operator, a spry, long-winded geezer, greeted us as if he'd been manning his post since 1893 without much company. He gushed that the rail spur—a branch from nearby Grand Central—had only been used once in all his time there; by the crusty commander of our troops in World War I, General Jack Pershing, six years ago.

As he finished his docent's speech the brass gates opened, revealing the president's waiting train. The Boss, First Lady, and the rest of our party were already boarding.

After winning hearts and minds upstairs, here he was, archfoe of those privileged few enjoying this extravagant convenience. The man they'd once spurned as a traitor to his class.

The wheel had come full circle.

Within minutes we were out from under the Waldorf, heading north through the night in a jubilant mood. At our only stop, at Croton-on-Hudson, Eleanor and her lady friends departed to continue their trip by car.

The Boss was soon to bed in his berth, and so went I to mine. After this marathon one-day crusade, the election itself was only sixteen days away. Yours truly and many others in our party came down with lousy colds after that frigid October dousing.

I wrote this in my diary before retiring: "Yankees and Roosevelts hate to lose, and he was determined on both counts. His Dutch was up, he was mad as hell, and my fears and misgivings about his health had vanished like the morning mist."

The Boss was going to bury Tom Dewey and nothing would stop him now.

This election was in the bag.

November 7, 1944, Hyde Park

Over the years of FDR's presidency, Election Day in the village of Hyde Park had evolved into a series of comforting, small-town rituals for its favorite son.

The Boss felt so invigorated after his charmed day storming New York he spent the campaign's last two weeks blazing a wider trail. Traveling by train across the Midwest and Eastern Seaboard, he gave formal speeches at night, and whistlestop rallies from the rear of his car by day. He'd started exercising again and felt strong enough to deliver those remarks standing at the back of the train car in his dreaded iron braces.

In Chicago he spoke, by my calculation, to the largest crowd of any American politician ever; three hundred thousand people sardined inside and out of Soldier Field, buffeted by icy winds blowing in off Lake Michigan. In New York, a speech broadcast live from a packed Madison Square Garden, and at the last stop to Boston a standing-room-only crowd in the home of the Yankees' eternal foe, Fenway Park.

The next morning, Sunday, November 5, we pulled into Springwood at nine. Aside from an hour going over mail that had piled up in his absence, the Boss rested all day and retired early. Looking forward, he said, to the next day's sentimental journey.

Our three-car caravan assembled on the Post Road outside town, outnumbered by squads of following press. On a delightfully crisp sunny afternoon, we made a three-hour ramble through the Hudson River Valley, just as he had during his first run for state senate thirty years before and every election since.

The highlight: A stop at Eureka Shipyards on the banks of the Hudson, where the Boss thrilled a crowd of workingmen with a bold prediction; tomorrow night, he promised, local Republican congressman Hamilton Fish III would finally be sent packing after a quarter century of abusing his seat to benefit America's filthy rich. The crowd loved it, so did we, and the Boss was spot on. The next day Fish was finally cooked. In his self-pitying non-concession speech, he blamed FDR, the New Deal, and, naturally, Communism. A farewell devoutly to be wished.

At 10:45 that night, Franklin offered a brief fireside chat and closed with a prayer. Tomorrow, the people would return their final verdict. In fine spirits, the Boss retired.

I caught a ride into town and enjoyed a final tipple in the bar of my hotel. I conducted an informal poll among friends in the press corps; they predicted a resounding win for the Boss.

So did I and so I slept like a newborn.

• • •

We left the house just after noon on Election Day; FDR, the First Lady, Anna and John Boettiger, and the dog of the hour, Fala.

A chorus of Hyde Park schoolkids serenaded us with a rendition of "America the Beautiful"—nearly on key. The Boss let them pose for a photo with their real favorite—Fala—before entering Hyde Park Town Hall to vote.

Mrs. Roosevelt collected her ballot from the town clerk, a New England spinster who'd seemed superannuated to me in 1936. As Eleanor entered one of the room's green-curtained booths, Anna wheeled the Boss to the desk. The deadpan clerk, probably a Republican, barely glanced at him.

"Name?" she asked, in a gravelly baritone.

"Mr. Eleanor Roosevelt," said the Boss.

That earned him a side-eye. Part of their routine. He smiled pleasantly. From behind the green curtain we heard a familiar voice.

"Franklin, this darned machine won't work."

"You're only supposed to vote once, dear," said FDR, before turning to ask, "Give her a hand, would you, John?"

John Boettiger diagnosed that a cameraman's cable had snagged the curtain from closing and quickly sorted it out.

"Sorry," said the Boss to the clerk. "You were saying."

"Profession?"

"Tree farmer," he said.

He winked at us. Anna nudged me. The clerk sighed.

From the booth: "Thank you, John, it's working now!"

FDR leaned in to ask, "Think she'll vote for me?"

"Somebody has to," said the clerk.

FDR laughed. "We've got to stop meeting like this!"

"You first," she said, handing him his ballot.

"You know, if I lose this time, I'm coming home for good."

A beat. "I'll keep you in my prayers."

The Boss threw his head back and laughed as he rolled to the booth beside the First Lady.

"It's spelled R-double-o-s-e-v-e-l-t, Babs," he said.

"That's not helpful," she said.

Another hearty laugh and he wheeled inside. Anna closed the curtain and laughed.

• • •

We held a five-dollar pool on the final electoral tally. Hopkins put his money on 442, then cabled Churchill predicting a landslide. If he was wrong Harry promised Winston he'd underwrite the British national debt and join the Presbyterian Church.

Harry didn't join us for election night as he was in Washington with his wife and daughter, battling a cold. The good news for Harry: In the last few weeks, privy to me and a few others, he'd worked his way back into the Boss's confidence.

Mrs. Roosevelt opened Springwood's doors at seven as staff and friends gathered for the watch party. I'd overseen the installation of Associated Press and United Press teletypes in the octagonal smoking parlor just off the dining room. Grace Tully remained stationed there, on the phone with our election HQ in the New York Biltmore.

After East Coast polls closed, the Boss settled in at the head of the dining room table, Anna at his side. Radio on, both with pen and pad in hand, tabulating totals. I shuttled back and forth from them to Grace and the teletypes, passing the Boss numbers as they came in.

Many gathered around the big console radio in the library, but moved freely throughout the evening, the whole house in a confident mood.

Returns from major cities, always the first votes tabulated, augured well. The Boss asked me to ring Hyde Park's mayor, one of his old law partners, Elmer Van Wagner, to tell him we'd be receiving neighbors and villagers—another ritual of Springwood election nights—at eleven, an hour earlier than usual. FDR considered it bad luck to make predictions out loud until results were certain, but his implication was unmistakable.

I found Dr. Bruenn in the music room during a lull and sat beside him. He gushed about how much he'd enjoyed the campaign, radiating the glow of a rookie volunteer on the cusp of victory.

"How does he seem, Doc?" I asked, as we watched the Boss working.

"Bill, I examine him daily, and did again tonight. His BP levels are lower than before he went out on the hustings."

I smiled. "Isn't that something?"

"Eating well, sticking to his diet, getting plenty of sleep, and the digitalis has done wonders."

I sneezed and blew my nose, a relic of the cold I'd been trying to shake since New York. Bruenn laughed and said he'd just gotten over his.

"All those miserable, rainy days, exposed to the elements and not a single symptom. Seemed stronger than about anybody else on the train."

I wanted to say, "Let's see how he feels tomorrow," but held my tongue, patted his back and went to check the wires. When I showed the latest numbers to the Boss, he put a hand on my arm and smiled.

"Don't tell anyone yet," he said quietly. "This one's over, Bill."

With that the Boss put down his pencil. This election, our country's first in wartime since Lincoln had won a second term, was done but for the paperwork.

We bundled up and went out to join the First Family on the front patio. At eleven, the Hyde Park torchlight parade came up the drive. For a small-town boy like me, a happy relic of days gone by. After marching around while the band finished "Hail to the Chief," they gave three hip-hip-hoorays and the Boss offered some cheerful remarks.

"We're rightfully superstitious in these parts about 'counting our chickens.' But I can tell you it looks as if I may be coming up from Washington to see you all again for four more years."

The loudest cheers came from some boys who'd scaled an old sheltering spruce beside the drive. I pointed them out to Anna, and she alerted her father.

"I love it!" he said, waving at the lads. "Used to hide in that same tree whenever Mother was on the warpath."

The crowd headed back to town and the party began to thin, guests drifting off to home, or upstairs to bed. I hung around with the old regulars in the dining room, listening to the radio deep into the night. At midnight, someone sat at the piano and we serenaded the Boss with his favorite tunes, starting with "Home on the Range."

The numbers told it plain, but tradition demanded that chickens not be counted until the loser conceded. Would it surprise you to learn we had to wait until 3:16 AM to hear Tom Dewey's measly attempt on the radio? It pleased us to no end to learn he was speaking from GOP headquarters in New York: at the Roosevelt Hotel.

Young Buster did not, however, have the decency to send the "tired old man"—who'd just trounced him 432 to 92—any personal congratulations as courtesy required.

The Boss asked me to send Dewey a telegram instead: "I thank you for your statement, Governor, which I have heard over the air a few minutes ago."

"I'll send it right away," I said.

"PS: I would've called him myself, but this tired old man is going to bed. With my dog!"

The whole room howled. With Fala in his lap, the Boss headed for the elevator.

"The bridegroom will be back on his cake by morning and all's right with the world," I said, walking with him. "Good night, Mr. President."

The Boss shook my hand. His smile had a sharp and satisfied edge.

"I still think he's a son of a bitch," he said.

Our staff celebration was still going by the time I made it to my hotel at four. Unable to refuse the entreaties of my colleagues, the night was completely at odds with the day by the time I reached my room at 6:45 AM.

I found a telegram from Harry inside my door, offering back to me words I'd often said to him:

"Like always, the only people who want him are the voters. PS: I would've won the pool on the nose if my own damn state hadn't disappointed me. Again."

January 20, 1945, Inauguration Day

By Election Day, Harry the Hop was healthy enough for full-time work and back in FDR's good graces. Here's how that happened:

A serious crisis among our leaders had threatened the Alliance in early October. With an end to the war in sight, disagreements about what the Big Three wanted in its aftermath emerged. With the Boss busy campaigning, Churchill had proposed he meet with Stalin alone in Moscow to sort them out. The Boss hastily approved, and sent our Soviet ambassador, Averell Harriman, to represent our interests.

Harry was the only one close to FDR who cried foul. First, he said: Churchill's postwar goals for the world—and his British Empire—did not align with ours. Russia's ideological imperatives most certainly did not.

Second: Giving Stalin the idea that whatever he worked out with Churchill in FDR's absence was A-OK with the Boss could set in motion unintended and disastrous consequences. Sending Ambassador Harriman to join them, without any veto power, sent a message that FDR—and America—supported any conclusions they might reach.

Harry suggested the Boss needed to reframe this and fast: Tell Churchill and Stalin they had every right to discuss any subject they wished. But for God's sake don't give them the idea you'll rubber-stamp whatever they come up with.

Because Harry was still out of the loop, the next day he received a call from a friend—I'll confess: me—that the Boss had drafted and was about to send a vaguely worded cable to Churchill implying exactly that.

Harry didn't hesitate. He called the duty officer in the Map Room and learned this cable was about to be wired to 10 Downing Street. The Hop took the kind of preemptive action that had earned him FDR's trust for the past sixteen years. Given his long absence, Harry possessed no authority to kill the cable, but he gambled that the duty officer didn't know that.

He was right; the officer heard Harry Hopkins barking a direct, urgent order at him and put a hold on the cable.

Harry then rushed to the White House, and I walked him straight in to see FDR, who was shaving. Harry immediately came clean about what he'd just done and why. To his credit, after listening carefully, the Boss admitted he'd been consumed with campaigning and signed off on that cable without thinking it through.

FDR finished shaving and killed the telegram to Downing Street. He and Harry then composed and sent to both Stalin and Churchill this message instead: He had no objection to their meeting in the presence of Ambassador Harriman, but their talks must be strictly a prelude for a third summit between all three of them in the New Year.

The Boss then rushed a confidential cable to the capable Harriman drawing the line he wanted held: FDR demanded the right to withhold judgment on anything they discussed until they were all face-to-face, as they'd so successfully done before.

Crises averted.

The Boss didn't say thank you to Harry afterwards—not that Harry expected him to—but from that moment on the Hop was back in the saddle.

This is what made Harry the indispensable man. No one else ever had the guts and audacity to risk the wrath of the world's most powerful men in service of a greater good. Just as he'd been first to look past the false face of boyish American hero Charles Lindbergh and see his turn toward Fascism coming. His ability to see through the fog of the world's most complex characters remained unmatched, great men, tyrants, and feckless narcissists alike.

Harry's return to form could not have come at a better time. In the next few months, the Boss would never need the Hop more.

• • •

On Saturday, January 20, 1945, President Roosevelt's fourth inauguration took place on one of the coldest days in memory. An inch of snow had fallen and frigid temperatures prompted the Boss to cancel the usual parade and most of the traditional festivities. That was the only chill in the air that day. After booting the Nazis from Paris, we'd driven Germany's armies back to its borders. With Soviets closing in from the east, a noose was drawing taut around the corporal's neck.

After the election, the Boss had trained to Warm Springs for Thanksgiving. He intended to stay until Christmas, his longest visit since the war began. I went along with Grace, the inevitable McIntire, Dr. Bruenn, and other staff, but Anna, Eleanor, and the family stayed in DC. So the Boss invited his two favorite cousins to join him.

This was my longest stay at Warm Springs. Vast improvements to every part of the operation since my last visit astonished me. Over one hundred patients were being treated, including many service veterans. FDR's cheerful presence lifted everyone's spirits, most notably at the Thanksgiving feast he hosted for all staff and guests. His energies had flagged in the aftermath of the campaign, but Dr. Bruenn and I agreed spending hours each day with his flock remained the best medicine.

Then, the highlight: a two-day visit I arranged for Lucy Rutherfurd and daughter Barbara. The Boss had always taken tender interest in Lucy's only child, and she adored him. FDR had recently taken his cousins into his confidence about Lucy. For the first time, without Anna there to take the lead, both became involved in our subterfuge.

Laura "Polly" Delano, four years FDR's junior, was a flirty socialite he'd known since childhood; birds of a feather of wildly contrasting plumage. Polly was the clan's certified eccentric, living a life as only headstrong, charismatic, and wealthy women can. Although a social doyenne, Polly didn't give a damn what anyone thought of her; her passion was breeding Irish setters at her nearby Hudson Valley estate. She dressed like a diva, dyed her hair purple, loved whomever she chose but never bothered to marry, and became one of the Boss's closest intimates. He loved her bright nature, appreciated her counsel, and relished a good gossip. Polly was all in favor of Franklin's relationship with Lucy, just as she had been their first time around. She never hid her feelings about Eleanor, whom she considered an earnest, humorless scold and a dreadful match for her favorite cousin. For the record, Eleanor didn't think much of Cousin Polly either.

FDR's more distant cousin, on the Roosevelt side, Margaret "Daisy" Stuckley, was Polly's opposite number; an empathic, modest spinster devoted to the Boss. They connected in adulthood, after Daisy's immediate family fell on hard times. Eleanor invited her to tea when FDR was recovering from polio. Daisy's heart went out to her glamorous cousin, but their friendship didn't fully blossom until he entered the White House.

From then on when the Boss visited Hyde Park, Daisy became a fixture, and an emotional bond formed that he and Eleanor no longer shared. I felt certain Daisy would have wanted more, had FDR asked, but that was not to be, and she wasn't the sort to assert herself. She did, however, bring another great love into his life when she gave him a puppy named Fala.

I saw his cousins as a matched pair of opposites, salt and sugar. The two had grown into an odd-couple double act, supporting their cousin in complementary ways, but both grasped what Anna and I believed: Lucy was FDR's ideal companion and these innocent hours they spent together were giving Franklin a new lease on life.

The Boss cut short this stay in Georgia when the housepainter scraped together every resource he had left for a last desperate throw of the dice. He chose a weak point in the line we'd established on Germany's western border: Belgium's Ardennes Forest, through which Germany had invaded France in both World Wars.

On the dismal, overcast morning of December 16, Hitler sent 250,000 men and 2,500 tanks at that line across an eighty-mile front, and they smashed right through our weary, inexperienced troops, straight toward the city of Antwerp. The Allies had captured Belgium's primary port a month prior; our armies in northern Europe now depended on resources flowing through its docks.

We learned the corporal's half-mad scheme later: cut off and surround British divisions north of Antwerp to create a second Dunkirk. Negotiate a separate peace with England to guarantee their safe return and buy himself time to stave off American and Russian forces closing in from west and east.

Entirely, utterly mad, as I come to think of it.

FDR headed home, monitoring news from the front as we traveled, but never lost confidence in General Eisenhower's leadership. The Battle of the Bulge, as we soon called it—for the 101st Airborne's heroic defense of Bastogne, around which the Nazis "bulged"—raged for days, becoming the largest clash of the entire war by every measure.

The day we returned to Hyde Park, the tide shifted our way when leaden skies over Belgium finally cleared. General Patton's lightning-fast charge of his Third Army into Belgium stonewalled the Nazis cold. Our utter domination of the air turned the last act of this nightmarish fight into a one-sided shooting gallery.

The First Lady invited me again to Christmas dinner with the family. I sat beside her at the far end from the Boss, who was flanked by John and Anna. To my right sat dashing brother Elliott, on leave from the Air Force, about to become a brigadier general. Beside

Elliott sat the third wife he'd recently and hastily wed—a glamorous Hollywood blonde named Faye Emerson, whose work to date on the silver screen, I'll admit, had eluded me. Elliott's mother wore the disappointment of his latest matrimonial escapade on her sleeve, no translation necessary.

An otherwise delightful if subdued occasion. Holding court as paterfamilias, FDR looked worn and weary that evening. At least he didn't mistake Elliott's latest bride, as I'd done initially, for the "other Hollywood Fay"—last name Wray—who'd decorously graced the oversized paws of King Kong.

We opened presents after dinner. I was touched by the Boss's thoughtful gift to me: a beautifully printed and signed copy of his D-Day prayer. One of only a hundred made, I later learned.

• • •

Four weeks later, we huddled together on the White House's South Portico at noon on Inauguration Day. An audience of fewer than five thousand had braved the weather to attend. The Boss strapped on his iron braces one last time and, with no overcoat, managed a short walk to the podium on the arm of General Watson.

After outgoing VP Henry Wallace swore in his successor, Harry Truman, FDR took his oath for the fourth time. He then offered the shortest inaugural speech on record, a simple call for resolve to finish the job before us. From my angle, I noticed the Boss's hands gripping the podium, his knuckles bone white.

The whole ceremony took only a quarter of an hour. The occasion, the trappings, his speech, all brief, solemn, and austere, stripped of adornment, in the spirit of a nation still at war.

On my way to the reception inside, General Watson quietly put an arm on me and pulled me into a private parlor nearby. FDR lay flat on his back on a sofa, collar open, trying to catch his breath, attended by his oldest son, Jimmy, and Dr. Bruenn.

The Boss had been gripping that podium so he wouldn't keel over;

angina again, throughout his speech. A nitroglycerin tablet Bruenn had given him was starting to work as I entered. FDR asked for a stiff whiskey. Bruenn gave the nod and I poured half a tumbler at the bar. He told me later the booze worked as a vasodilator, increasing blood to his heart, medicinal.

We were aghast but the Boss treated the episode as a lark, chatting throughout—as he sipped whiskey—about a similar moment Cousin Ted faced during the 1912 campaign. As he spoke from the rear of an open car, on the way to address the Bull Moose Party's convention in Milwaukee, a madman fired a shot at Ted point-blank. Slowed by the fifty folded pages of his speech and a metal glasses case, the bullet lodged between his ribs. Teddy's white shirt was drenched in blood, but instinct told him it was a surface wound. He refused to go to a hospital, insisting they head to the hall so he could accept its third-party nomination for president.

"He gets there, opens his coat and vest to show them his bloody shirt, and tells them he'd just been shot," said the Boss. "Talk about grabbing an audience. Gives the whole speech, hour and a half—lightheaded from loss of blood—before he'll go to the hospital."

FDR drained the whiskey, his color returning from the ashen shade I'd seen on entry. He insisted he was ready to mingle and, with a laugh, waved off Pa Watson's attempt to discourage him.

"What am I supposed to do, Pa? Skip lunch with these nice folks who came to see me over an attack of the collywobbles?"

Seeing Bruenn didn't disagree, I offered no objection. FDR's faithful valet entered moments later, lifted the president into his chair, and tenderly retied his tie.

"By the way," said FDR, "that bullet stayed in Ted's ribs the rest of his life. Too close to his heart for surgery."

His valet pushed the Boss out, Jimmy and Pa Watson flanking him.

"Oh, did I tell you, Pa?" said FDR. "Just before he gives the oath Justice Stone leans in to say: 'Tell me, Franklin, isn't this getting just a wee bit monotonous?' Ha! Don't you just love it?"

He laughed, and I saw Pa Watson fail to hide a smile. The Boss headed into the largest reception he'd ever hosted at the White House; two thousand folks were waiting to see him, everyone from Bernard Baruch to Orson Welles and Rita Hayworth. As they wheeled out, Bruenn and I lingered in the parlor.

"Twenty-six years later," said Bruenn. "Still chasing Teddy's ghost. Is that what's driving him, Bill?"

"That's part of it. Not all."

Yalta

Two days later the president of the United States disappeared. All appointments canceled for four weeks, without explanation. Rumors abounded. The secret was so closely held even I didn't know where he was headed. All I knew was that FDR and his party left Norfolk at dawn.

Harry Hopkins had worked out the details for the Big Three's second summit. He'd left to do advance work in Europe days before, on the maiden flight of America's first official presidential plane. We called it the Flying White House, but its exalted security status earned it the code name Sacred Cow.

Harry kept an account of his journey that he later shared with me. He spent two days in London prepping Winston Churchill, then flew to Paris to soothe the perpetually vexed General de Gaulle, now calling the shots—ex officio—for France.

For Harry's courtesy, the Grand Asparagus lectured him ad nauseam on the slights he'd received from his "so-called Allies," whose blood had just sanctified and saved his beloved France. Not all of Harry's legendary charms—which had won the trust of Uncle Joe Stalin—could get through to this imperious caesar.

Harry then conferred in Paris with a buoyant General Eisenhower. His focus had turned to our coming assault on the German homeland across the Rhine. Ike possessed all the ease and confidence earned as a military leader that the graceless de Gaulle lacked.

Harry flew on for an overnight stay in Rome, where he met with Pope Pius XII. I was astonished to learn my friend, the extravagantly lapsed Iowa Methodist, then experienced in the Vatican something he described to me, the devout Catholic, as a religious epiphany.

I learned this later: Before leaving Harry had felt so fragile he'd written his daughter Diana on the eve of departure. He told her Mrs. Roosevelt had promised to look after her should he not return, and included a copy of his will. A will that made it clear the second most powerful man in America had hardly a penny to his name.

• • •

I determined by their absence who had boarded ship with FDR: McIntire, Bruenn, Pa Watson, Steve Early, our top military brass, and, crucially, making her first trip abroad with him at last, Anna.

Having achieved every ambition the Boss could aspire to, one remained: finishing the job. Twenty-five turbulent years had erased the memory of every statesman who'd failed to resolve the First World War. They'd succeeded only in making it the opening act for ours.

The Big Three would meet again, that much I knew: Stalin, an enigma and an unrepentant butcher. Churchill, for all his brains, guts, and courage, determined to preserve the British Empire. He lacked everything but vision. (De Gaulle, despite his tantrums, had not been invited.)

Which meant FDR had to lead and carry the day. Neither he nor Harry were in peak form. What the Boss did now to settle accounts for our last quarter century would surely define his legacy.

But who am I to ponder the imponderable? I simply asked God to give him strength, courage, and wisdom.

• • •

We threw ourselves into work at the White House without a word from FDR for a week. His ship—I'd learned he was aboard the heavy cruiser USS *Quincy*—traveled under destroyer escort and strict radio silence, as German U-Boats still roamed the Atlantic.

A week at sea, FDR celebrated his sixty-third birthday. Along with his morning coffee Anna greeted him with presents, an assortment of quirky gadgets, including one from Lucy: a sturdy cigarette lighter that could withstand stiff ocean breezes. Anna hosted dinner that night without a hitch, a rehearsal for the work awaiting her at the summit.

• • •

I spent FDR's birthday with the First Lady, filling in as she so often did, for a packed schedule of ceremonies. The Boss's favorite charity—one he'd launched a decade ago, collecting coins to help victims of polio—had grown into a powerhouse called the March of Dimes. (In case you've ever wondered why FDR adorns our humble ten-cent piece.) Rushing to multiple events to honor him and the work of Warm Springs, Eleanor worked each room we entered.

We returned to the White House to attend a lunch honoring the Boss and our war bonds campaign. Eleanor posed for pictures with every "sales rep" in attendance, a bevy of Hollywood stars with whom I tried my best to mingle. At close range, I found them a not-so-glamorous bunch, nor camera-shy either. With one exception: the delightful eight-year-old star of *Meet Me in St. Louis*, Margaret O'Brien.

One observation from the day: Eleanor was deeply upset she hadn't been allowed to go with FDR to the summit. Between events she told me that because of the blackout she'd been unable to even send a birthday message. I drew her out and learned Franklin had initially invited her to come, only to decide at the last minute Anna should go instead. She seemed to want to elaborate but checked herself and stopped.

"Seems to me, these past months," I said gently a moment later, "that Anna's learned to manage and look after him quite well. More than the boys could do."

After a pause she said, "I suppose that's true."

"He depends on you to represent him here when he's away, and you do in so many ways. I know he feels there's no one else who could manage that."

She nodded thoughtfully. "That's also true, yes."

"Perhaps, given difficult circumstances overseas, he feels that—"

"Daughters are less complicated than wives," she said, not happily.

I waited: "Anna mentioned the prime minister's daughter Sarah is coming with him."

"Clementine is not going, yes, that's true."

"What about Ambassador Harriman?" I asked, already knowing the answer.

Eleanor sighed. "His daughter Kathleen's going with Averell as well."

I said nothing more. Moments later she gave a more articulate sigh. I knew this exclusion cut to the heart of her eternal predicament:

Eleanor Roosevelt was as qualified to lead the United States as any man who'd ever done it, including her husband. She'd served our people as long as he had, strong, tireless, and capable in every task she'd taken on, whether on FDR's behalf or her own. A barrier to high office not even the most remarkable woman in our history could breach remained in her way.

Despite their innocence, her husband's meetings with Lucy that I'd helped arrange sat with me like a belly full of razor blades.

She remained graceful and tactful with everyone she met, high or low, throughout the day, which didn't end until she delivered a scripted radio message of appreciation from FDR to the nation for its kind remembrances.

She hadn't spoken to him since he left and would only do so a handful of times for the next five weeks.

• • •

We watched him in newsreels before we saw FDR again in the flesh. Near dawn on Wednesday, February 28, the First Lady and I met his train at the Fourteenth Street Station, after departing the *Quincy* at the Norfolk navy yard.

I went aboard. As I shook the Boss's hand my first thought was he looked better than he had in months. The voyage home had given him time to rest, a healthy tan, and an earned feeling of accomplishment. Deeper shadows made this a far more somber homecoming.

Also meeting us at the station: the wife of General Edwin "Pa" Watson, our beloved chief of staff. After a brief reunion with Franklin, Eleanor stayed behind with Mrs. Watson while FDR, Anna, and I went on to the White House.

Two days into the *Quincy*'s nine-day voyage home from a place called Yalta, where Stalin had hosted the summit at a war-torn resort in Crimea—General Watson suffered a sudden massive stroke. Pa lingered for two days and died without regaining consciousness. Anna told me FDR holed up in his cabin alone, depressed and inconsolable.

General Watson's casket was taken off the train and loaded into a hearse at Fourteenth Street. A devout Catholic, his widow rode with family members and their monsignor to a private church memorial that morning.

That afternoon with scudding clouds and a cold, steady downpour, Pa was buried with military honors at Arlington National Cemetery. At Mrs. Watson's request, along with Grace and Pa's loyal staffers, I stood under the grave site canopy with his widow and family.

FDR, Eleanor, Anna, and John watched from the Boss's car parked nearby. A bugle playing "Taps" never sounded more mournful. A more perfectly dismal occasion would be hard to conjure.

• • •

That afternoon, as we caught up on mail and signings, the Boss gave me a rough précis of the Yalta Conference. Late that night, after her parents had retired I sat with Anna and heard the rest of the story, a tale of courage and resolve, with a conclusion that left me in despair.

"What has he told you?" she asked as we sat before a fire.

"Just headlines, most of which I'd heard from Harry's letters. He spoke more about you. How grateful he was you were there. Not only did you see to every need, you managed his days to the last detail. Said he couldn't have done it without you."

She looked surprised. "Honestly?"

"He said you were 'remarkable,' Anna. You won over every person there. Churchill adored you. You got on with his daughter and Kathleen Harriman famously. You apparently had even Uncle Joe in the palm of your hand."

She smiled ruefully. Wiped away a tear.

"Did he . . . not tell you these things himself?" I asked.

"Some. Not all. You know how he is."

"Well, it's always seemed to me as if . . . words aren't needed much between you."

She sort of laughed. "Awfully nice to hear 'em every now and then, you know?"

I said that I did. She seemed in a mood to share, so I waited, then listened.

"We were never the same after his paralysis. He'd lost so much but never let us see it. People forget—well, you didn't—what a powerful, vital presence he'd been. How he'd throw himself at any challenge. Even after the illness, he'd get down on the floor with us, crawl around, show us how to slide down the stairs, making a game of it. I didn't realize, till years later . . . it was a fire drill."

"A fire drill."

"The only thing I think he was really afraid of."

"I see. Because of his legs."

"Even before he got ill. All my life, really."

Something hooked me, so I tugged the line. "Do you know why?"

She shrugged. "Maybe Mother or Cousin Polly would. Everything I did in Yalta, Bill . . . well, it was just common sense. I managed things, like I'm used to doing here. A lot happened that didn't make the newsreels. I'll tell you about it, if you're interested."

Of course I was.

"The crossing went fine. Watched movies every night, he napped, read, sat in the sun, enjoyed the crew. When we sailed into Malta, Churchill stood on the quay waving at us. He and Sarah came aboard. Spirits high, delighted in each other's company, great fun. We hosted them for dinner while we waited for the Sacred Cow to be serviced and fueled for the flight to Yalta. Harry'd flown in on it earlier that day, from Naples."

She took out a cigarette and I lit it for her.

"Harry didn't come to dinner?" I asked.

She shook her head. "I broke up the party at ten so he could rest before the trip. Went to pack. That's when Harry showed up. About ten-thirty. He'd been there all day but this was the first we'd seen him. His son Bob was with him, you know him, right, the photographer?"

"From Eisenhower's detail, yes."

"Terrific kid. Ike gave him leave to cover the summit so he met Harry in Italy. They came aboard together. Ed Stettinius was with them."

Ed Stettinius had weeks earlier become our secretary of state. He and Harry had flown down from Naples; both were going to the summit.

"How was Harry?" I asked, uneasily.

Anna hesitated. I saw a wince of distaste. "He'd obviously been drinking, Bill; came in loaded, demanded another one. Bar was closed, so I gave him a shot from a bottle I kept for Dad. Had to tell Harry to keep his voice down; he wanted to see Dad and I had to tell him no. He was belligerent, kept asking me if Dad had read the briefing books he'd prepared for the crossing. I said of course he had, but I don't think he believed me. I went to grab something to pack. When I came back, Harry was gone, along with his son. And the bottle."

I felt a chill.

"Did you ask Stettinius about him?"

"He said Harry'd been drinking in Naples and got so violently ill on the flight to Malta Bob had to put him to bed. Stettinius thought it was dysentery. Harry told him he'd been running on cigarettes, coffee, and booze the whole trip, and it was catching up with him."

"I see. Did he fly with you to Yalta?"

"I didn't want him on board with Dad. Not like that."

The full Allied congregation, almost seven hundred people on twenty aircraft, took off from Malta at midnight escorted by squadrons of fighters. Seven hours later they touched down near dawn at an airfield in Crimea near their destination, Yalta.

She said they had lowered FDR by elevator and he was greeting Soviet dignitaries on the tarmac when Harry came over to shake his hand. She showed me a photo Bob had taken of them. Harry looked dreadful, pale, eyes protruding, skin taut across his skull. The Boss smiled, cheerful, if a bit frail, but beside his cadaverous best man he seemed glowing with health.

Their motorcade took five hours over eighty miles of rough mountain roads to Yalta. Anna kept Harry out of their car, to make sure FDR saved his energy. Our delegation was staying in the Livadia Palace, summer retreat of the last tsar, Nicholas II. This wasn't summer. The palace was frigid and drafty, no central heat. Two hundred Americans had to somehow share six bathrooms. Many fell ill. Harry was a mess when he arrived.

Anna thought Harry looked like death warmed over.

The conference began; days of hard-nosed negotiations followed by elaborate Russian receptions and formal dinners. Harry spent every evening in bed, mustering just enough energy to join afternoon sessions with the Big Three. He sat silently behind the Boss, watching and listening. They passed notes back and forth, poker-faced; Harry sober and observant.

"He looked like hell but when everyone saw him back in the saddle that first day, people from all sides—Brits, Russians, Americans—began dropping in on Harry, in bed and his pajamas. I shielded Father from distractions, but I couldn't do that for Harry. To be honest it worked better this way and put Harry where he could do the most good; taking in everyone else's position, which he then filtered back to Dad."

"How'd they reach the finish line?"

"Dad had two objectives. Both came easier than we expected. Stalin promised to declare war against Japan soon as Germany's defeated. And he agreed to support and join the United Nations, once the charter's written. Then they hit a sticking point on voting rules."

I'd heard from a friend at State this concerned the number of General Assembly votes allocated to the Big Three. The Brits still controlled their surviving colonies, and the Soviets had gobbled up Eastern European states they'd liberated from the Nazis: England demanded three extra votes and the Soviets sixteen. Putting us—with just one vote—at a massive disadvantage. And Churchill was backing Stalin.

"In their last meeting, Harry played an ace. It was getting heated, so he passed a note to Dad. Suggested they kick this down to a subcommittee—where Harry felt we could prevail, without having to take on Churchill or Stalin face-to-face. That subcommittee, as Harry had predicted, gave us what we wanted.

"Churchill got one vote for India, Stalin two for Ukraine and Belarus. Both then, off the record, agreed to give us two extra votes to balance the scales. Father and Harry think the United Nations has a real chance now. Stalin turned out to be a man they could make a deal with."

But a final issue remained: the fate of Poland. In their 1939 pact, Hitler offered to split Poland down the middle with Stalin like a coffee cake. A week later their joint offensive crushed Poland from both directions.

"Given that Stalin had already annexed his side of Poland," said Anna, "and grabbed half of Germany as they advanced on Berlin, Churchill said we had no choice but to give Poland to the Soviets after the war.

"In the last hour FDR convinced Stalin, on paper, to include former Polish officials who'd fled to London in Poland's new government."

An agreement not worth the paper it's printed on. I didn't say it, but suspected she felt the same way.

"Given the lousy cards we'd been dealt," said Anna, "and the concessions Stalin had already given us, Dad felt that was the best we could do."

"So all three got what they wanted."

"Even Harry seemed surprised. He said these things aren't successful unless all parties leave feeling they could have gotten more."

Newsreels, and Bob Hopkins's fine photos, had been released as the conference concluded, and reached us at the White House. Presenting the summit as a triumph, film and images showed the Big Three seated together in a jolly mood. Initial response to the statement they issued on the Yalta Conference suggested they'd sold their pitch.

I thought Churchill looked diminished in these images. The Boss was thinner, older, and exhausted, but his confidence made up for a lot of that. I caught a furtive glimpse of Harry in the back of a newsreel shot, so lean and wizened I hardly recognized him.

Uncle Joe sat there grinning in every shot like the Cossack that ate the canary. The major failing of the Conference—Poland's fall into the hands of the USSR—would come to be seen as Yalta's great failure. One that caused the Polish people unimaginable suffering. But we didn't know that yet.

"So you'd say the Boss was pleased with Harry's performance."

"As we packed to leave, he said Harry played an essential part in pulling it off," she said, refilling her glass at the bar.

"Did he tell Harry that?"

She shook her head. "That wasn't the end of it."

After trekking back to the same Crimean airfield, FDR, Harry, Anna, and a smaller party boarded the Sacred Cow for a flight to Egypt. Once on the ground they billeted aboard the *Quincy*, which had sailed ahead to the Suez Canal. FDR had decided to make a quick small-caliber diplomatic visit, one Harry put together last minute, on behalf of the United Nations.

For the first time in history an American "monarch" met face-to-face with an Egyptian one, King Farouk. Their meeting on the *Quincy* was colorful, exotic, and mostly ceremonial. When FDR told Churchill—at dinner the night before in Yalta—he was meeting with the ruler of what was still a British colony, Winston pitched a fit. He impulsively decided he would go see the king as well, in case FDR was up to something.

When Harry heard this childish reaction, he urged the Boss to soothe Churchill before he blew a gasket. FDR agreed; arrangements were hastily made. They sailed up the Suez the next morning to host Winston for lunch on the *Quincy* near Alexandria.

They quickly unruffled Winston's tail feathers: Harry convinced him the UN was their only reason for meeting Farouk. The Boss broke the ice with picaresque stories of the king bringing his retinue aboard, including harem, palm frond–waving slaves, the royal astrologer, and eight sheep. His way of saying he had no reason to meddle in Egypt's relations with England. Between that and the flowing bubbly, Winston relaxed and they enjoyed a pleasant lunch on the *Quincy*.

"We said goodbyes to Winston and Sarah and sailed off on the *Quincy* for Algiers," said Anna as she poked at the fire. "Harry'd arranged a meeting with de Gaulle, but at the last minute the Asparagus worked himself into a snit over some nonsense and snubbed us. So we put in to resupply for a day before heading home. But something happened on the way to Algiers."

She finished her whiskey and poured a little more.

"Seas were rough the whole way. Harry stayed in bed the whole day before we reached Algiers. Came out late that night, pale as a sheet, and begged to speak to Father alone. I walked him in.

"Harry told Dad that given everything they'd done, and what the heavy seas was doing to him now . . . he couldn't face nine days crossing the Atlantic in winter."

"He was never a sailor on his best day," I said, apprehensive. "Not with his stomach."

"But Harry didn't ask permission. Just said he was getting off in Algiers to rest and fly home. Father didn't even answer. He just stared at him, Bill. Finally, Harry walked out."

My heart sank.

"We'd been riding high, Bill . . . Father said he'd been counting on Harry to help write his report on Yalta for Congress. Looking forward to his company. He groused about Harry's 'episodes,' that he only used them to duck out and avoid him. I said I didn't think that was fair and he clammed up. Then he asked me to try to talk Harry out of it."

"How'd that go?"

"I went to his cabin. Harry looked dreadful. Said he was sorry, he was just too sick to go on. He broke down. He'd lost eighteen pounds in three weeks; he wasn't lying, he was at the end of his rope."

I believed that was true.

"He begged me to call London, have them fly someone in who could help Dad with the report, but he simply couldn't do it. He'd given his life to all they'd worked for and . . . he just wanted to see his wife and daughter . . . 'cause he was afraid he was going to die. He was terrified of being buried at sea. . . . What was I supposed to say?"

I didn't know how to answer.

"I went to Pa Watson. Asked him to find someone in London, fly 'em down and meet us before we left Algiers. He went pale as a sheet but said he'd handle it. On the way back I found Dad outside, in his chair and cape, in a cold wind, staring at a distant storm."

She sat beside me: "I told him Harry wouldn't budge. Father didn't move, didn't even look at me. Just sighed softly and said, 'Let him go.'"

I put my head in my hands. All the desperate work Harry had done to put himself back into FDR's good graces . . . down the drain.

"Next day we anchored in Algiers. We were going over papers at

Father's desk. Harry knocked, bag in hand; I think he'd come to apologize. Father looked up, stuck out a hand, and coldly said goodbye. They shook hands and he cut Harry dead, not another word, just went back to work. I walked Harry out. He couldn't even speak, just boarded the tender alone and left."

I knew the rest. Harry flew home days later. By the time the *Quincy* docked in Norfolk and FDR reached the White House, Harry had checked into Mayo Clinic, where he remained in intensive care, desperately ill. For the last time he'd stepped away from the job that for the last twelve years had been slowly killing him.

In his weakest hour, my best friend Harry, who'd predicted FDR would abandon him if his health ever failed—which I, in my wisdom, swore he'd never do—had been dismissed by the Boss for good.

Then a second disaster: Two days after the *Quincy* left Algiers, Pa Watson was felled by a stroke, lingered two days, and died.

The Boss had asked me after Pa's funeral if I could take on his job and work double duty as appointment secretary. I said yes, of course. But the old guard was slipping away.

Harry Hopkins and FDR never saw or spoke to each other again.

March 1945

The month of March, teasing us with glimpses that foretold an early spring, passed rapidly. I found that combining my usual work with keeping FDR's appointments resulted in a workable economy of purpose. Anna and I spent mornings with the Boss in his bedroom, sorting mail, congressional business, confirming the day's schedule. We adjusted his workload on the fly, day to day, according to his stamina.

Two days after his return, FDR offered his report on Yalta in person to Congress, and for the first time ever he faced them sitting down. In simple words offered without self-pity, he told them why: He was no longer strong enough to stand.

I noticed tears in the eyes of his cabinet and staff around me. I'm sorry to say the address FDR then gave, one he'd written alone on the voyage home—an hour long, often meandering—lacked the power of persuasion Harry the Hop would have given it. For all that, the Boss was kindly received on his last visit to Capitol Hill. With victory in sight his conciliatory tone reflected perfectly the country's mood. Our politicians seemed eager to help him to that end.

• • •

FDR's daily focus now centered on the war, following avidly the progress our forces made in both theaters:

By the end of March, all of the Philippines was back in our hands. After six weeks of desperate fighting, Marines captured the island and airfields of Iwo Jima. We hoisted our flag on its summit, a moment captured in an iconic photo—albeit one, I learned, re-created for the camera moments after it happened by military PR men. One last Japanese stronghold stood between us and their mainland: the island of Okinawa. Operation Iceberg began there on April 1.

In Europe, General Eisenhower and the First Army captured the last bridge the Nazis had left across the Rhine before they could destroy it. Ike marched six divisions across the bridge at Remagen into western Germany and the target-rich industrial Ruhr Valley.

Two weeks later General Patton drove a division of the Third Army across that border; this conquering general paused to take a piss in the Rhine. Eisenhower stepped up the pace of our offensive. With Russians closing on Berlin from the east, the last battles to stamp out the corporal's madness would be fought on German soil.

FDR's second preoccupation remained this: avoiding the mistakes he'd watched a sick, weakened President Wilson make in 1919. In haste to realize his starry-eyed League of Nations, Wilson failed to blunt the retribution France and England exacted on Germany. A tragic misstep that led directly to the rise of Fascism and the Second World War.

FDR's solution to this job aligned with his first: drive the Axis Powers to their knees in unconditional surrender and ensure the peace that followed would last. Germany this time would be rebuilt into a country fit to rejoin our family of nations. FDR believed we needed a sturdier global political body. One that in real and practical ways would achieve the lasting peace that Wilson's League had dismally failed to do.

His more muscular version of world governance was about to draw first breath. All forty-seven nations of our Second World War alliance had accepted FDR's invitation to sign as charter members. At the end of April, he would preside over the first convention for representatives of our United Nations in San Francisco. FDR planned to deliver a commencement address to the delegates and for broadcast on radio around the world.

Win the war and then win the peace. Then and only then would the job be finished. Once accomplished, Anna told me he'd talked of retiring from office, going home to Hyde Park. To that hope I added mine in prayer.

We traveled to Hyde Park in March twice—both times raining pitchforks—and rallied family and staff to give their all in support of these objectives. He met twice more with Vice President Harry Truman, in meetings with congressional leaders. Although FDR greeted Harry warmly both times, he never spent a moment alone with the man now occupying the loneliest on-deck circle on earth.

During March we observed two anniversaries at the White House. The first came on March 4: the twelfth anniversary of FDR's first inauguration. Honored this year more in quiet resolve, by those around him, than celebration.

The second came two weeks later, March 17, St. Patrick's Day and the fortieth wedding anniversary of Franklin and Eleanor. A quiet Saturday for the First Couple and a relaxed lunch in the White House residence. A larger, more formal dinner in their honor was held that evening for dignitaries, followed by a Hollywood movie. A rather ordinary thriller enlivened by the remarkable Charles Laughton. The Boss whispered to me during opening credits he'd been eager to see it ever since Stalin told him at Yalta that Laughton was his favorite movie star.

And so, another milestone passed in the lives of this extraordinary American couple.

• • •

I am free to tell you that in the days prior to this—April 12 to 15—the First Lady was away on business in North Carolina. In a visit I had arranged, after FDR learned of Eleanor's trip, Lucy Rutherfurd came to town.

Lucy spent the first two evenings at the White House dining with FDR, Anna and John, and guests including Canada's prime minister. All discreetly asked, by Anna or myself, and all agreeing without hearing a reason why, they should not mention Lucy's presence.

Lucy stayed at his sister's house in Washington. Each day the Boss drove there in his own car to pick her up. I rescheduled his appointments so he could spend mornings with Lucy, and lunches they enjoyed with Anna. After lunch they took drives in the Maryland countryside, bracketed discreetly by Secret Service. Seeing them off each day at the motor pool, the Boss looked animated and full of life behind the wheel. I couldn't help but recall the first glance I'd had of them together, driving along the Potomac, twenty-seven years ago.

On Lucy's final evening, the Boss spent three hours dining with his dearest friend alone. I waited in the parlor outside before escorting Lucy near midnight to a waiting car. She told me she'd given FDR a special gift:

A formal sitting with a close friend of hers, a gifted Russian-born portraitist who earlier had produced an in-person watercolor of Franklin that he not only sat still for but actually liked, a rarity. They decided her artist friend, Elizabeth Shoumatoff, would accompany Lucy to visit FDR and paint this new work during our upcoming visit to Warm Springs.

The First Lady returned to Washington the next day. Two days later, we celebrated their anniversary. To this couple we all owed so much, I sent two dozen yellow roses, Eleanor's favorite flower. Although given to both, privately I meant them for her alone. Honoring my friendship with the woman I'd known as long as her husband and admired as much if not more.

As to what other emotion moved me to do so, I leave for you to decide.

We made his final trip to Hyde Park on March 24. The early spring we'd hoped for delivered its promise. Flowers budding in the garden, wintering birds returning early to nest. Not yet time for the stands of lilacs near the river to bloom, but that felt near.

Anna told me Franklin had invited Eleanor to join him for the UN Conference in San Francisco. They afterwards planned a voyage to London to visit the Churchills and the royal family, who'd invited them to stay. Eleanor had ordered new clothes; they spoke of embarking from there on the world tour they'd always dreamed of. FDR had told Anna he hoped to visit the front with Churchill and Eisenhower. When she brought up security concerns, he took her hand and whispered: "Don't tell anyone, dear, but don't you worry; the war in Europe will be over by May." She took this to mean he would then resign from office.

As we worked through the mail our last day in Hyde Park, the Boss seemed blissful, as always on the eve of a trip to Georgia. He said all he planned to do when we got there was "sleep, sleep, sleep."

We boarded the train that evening for Washington. After a packed morning in the Oval—the Boss delighted to see the wisteria on the South Portico had flowered in our absence—we went back to the station below the Bureau of Engraving that afternoon.

Next stop, Warm Springs.

Warm Springs

We arrived on Good Friday, driving from Atlanta on country roads adorned with spring foliage, an idyllic, warm and sunny spring day. The usual staff came with us, along with Dr. Bruenn—no McIntire this trip; he was busy—FDR's cousins Polly and Daisy, and faithful Fala. Eleanor stayed behind to open Springwood for the summer. Anna had been scheduled to come, but at the last minute young Johnny came down with severe tonsillitis. Anna and John were taking turns by his bedside at Walter Reed Hospital.

The whole town and the patients in residence turned out to greet FDR as we drove in that afternoon. The Boss then drove himself and the cousins up the hill to the beautiful cottage we called the Little White House and retired for the day.

I ate with Dr. Bruenn in the dining hall that night; down-home Southern cooking, an exotic treat for my beige Yankee palate. Afterwards we strolled the gardens and sat near the mineral pools, lights reflecting off the waters at twilight. I lit my pipe, Dr. Bruenn smoked a cigar, and we sat watching stars wink on overhead.

"How does he seem to you, Doc?" I asked.

"Holding steady. Being here will do him a lot of good, don't you think?" When I didn't respond he asked, "How does he seem to you?"

I paused thoughtfully and decided to just say it: "I think he's slipping away from us . . . and no earthly power can keep him here."

We heard laughter from one of the guest cabins nearby.

Bruenn took that in, then in a measured tone: "Tell me why you think so."

The fading light gave me cover. I was saying what I'd never said to anyone.

"I understand your position, Doc. Your obligation's to not admit defeat. I've no quarrel with that."

"How long have you felt this way?"

"Before the election. For certain? Since our visit here in December. I mentioned my concerns to you then."

Bruenn took in a sharp breath. "You said he seemed exhausted."

"Beyond exhausted."

Bruenn stood and paced, agitated.

"I've said nothing else to anyone. With staff, family, the Boss himself I've maintained the bluff—"

"You see him every day, for hours—"

"That's how I know—"

"But you haven't said this to me—"

"It doesn't matter, it won't change anything. And I'm not the only one who thinks so."

He paused. "Who?"

I hesitated. Since we'd traveled with him on the train, and had just seen him at dinner, he guessed it: "Doc O'Connor?"

"That's right."

Basil "Doc" O'Connor—a lawyer, not a doctor—had been FDR's legal adviser for decades. He'd entrusted Doc to administer Warm Springs Foundation since its founding.

"We both felt it, last summer. His indifference to the election. He didn't seem to give a damn about it—"

"He ran a flawless campaign—"

"After Dewey fired him up, yes. That 'tired old man' stuff, going after Fala, all their nonsense. His instincts and adrenaline kicked in—"

"But you were with him, so was I, he campaigned like a lion."

"Yes," I said, lowering my voice. "Yes, he did, Doc. For six weeks.

And at the end of each day, he had nothing left. He gave it everything he had and now he's paying the price."

Bruenn struggled. "Why is he hanging on?"

"Finish the job: win the war. Win the peace."

He thought a moment. "Is there any chance he'd step aside?"

I shook my head. Bruenn looked devastated. I felt guilty saying as much as I had.

"Doc, he wouldn't even be here now if you hadn't stepped up when you did."

He grimaced, rubbing his forehead. I stood. We walked back toward our residence hall.

"I never did find his medical records in the archives," he said. "Where McIntire said they'd be. No trace."

"Surprised?"

"I guess not."

"We'd never be able to prove it, so . . . what's the point?"

We stopped in front of the hall. Someone was playing piano inside, people were singing.

"His condition's grave, yes, I give you that," said Bruenn. "But I don't think it's hopeless."

I looked at him in the dying light. "No offense . . . is that your science talking, or your heart?"

"There's more I could do, Bill, if we just . . ."

He trailed off. In his own kind way, he was echoing Eleanor's conviction that FDR could just will himself to go on. There was always more one could do. But this was his wife's blind spot too; her inability to perceive limits, or allow exceptions, for human frailty.

That's why the Boss had gently suggested he travel to Warm Springs without her; Eleanor would join him in two weeks, and they'd leave for San Francisco. So Anna and I had made arrangements for Lucy to visit. Help him relax and be himself in ways his wife, alas, could not.

I offered my hand. "I take no pleasure in telling you this. You're as fine a man as you are a doctor." He thanked me. I lowered my voice.

"He knows all this. He's staying the course because this is how he wants it. His terms."

I believe, as we parted, he understood my point of view. But we did so with heavy hearts.

• • •

We went to the Little White House together the next morning. I lugged a bulging mailbag just arrived from Washington. Doc gave the Boss a once-over. We both thought he looked better after a good night's rest. He worked through our daily chores with cheer and good humor.

When we returned for cocktail hour at five, the contrast was stark. Once again worn, gray, and weary. Didn't offer or ask for a cocktail, just wanted to rest.

We huddled outside with Cousin Daisy and Grace. The Boss was steadily losing weight—twenty-five pounds the last three months. Little appetite. Daisy offered to give him oatmeal and cream—what she called gruel, something he'd loved as a child—to jump-start his appetite between meals. Grace suggested we try engaging him with hobbies he'd brought along; his stamps, boxes of his books we were sorting through for the library.

So Daisy gave the Boss "gruel" before dinner and he perked up. She told us he talked of retiring once the war was won and the United Nations up and running. I phoned Anna each night after dinner with a daily brief. She gave me good news on Johnny; they were using the new wonder drug, penicillin, and his tonsils were improving. Anna didn't say so, but I could hear that not being with her father while her son lay ill was tearing her in two.

The following day was Easter Sunday. We signed mail and after breakfast the Boss said he felt well enough to attend services that morning, and we drove down with the cousins.

The chapel was filled with lovely sprays of spring flowers. Franklin looked frail, stationed between Polly and Daisy. I sat behind them. As we sang hymns he sounded weak as a reed. Once he dropped his hymnbook, another time his glasses.

I offered my own prayers that Warm Springs could renew him.

The next day my prayers found a foothold. His strength and spirits rallied. He'd spoken to Lucy the night before by phone, and she was arriving that afternoon, April 9. Accompanied by her artist friend Elizabeth Shoumatoff, and her assistant, Nicholas Robbins. Polly, Daisy, and the staff prepared the cabin next to FDR's for the women; Robbins would stay at a hotel in town.

FDR had promised Lucy he'd drive out to meet them and guide them in. The Boss took Daisy and Fala with him in the car, along the road he knew they'd be using. Two hours later—having lost their way—Lucy drove into a town fourteen miles north of Warm Springs and saw a crowd outside the drugstore, gathered around an open coupe. There sat the president behind the wheel enjoying the attention and a Coca-Cola.

Daisy said she saw pure joy on their faces when Lucy and Franklin spotted each other. He patted the seat and she hopped in beside him for the ride to Warm Springs.

The particulars that followed matter less than this: The next forty-eight hours passed in a way I hoped would never end; a sublime night and a perfect spring day and evening shared together in this sublime, healing place. His cottage filled with laughter and a bliss these two souls had only ever found with one another. Etched in my memory. All of us fortunate enough to share those days felt the same; I know, because I asked them.

As I worked with the Boss on the mail the next morning, Lucy sat with us, attending to him. Franklin and I then scratched out a radio speech for the following day, April 13, to commemorate Thomas Jefferson's birthday.

Both afternoons, after lunch in his cabin, FDR sat for Madame Shoumatoff, wearing his navy cape and an elder statesman's gravity.

She sketched his outline then began to fill in her canvas. Shoumatoff was a taskmaster, brilliant but demanding; taking precise measurements with a tape, insisting he hold still if he fidgeted. I wondered if she bossed all her big-shot clients this way and worried the Boss might lose patience, but Lucy kept his spirits bright and cheerful.

Shoumatoff directed Mr. Robbins to take photos from various, specific angles, reference points to complete the portrait at home after his sitting. He also took a photo of Lucy and Franklin together, holding hands. That image, subsequently lost, remains in my memory.

That afternoon the Boss felt invigorated. We worked on his schedule for San Francisco and beyond, then finalized the Jefferson speech with Grace.

After a nap before supper he took Lucy, Daisy, and Fala for a drive to the top of Pine Mountain and his favorite spot, an overlook on the summit called Dowdell's Knob. Mike Reilly settled FDR on his favorite bench and told his team to hang back. Daisy took Fala for a walk, giving them privacy. Franklin and Lucy watched a majestic sunset paint the Appalachians marching away to the west.

When they returned, as he'd done each evening, the Boss called Anna. She told him Johnny continued to improve. Franklin told her he was looking forward to a barbecue Warm Springs was putting on for us tomorrow evening. He ate a hearty dinner, conversation and laughs flowing freely. Dr. Bruenn arrived at nine, a curfew check to make sure he got his rest. The Boss put up mock resistance, asking for more time in a sweet, childlike way, but at Lucy's affectionate insistence he complied. Lucy tucked him in, the last to say good night before retiring herself.

He'd asked me to look over the Jefferson speech, which I did before turning in. This passage caught my eye:

"Let me assure you my hand is the steadier for the work that is to be done, that I move more firmly in this task, knowing that you—millions and millions of you—are joined with me in the resolve to make this work endure. The work, my friends, is peace. More than an end of this war—an end to the beginnings of all wars. I ask you to keep your faith . . . the only limit to our realization of tomorrow will be our doubts of today. Let us move forward with strong and active faith."

These, the last words he would ever write.

April 12, 1945

The mail pouch had been delayed so I didn't arrive until half past eleven. The Boss was up and dressed—double-breasted gray suit and college tie—stationed in his favorite chair by the stone fireplace at a card table he'd been using as his desk, chatting with Lucy. His color had returned. He looked happy and full of life.

The pouch was full and I asked if he'd rather hold off until after lunch. He insisted on signing right away. As I laid out the laundry Madame Shoumatoff arrived, set up her easel, and began her work as we did ours. Lucy helped Franklin slip on his navy cape. The ever-present cousins sat nearby, Daisy knitting, Polly watching the artist.

"I've been meaning to ask, madame," I said. "Do you have a title in mind?"

"I think I will call it," said Shoumatoff, *"The President with a Cape On."*

Courtesy of her Russian accent, the last words ran together. The Boss and I glanced at each other; his sly look told me the same thought had occurred.

"The President with a Capon," said the Boss, fiddling with his cape. "Hmmm. People might think I'm hiding a small chicken under here."

I stifled a smile, and saw Lucy do the same.

"May I offer an alternative, madame?" I asked. "*The President . . . Wearing a Cape.*"

Shoumatoff stopped to consider it. "Yes. Okay. Good."

But the Boss didn't let it go. "A reporter friend of mine—who shall remain nameless, *Bill*—once described Herbert Hoover to me as a 'fat, timid capon.'"

"Maybe you should be holding Herbert Hoover on your lap," said Lucy.

We all laughed, except mirthless Madame Shoumatoff. I set the day's last bill in front of FDR, and he borrowed my pen to sign it.

"Forgive the intrusion, madame," I said. "This is the last."

"Lucy, dear, look," he said. "Always wanted to show you . . . this is how the president makes a law."

He signed with his old flourish, struck a mock heroic pose, his pen as a sword, and said: "Pour l'éternité. Comme gravée dans la pierre. Une puissance incroyable!"

She responded with more French I didn't understand—that was the point, a language they spoke that we didn't. Both laughed. He signed his name, the date, and the word "Approved," as I'd watched him do a thousand times. He handed me back the pen and the bill.

"There, now," he said. "That job is done."

As I waited for the ink to dry I packed my bag with the finished mail.

"Meet us up at the barbecue round four-thirty, Bill, and please bring Dr. Bruenn if you'd be so kind."

I said my goodbyes and headed out as staff came in to serve them lunch.

"Oh, Bill, one last thing: Tell the postmaster I approve that latest design, and I'd like a sheet of our first UN commemorative stamp, pay full price, on the twenty-fifth in San Francisco. Want to show 'em off to everyone."

"Will do, Boss."

I drove to the dining hall and had just finished a bowl of soup—not more than fifteen minutes later—when I was called to the phone. It was Mike Reilly.

"Get back here fast," he said, and I heard it in his voice.

I reached the cottage in under five minutes, checking my pocket watch as I hurried in: 1:30. The Boss's valet Arthur Prettyman sat alone, head low, weeping. Shoumatoff and her assistant were hastily packing up; Daisy and Polly sat in the den and both reached for me, hands cold as ice.

"He said, 'I have a terrific pain in the back of my head,'" Daisy said. "I was closest to him, I'm the only one who heard."

"He looked at us," said Polly. "After they carried him in and set him on the bed. Looked at each of us. But I don't know that he saw us."

The bedroom door was open. Dreadful labored breathing from inside told the story. Mike saw me and waved me in.

A phone in his hand, Dr. Bruenn sat on the bed—talking with McIntire—beside FDR, flat on his back, motionless, covered in blankets, eyes closed. No sign of life other than shudders of that awful mechanical breathing. Lucy sat on his other side, holding his hand. Both glanced at me. Neither spoke.

I struggled to order my thoughts. There were things to do, too many. I kept looking at my watch, noting the time, doing my job again, but it kept me from anguish. I looked upon FDR one last time, the Greek profile, the noble forehead, and knew this was goodbye.

Mrs. Roosevelt and Anna weren't here, but I thanked God for Lucy. I left the room. Mike asked me to call Steve Early at the White House, tell him the Boss had fainted before lunch and was being treated in his bedroom. I returned from that call to sit and wait with Daisy and Lucy. Grace had arrived in my absence, sitting with them, holding Daisy's hand, moving her lips in silent prayer. It was 2:09 in the afternoon.

Others came and went. A specialist from Atlanta, summoned by McIntire, rushed in, medical bag in hand. Time stood still, but the hands kept moving on my watch.

Lucy emerged from the room at 2:20, eyes full of pain. I moved to her, took her hands, said the nearly useless things one can.

"Bill, we knew this day would come," she said softly.

"Yes."

"You just never think it's going to be today."

I could only nod.

"Elizabeth's packed the car. We need to go, Bill."

"That's right."

Her voice fell below a whisper. "We'll make sure, of course, all of us: No one must know we were here."

"No one will."

She covered her mouth. "I told him . . . I don't know if he could hear me . . . no regrets, and . . . I told him I just wished we'd had more time. The world needed him more than I did . . . and I'm so grateful for what little he could spare."

A car pulled up outside. I walked Lucy out. Shoumatoff sat in the back, her assistant, Robbins, behind the wheel. Mike Reilly opened the passenger door. I squeezed her hand one last time. Lucy took one backward heartbreaking glance, got in, and I watched them drive away.

I walked inside and waited. Bruenn came out of the bedroom at exactly 3:00. Waved me to follow him to the terrace. We spoke in whispers.

"It's a cerebral hemorrhage." He said other things; I heard the word "massive."

He was called back inside. I returned to the living room. We resumed our vigil. Cousin Polly rambled nervously, saying Franklin had never been afraid of anything, not his infirmity, not even dying. Only fire.

The involuntary breathing stopped at 3:31. Bruenn stepped out four minutes later, closing the door behind him. He told us quietly that FDR was gone.

Thus, a good man met the fate that awaits us all. And so, in the quiet beauty of the Georgia spring, like a thief in the night, came the day of the Lord. The weight of the world he'd carried, that no one man could bear alone for long, had finally lifted. I noticed a sudden stillness in the air around us; even the birds had gone quiet.

I closed my eyes to say one silent prayer: "Lord, make me know mine own end, and the measure of my days what it is; that I may know how frail I am."

Then, work: Bruenn called McIntire in Washington. I picked up another phone and asked them to put me through again to Steve Early at the White House, the friend who'd brought me in twelve years ago. Since we'd spoken earlier Steve had notified the First Lady and been standing by since.

"He's gone, Steve," I said.

I mentioned the time of death and the saltiest man I knew wept bitter tears. We did our best to stay on task. We would notify press at the same moment and announce it simultaneously; Steve to the press corps in Washington, me to the wire service men here in Georgia.

Next I called Doc O'Connor. He was already at his desk poring over FDR's will. First things first, he was looking to see if he'd stipulated burial wishes. I said I could save him time, because Franklin had told me, and I told him. Doc found the passage confirming it.

"You and I knew this was coming," said Doc O'Connor.

I agreed. No need or desire to elaborate.

Steve Early's first call went to Mrs. Roosevelt. After hearing from him earlier, Eleanor had stayed at the luncheon in Washington she was supposed to address. Fate had improbably seated her next to Woodrow Wilson's widow.

Word of FDR's collapse spread through the grounds and the wire reporters showed up at the door before I could summon them. I broke the news, then brought Bruenn over to give them a medical statement as well. Enough to issue their initial bulletins.

Neither of us ever breathed a word that Lucy Mercer Rutherfurd or her friend the artist had been with him when FDR was stricken. I told them that instead, at the dreadful moment, an artist named Nicholas Robbins had been sketching the president.

My next job was to find a local undertaker.

Home to Hyde Park

Three days later we buried FDR in the Rose Garden at Hyde Park, inside the hemlock hedge. The Boss had told me years ago that's where he wished to stay, a stone's throw from Springwood and his library.

At 9 AM the day after, as the world coped with the shock, we made ready to convey his body home by train—his casket rested in the living room—when the switchboard said I had a call from Rochester, Minnesota.

"Hello, pal . . ."

It was Harry. Jesus wept, I hadn't had a moment to call him. I asked him how he'd heard.

"Chip Bohlen at State," he said, thin-voiced. "When he was stricken, but before the chief left us. Called back to tell me that as well."

At least he hadn't heard it on the radio. I apologized the news hadn't come from me, but he waved that aside.

"No, no, none of that now, you had your hands full. You holding up?"

I told him the First Lady, Steve Early, and McIntire had flown down last night, arriving at the cottage after midnight. Eleanor's composed, dignified presence had done wonders to comfort the grieving. I said I was so consumed with all that needed doing I didn't feel much of anything; in a word, numb. I'd turned in around 2:30, but couldn't call what I did sleeping.

"Meditating, I guess," I said.

Harry told me he'd wired Churchill once the news was confirmed. By then it was the middle of the night in London, and he hadn't yet heard back.

"Bill . . . I've been thinking all night . . . I mean, of course it's an incalculable loss . . . but I'm filled with gratitude," said Harry, and I heard it; he didn't sound sad at all.

"Say more about that."

"We've been a part of something great, something we'll take with us the rest of our lives. And we know it's all true, Bill, what so many believed about him . . . what made people love him. There were little things, sure, for those of us around him, unimportant things that could get us all worked up. Even less important now . . . I think he knew how little and unimportant they actually were, don't you?"

I said I agreed.

He spoke just above a whisper: "But in all the big ways, all the things of real, permanent importance that matter . . . he never let the people down. That was the work. That's what you and I can hang our hats on."

I can't remember what I said to him next, if I could say anything at all.

I hung up, and for no particular reason realized that today was Friday the thirteenth.

• • •

A military honor guard two thousand strong had been hastily called in from Fort Benning. They assembled at attention on both sides of the road, from the president's cottage to the entrance gates. The First Lady, Grace, the cousins, and Fala, in Mrs. Roosevelt's lap, followed the hearse in a black sedan. Steve Early, Doctors Bruenn and McIntire, and I rode behind them. All the patients in residence had gathered outside—on crutches, in chairs, some on stretchers, all in tears—to pay respects as the hearse passed.

A military band struck up, and we stopped long enough to hear a heartrending version of "Nearer, My God, to Thee" played through tears by a favorite of FDR's who'd performed for him often down the years.

We drove through the gates of Warm Springs to the steady beat of military drums. Two hours later we were aboard the presidential train and underway from Atlanta. We traveled at a measured pace, no highballing; the railway version of a funeral cortege. Throngs of people massed along the line into the countryside. Tens of thousands gathered to watch him pass during the long day and night that followed. I watched them, alone with my thoughts, from the window of my compartment in the car.

Everywhere grief and reverence.

Once in a while I glanced behind me. In the parlor a massive bronze casket I'd ordered less than twelve hours ago rested in its center, draped by an American flag. At each corner a full-dress soldier stood at parade rest—three teams drawn from all branches of service, in eight-hour watches. FDR's personal honor guard maintained their vigil during our entire seven-hundred-mile journey.

The same room, the same space where day and night our circle sat and ate and drank and talked and laughed and lived our lives with him all those many years.

• • •

Two hours into the journey, I got up to find Mrs. Roosevelt, who'd sent word for me. She was riding in the car ahead. I hadn't wanted to intrude when she'd arrived the night before. Alone, in black, gazing out at the crowds, she looked up, smiled softly, took my hand, and asked me to sit beside her. My condolences were few, none came easily, and she waited till I finished.

"I knew what had happened, Bill, the moment Steve called," she said. "Strange, isn't it? I knew after the first call, but you have to hear the words, don't you? Ross and Steve met me at the White House. I wired the boys. Asked Steve to send a car for Anna at the hospital with Johnny. I told them all their father did his job to the end, as he would want us to do now."

I told her all his staff felt the same.

"Steve reached Mr. Truman," she said. "I asked him to come quickly and quietly. I felt it best I tell him myself."

I hadn't found a moment to even think about this. The chief justice swore in our new president two hours after Eleanor broke the news to him, at seven that night, less than three hours after FDR died.

That allowed me to put something together; before seven I'd gotten a frantic call from the head White House usher asking, without saying why he needed it, where he could find a bible. I kept an old Gideon's in the top desk drawer of my office and that was the one they used.

Vice President Truman promised the First Lady that in the days ahead the full power of our government would be hers to use in any way she needed. By the time Truman took the oath, now a private citizen, Eleanor was in the air on her way to Georgia.

The lesson, somehow comforting; no matter how unexpected the moment, succession is quiet, orderly, and the continuity of our system of government proceeds.

"Anna stayed behind to make arrangements," she said. "May she call on you for help as needed?"

I told her yes, in any small way I could. She took a deep breath.

"Bill, the arrangements, the help you always provide . . . I don't mean just today . . . I can't adequately express my appreciation."

I found it too difficult to speak.

"I'm grateful you were with him, at the end . . . and I want to ask . . ."

She halted. For the first time I saw distress as she asked, without looking up.

"... did he suffer, Bill?"

I needed a moment. "I'd stepped away, not long before ... and was called back." I chose words carefully, truthfully. "It's my belief that, no, ma'am ... I don't believe he suffered. I believe ... he was gone within moments."

She took that in. It seemed to offer comfort.

"I've never been afraid of death," she said. "I've seen too much of it. I'd accepted the possibility that his time was short. I presume he did, too. But we were always looking ahead, you know, speaking of the future; that was just the way he was. We never spoke about the end, not a single word, in forty-two years. How can that be?"

She'd asked a question no one could answer. I didn't feel she expected one.

"Now, please tell me, Bill ... is there anything I can do for you?"

I could only shake my head—in wonder, really.

"One last thing ... did he ever speak to you about instructions for his burial?" she said, tears forming in her eyes.

I held out my hand. She took it, without looking up, and quietly composed herself. I told her I'd spoken with Doc O'Connor, and what he'd found in the will. I also mentioned the Boss had left another document in his bedroom safe at Springwood that might be useful.

"So ... the Rose Garden, then," she said. "Thank you, Bill."

I excused myself, returned to and stayed in my berth alone into the night. Continuing my vigil. Crowds along the tracks grew larger each mile we traveled. As darkness fell, I realized the car had been lit in such a way that they could see his honor guard and the flag-draped casket as we passed.

Short of sleep, I retired at ten. By then a new shift of the honor guard stood watch, but nothing about their solemn dedication changed.

• • •

What had changed was this, although I wouldn't know it for a few more hours.

When Mrs. Roosevelt arrived at the cottage that night, Grace and the cousins stayed up to meet her. Eleanor sat with them and heard their accounts of what happened. Daisy told her she noticed something was amiss when FDR fumbled his glasses off and gestured toward his head.

Then this: Laura "Polly" Delano, Franklin's gossipy cousin, proceeded to tell the grieving widow the name of the artist who'd been painting her husband's portrait. And that Madame Shoumatoff had arrived three days ago in the company of a friend with whom she'd shared the cabin next door. The woman who'd asked her to paint Franklin's portrait in the first place.

Lucy Mercer Rutherfurd.

Dear God. An unimaginably cruel betrayal.

• • •

I went to see Mrs. Roosevelt in her car at ten the next morning. I hadn't slept much; I don't believe she had at all. I'd received a wire from the White House asking which hymns should be included in his memorial service, which she gave me. To the presiding bishop she asked me to send a passage from Franklin's First Inaugural she wished included. She also told me she'd spoken with Doc O'Connor.

He told her they'd opened the safe at Springwood to find the letter Franklin left. Addressed to her. In it he described the marker he wanted for his grave, one that Eleanor agreed seemed appropriate: a large, unadorned rectangular block of white granite, drawn from a Vermont quarry that had supplied the stone for many of Washington's original buildings.

"He didn't mention an inscription, aside from dates and so forth," she said. "He actually requested there be none at all. . . ."

That seemed in character, but she asked if I thought Franklin would mind if it were engraved with a short epitaph, which she shared with me. I said I believed he wouldn't object at all if this was her wish.

She looked at me gravely a moment and said, "Bill, we must all now do the things we cannot do."

I soon learned FDR's will had also stated that, when her time came, it was his wish Eleanor share his resting place in the Rose Garden.

• • •

At quarter to ten the next morning we backed slowly down the tracks into Washington's Union Station. Anna and John, Elliott and his new wife boarded through the rear of his car. I stepped back as they greeted their mother and paid their respects at the casket. The air felt weighted. Anna's hand lingered on that flag.

An honor guard arrived and conveyed his casket with strength and dignity from the train to a waiting caisson drawn by six white horses. Vehicles and companies of soldiers formed behind it. We loaded into our assigned cars.

Under blue skies and early summer heat, with solemnity, his family and associates, friends, and former foes rode together between the caisson and his military escort. Passing crowds vaster than any I'd ever seen in our capital, we enacted rituals of grief, made luminous by myths of antiquity as old as Rome or Greece.

Soldiers lined each street and corner on our route from the station to the White House gates. Warplanes rumbled in formation overhead. In the crowd, hats over hearts, salutes held, sobs the only sounds I heard beside the soldiers' heavy cadenced steps. Refrains of Chopin's funeral dirge from military bands accompanied us throughout, played to a low, doleful roll of muffled funereal drums.

I looked at Eleanor and Anna side by side in the car before me. As I glanced up at the buildings around us, windows filled with spectators, a memory came:

As a six-year-old in 1865, Teddy Roosevelt and brother Elliott, from a window of their grandfather's townhouse in downtown Manhattan, had watched the funeral cortege of Abraham Lincoln wend its way through New York.

Eleanor's uncle Ted and her father, the future lost and lamented Elliott Roosevelt.

• • •

His guards carried the casket into the White House and wheeled it down a long red carpet to where he would lie in state in the East Room, beneath Stuart's portrait of George Washington. Eleanor led us inside to the door of the East Room, where she spoke with the head usher. I learned she'd asked for a moment inside alone, before his honor guard took up stations again.

As the doors closed behind her, I found a moment to speak with Anna, our first since his passing. She grasped my hand, told me how pleased her mother had been with the arrangements, and how grateful she'd been for my presence.

"I know better now why he called you the Bishop," she said.

She went upstairs to the residence with John. The head usher later told me he'd been the only witness to this moment inside the East Room: Eleanor requested Franklin's casket be opened. She gazed at her husband awhile, drew the wedding band from her finger, and placed it on his. Then she turned and left the room.

The service was scheduled for four that afternoon. Eleanor went up to the residence to rest. I walked alone to my West Wing office and wrote in my diary all I could recollect of the past three days.

• • •

Filled with flowers and orderly rows of gilded folding chairs, the East Room—where Lincoln once lay in state—now lent itself to a similar occasion. Two hundred in attendance, seated by ushers according to protocol, the congregation overflowed in both directions to adjoining rooms. A final roll call of the Roosevelt years assembled: FDR's cabinet, Supreme Court, joint chiefs, congressional leaders, foreign dignitaries, many of them future delegates of the United Nations. Even Governor Tom Dewey appeared in a back corner, genuinely solemn.

I saw a frail, gray, stooped figure shuffle slowly in and stand close to the rear. I didn't recognize Harry until I saw his wife, Louise, take his arm.

President and Mrs. Truman and their daughter, Margaret, almost unnoticed—no one thinking to observe protocol by standing—entered and took seats across from Elliott, John Boettiger, and other family members in the first row. This oversight of etiquette seemed entirely unintentional; I doubted the new man himself could comprehend our reality just yet.

The bishop stepped forward, raised his hands, and the congregation stood as one. Ushers led Anna first, then Eleanor, veiled and in black, down the center aisle to their seats in front. Both composed and stoic but to my eye under a mounting strain. Everywhere tears and plentiful, eloquent grief. We remained standing for the first hymn. I glanced back and saw Harry clutching his chair, inconsolable, racked with sobs that looked as if they'd break him in half.

Bishop Angus Dun, recently installed at the archdiocese, conducted the twenty-minute service with a gravitas surpassing his youth. He closed, I was pleased to hear, with the passage Eleanor had requested I send him from FDR's First Inaugural:

"Just as the president bore testimony to his own deep faith, let me assert my own belief that 'the only thing we have to fear is fear itself.' As that was his first word to us, I'm certain he would want it to be his last. We should go forward, and look forward without fear, without fear of our allies or friends . . . and without fear of our own insufficiencies."

Amen.

On our way out I met Postmaster General Frank Walker and

recalled I'd never had a chance to carry out the Boss's last directive: the sheet of stamps commemorating the UN Conference he'd asked me to buy. Frank seemed deeply moved. I asked him to place the order at my expense. I wanted the stamps as a keepsake.

I stopped beside Harry, still seated, ravaged. He stood and wrapped his arms around me, a wraith in my arms. He spoke in a faint rasp, told me President Truman had asked to visit with him in the Oval before the service. He didn't tell me why or what they'd discussed. Utterly spent, he said he was going home to bed.

"Chief's work is finished, Bill," he said last, in that cryptic way of his, "but ours may not be."

• • •

At ten that night, FDR's casket again in the parlor car protected by his honor guard, we made our final departure from the Bureau of Engraving and Printing. The last leg of his journey home to Hyde Park.

Seventeen extra cars had been added to carry the congregants. I said an early good night to Mrs. Roosevelt. Returning to the parlor, I passed Anna and John at the window of her father's stateroom. A study of sadness in repose, she saw and waved me in. Anna squeezed John's hand and whispered to him. He kissed her, shook my hand, and left us alone.

"Mother told me about the crowds on the way," she said, nodding at the window. "Look, Bill."

Sure enough, as we rolled through the capital in darkness, people lined the tracks, three or four deep, to solemnly watch him pass.

"It was like this all the way from Georgia," I said.

She wanted to tell me something. I waited.

"They gave me father's berth," she said.

"So I see."

"Who made the assignments, do you know?"

I told her I didn't.

"I would've thought they'd put Mother here," she said. "But then again . . ."

She might've said, "Perhaps because they hadn't shared a bed for so long," or words to that effect. She saw I could tell what she was thinking.

"Mother knows, Bill," said Anna. "She asked to see me alone, at the White House, after the service."

Before I could respond she said: "Cousin Polly. When Mother got there that night."

I was struck dumb. Incomprehensible.

"She blurted out everything; Shoumatoff, Lucy, his final days, all of it. I can't believe it."

My heart sank. I was the one who'd publicly named Nicholas Robbins as the artist who'd been painting his portrait.

"My god, Bill. To betray them both in such a mean way; that small, miserable, awful woman—"

"Why?"

"Oh, I asked her that, I cornered her as soon as I left Mother: 'How could you? How could you do such a thing at a time like that.' . . . Pretty sure you can imagine her reply."

"Because she didn't want Eleanor to hear it from somebody else."

"Damn busybody never could keep a secret, from anybody. I could've screamed, but Mother composed herself, God knows how, then pressed Polly for specifics: Where? How many times? Who arranged it?"

Much worse. "She told her it was you."

"That's right. All of it. She and Mother never got along, you know, not in forty years. All the good Mother's done for people and all Polly cares about are her damn dogs, never worked a day in her life. She took pleasure in it. This was vengeful."

She took out a cigarette and I lit it for her. She shook her head, one crossed leg fidgeting on the other.

"I'll speak with her," I said. "I'll tell Eleanor it was me, that he asked me to do it, and I made all the—"

"Bill, no, I asked you. To help *me*, not him—"

"I can tell her Polly had it wrong—"

"Can't let you do that. I came clean, I already told her it was me, I told her why, and I did not mention your name. This is between Mother and I and that's where it stays. She needs you now. You've got the library to look after together, the disposition of the house, all his papers. She can't do that alone."

I put my head in my hands. A more thoroughly rotten feeling possessed me than any I could ever recall. She leaned closer and lowered her voice.

"We did nothing wrong. It was an impossible proposition. It was innocent and kind, you know that. They shared a closeness he never felt with anyone. In a better world they should have been together all along."

I didn't doubt this was true.

"This was my decision. He was dying, Bill. If we gave him a few hours of warmth or comfort from a love he thought he'd lost, I wanted him to have it. I believe it was keeping him alive, I do."

I agreed. FDR had given his life to win this war, as sure as Harry's son or the hundreds of thousands of others who died for their country had done.

"He wanted to finish the job," I said. "Nothing anyone did or said would stop him."

"That's right, and to deny him this kindness when he was failing would have been unforgivably cruel. But not as much as it was for Polly to tell Mother the way she did, and when."

I said how deeply sorry I felt. That I hoped her mother might find a way to the grace of forgiveness.

"I don't know. I said all of this to her and maybe I got through at some level. She was terribly cold and angry with me. I can't blame her. I know her. She won't ever forget it."

"Don't underestimate her," I said.

She stubbed out her cigarette, put a hand on my arm. I looked into the parlor, the tableau of casket and honor guard.

"I can't bear it and I have to live with that. But I don't regret it, not for a minute. All I can hope . . . I hope I haven't lost both my parents today."

Anna looked resigned, but I knew whatever price she paid would never include self-pity. She went off to look for John. I felt this certainty as I watched her go:

Anna was a Roosevelt, as strong and gifted in her own way as her remarkable parents, and any others in their lineage.

I went back to my berth.

I tore out all the pages that mentioned Franklin and Lucy from my diary and destroyed them.

The Rose Garden

The train pulled in at 8:30. I climbed down first, alone, and started up the hill through the woods on foot. An early chill still misted the Hudson. I was soon offered a ride by a passing car: Mrs. Henrietta Nesbitt, of all people, the tyrant who'd ruined FDR's—and everyone else's—appetite at Springwood and the White House. Franklin had put Eleanor in charge of the house, and she'd hired Nesbitt because they were friends—she had no culinary training and never felt an obligation to acquire any. We'd hardly ever spoken but I remembered the nickname Harry had given her years ago: Eleanor's Revenge.

No wonder the Boss cherished Hyde Park eggs; the one food on earth not even she could find a way to wreck.

The things that come to mind at times like these.

I followed the gravel path through a gap in the hedge bordering the Rose Garden. A sight jarred me, near its center, where the Boss had once shown me where he wanted to rest: his open grave.

Faithful Mr. Plog, the ageless groundskeeper who'd served FDR and his father before him for fifty years, was inspecting the work. I shook his trembling hand. Tears streaked his weathered face. Like all of us, he loved the Boss.

I'd wanted to be first to arrive, giving me time I needed to order my thoughts. The shape and patterns of his life. Beginning here, now ending here, a stone's throw from the room where he'd entered it. Rhythms and rhymes, a myth to suit the scale and scope of his story, for the man, his family, our country, and the world.

Mourners from the train and town, high and low, began to arrive. I stood at the edge of the eastern walkway, greeting General Marshall and his aide, who settled beside me. Soon there were close to three hundred of us, most of whom had been in the East Room yesterday.

Not Harry the Hop, though. He'd been too weak to come and I knew why. This day might have finished him.

The Trumans and their daughter entered, with their own Secret Service detail now. Colleagues of his followed I did not recognize, a changing of the guard underway. We all gathered and stood in solemn silence.

Muted strains of the West Point band reached us as a horse-drawn caisson climbed up the hill from the train; Chopin's Funeral March so grand. The music ended as his escort of West Point cadets in their dress grays entered and took up around the hedge, enclosing us.

Now came the procession, led by the rector of Hyde Park's St. James Church, near eighty, of faltering step. Eight burly soldiers carried in the great bronze coffin. Behind them came Mrs. Roosevelt, Anna and John, Elliott and his wife, and the wives of Jimmy, Franklin Jr., and John, the men still on their way from distant wartime posts.

The rector read committal words from the *Book of Common Prayer*, a stiff breeze off the river fluttering his cassock. My gaze drifted toward the Hudson where I saw movement; the lilacs, waving in the wind, now showing their blossoms the Boss so loved.

Whitman's first line of his ageless tribute to Lincoln came to me, "When lilacs last in the dooryard bloom'd," and a shiver ran through me as I realized:

Today was April 15. Lincoln died eighty years ago today.

The soldiers lifted and held the flag taut above the grave as the coffin was lowered. From behind them, evenly spaced, came staccato reports: seven soldiers firing three times skyward. Their salute echoed across the valley before fading.

A lone bugler sounded "Taps."

Like the Great Emancipator, the Boss's work is done. I prayed for strength for all who would now carry on. And to not make a mess of things like those who followed Lincoln.

As the coffin disappeared, I felt nothing but pity for his enemies, bearers of false witness, slanderers who said he bought votes with the relief he gave to those who'd suffered at their hands, and for all traitors to our precious, fragile idea of democracy.

I thought not of the statesman who'd redeemed his people from economic despair, or the commander who saw the threat to freedom in the Nazis' evil and led the world to the brink of their destruction. All that, in this moment, was far from my thoughts.

I thought only of the man whom it had been my privilege all these years to know and serve. Who during that time had been generous in his praise and patient with my shortcomings, which are many and great. Who gave me his trust and confidence so that I count my association with him as the chief blessing of my life.

May he rest in peace—with Lazarus.

Afterwards

We trained back to Washington hours after the reception. Mrs. Roosevelt and the family, and the old guard, rode in his car. Calm and composed, gracious and thoughtful as she had been since Warm Springs, Eleanor asked if I might notify the White House to prepare a family dinner for that evening.

"One of our last nights there together," she said. "There will be nine of us, Elliott and his wife, the boys' wives, and of course John and Anna."

That made eight. Hearing Anna's name on the list—and the kind way she said it—gave me hope.

"Of course, you'll join us too, won't you, Bill?"

I couldn't speak for a moment. "I wouldn't miss it for the world."

• • •

The next morning I walked from my apartment to the West Wing at the usual time. A strange feeling as I entered, already so many new faces in that busy hive doing the day's business. Almost impossible to imagine FDR's time was done with another man in charge.

I was packing my office into a few boxes when I took a call: President Truman wished to see me. I went at once to the Oval, waited scarcely a moment before the door opened and I was ushered in.

President Truman walked right to me, offering his hand. Although I'd seen him at both memorials, we'd only met that once during his lunch with FDR.

"Mr. Hassett, glad to see you. Thank you for coming. And my deepest sympathies to you."

"Thank you. Mine to you, sir—and it's Bill, please, Mr. President. How may I help?"

He took me in a moment, an open and friendly look that felt sincere. "If you don't mind a personal question, Bill, what are your plans?"

"I'll be closing my apartment, heading to Vermont in the next few weeks. An old family home there I've been planning to restore in my retirement."

"Retirement," he said.

"Yes, sir."

He smiled kindly. "I didn't really know President Roosevelt. Not nearly as well as you did. We spoke only once, just the two of us. I thought, as you probably did, he'd live forever."

Something about his compassionate, affable manner unleashed the grief I'd been holding off. I could only nod. He laid a sympathetic hand on my shoulder, another warm gesture I didn't expect.

"I was in my office. Mrs. Roosevelt called me to the White House. I hurried over. Your friend Steve Early was there. She walked to me, put her arm around my shoulder . . . and told me Franklin was dead. A shock like I've never known. I said what you say . . . 'Is there anything I can do for you?'"

He fought back tears. "And she said . . . 'No. Is there anything we can do for you.' At that moment, Bill."

He took out a handkerchief, unashamed, took off his glasses to dry his eyes. At which point I will say it seemed we understood each other.

"I didn't expect to be called to this job. Not this way, not how it happened, or when. Nor did I want it . . . but he did say this much to me, that day we had lunch, the day I met you. He said should I ever be asked to shoulder the crushing responsibilities of this job . . . I would need all the help I could get."

"He said 'crushing'?"

"Yes. Judging by what I've faced the last few days, he's right. And I intend to assume these obligations the only way I know how, head-on, straightforward."

I could see he meant it.

"Harry Hopkins and I—you may not know this, Bill—we've been friends since 1933. I was a judge in Jackson County and state director of federal reemployment. Harry was in charge of the WPA, a very busy man, as you know. But he always found time for me when I asked or needed help. I've never forgotten that."

I told him that sounded familiar, maybe Harry had mentioned it to me.

"I trust Harry Hopkins like few men I've known. I'll ask his help again if he's able. He told me I'd want my own people around if this job ever fell to me. President Roosevelt gave me the same advice. That day at lunch he took me aside and said there was one man here he considered indispensable. He said I needed you."

I didn't know what to say. Surely FDR had been talking about Harry. But no. Truman's frankness invited mine.

"Mr. President . . . I consider it an obligation, implicit in my loyalty to the late president, to help his successor to the best of my ability."

"I'm mighty glad to hear it. Hopkins told me you'd feel just as he does, by the way."

So that's what Harry'd meant at the memorial. They'd already talked about this.

"But I want to make it plain, sir," I said, "I wouldn't expect any role I undertake to be permanent. I agree with both my friends; you should have your own people around you, so I'll step aside, at your pleasure, to make way for—"

"No, no, no," he said, grinning as if we'd known each other years. "When you get to know me, Bill, you'll find I trust my judgment.

I like to make up my mind about things and get on with it." He offered his hand. "I need you. I want you to stay."

We shook on it.

So much for my retirement.

• • •

I returned to my desk, unpacked my boxes, told my secretary to put her transfer application on hold, and went right back to work.

All so very strange. Four mornings ago, I was sitting with Franklin in Warm Springs. The transfer of authority was now as complete as it was swift. The work of government continued without interruption. And here I sat, back at my desk, and FDR sleeps in the Rose Garden.

First order of business: sort thousands of messages of condolence coming into his office. President Truman was right: He had a dreadful weight to carry, and maybe I could help. It wasn't as if I didn't know how to do my job.

Here's how close the Boss had come to finishing his:

Exactly two weeks later, on April 30, 1945, with Russia overrunning Berlin and Ike closing in from the west, the corporal shot himself in a squalid bunker beneath the Reichstag.

• • •

Our old friend Ed Murrow, America's most trusted reporter, who'd chronicled the war from London, was not the voice who announced FDR's passing. Nor did he attend the funeral. Ed had been in Germany on secret assignment.

The day we buried the Boss, Ed broadcast a horrifying first-person account of the liberated Nazi death camp at Buchenwald. Ike had confronted the same malignance the day FDR died, at a camp he toured called Ohrdruf. Both men told me later the horrors of those defilements scarred them in ways that never healed. Murrow had to burn his uniform because he couldn't rid it of the smell of death. Dozens more of their dark satanic mills would be discovered in the weeks and months to come.

Ike ordered that films and photos document these hell places, to reveal their unspeakable evils to the world. Every Allied nation agreed; the limitless nightmares the corporal and his fiendish cabal had unleashed upon humanity must never be forgotten. The final toll, as the world now knows, was counted in millions.

In August, four months later, we settled accounts with Japan, and you know how. Thus ended the story that began the day Churchill handed over his Tube Alloys project to FDR at Springwood in 1942.

• • •

Harry the Hop was right about most things; like me, his job wasn't done either. In the aftermath of FDR's life and the waning days of war, relations with our "friend" Joe Stalin slipped sideways, portending the Cold War to come. President Truman tapped the only man he thought might talk sense to the "Man of Steel." Rising from his sick bed, Harry, Louise, and a translator left for Moscow three weeks after the corporal smoked his gun.

Drawing on his own relationship with Stalin, and the dictator's residual respect for FDR, Harry secured agreement that, for the moment, stanched the bleeding in American–Soviet relations. Horse trading one-to-one with Uncle Joe to hash out the thorniest issues, Harry's work was hailed in all quarters as masterful and timely.

As Harry and Louise made their way home, they spent four days in Paris; Ike gave them use of his suite at the Hotel Raphael. And so, long delayed, they had their honeymoon. Louise Hopkins, who as editor of *Harper's Bazaar* before the war had been the toast of that ancient and civilized citadel, finally shared the City of Light with her Iowa greenhorn husband.

In September, for his tireless work on behalf of America for more than thirty years, President Truman awarded Harry our highest civilian honor, the Distinguished Service Medal. At his dinner that night, I sat with Harry one last time. He was little more than skin and bones, but this honor thrilled him, and his words, eyes, and inner fire still burned with a desire to serve.

He entered the hospital for the last time in November, steadily weaker, until lapsing into a coma days before he left us on January 29, 1946. Only fifty-five, he died virtually penniless. His last words to me, offered without complaint:

"You can argue with fate, pal, but you can't beat destiny."

• • •

Anna and I worked hard to contain the damage Cousin Polly had done the day FDR died. One bulldog reporter caught a rumor on the wind and only four days after the president's death found his way to Elizabeth Shoumatoff. Madame granted him an interview and openly admitted that, yes, she'd been the artist painting his portrait at Warm Springs that day—not Nicholas Robbins, the artist I'd identified.

"What of it?" she added haughtily.

When he pressed her on why she'd fled and concealed her presence from the public, Shoumatoff shamed him for suggesting it: No one ever asked her about it! She'd left when FDR took ill out of respect and common decency. What did it matter that a person as insignificant as herself had been doing her job when he was stricken?

To Madame's eternal credit, the tough-hided Russian aristocrat never gave up her dear friend Lucy. Not one word. The trail went cold and, thankfully, no one ever doubled back to ask me how I'd "confused" the two artists.

Anna kept me up-to-date on Madame Shoumatoff; she solidified her reputation down the years as one of the premier portraitists of royalty, presidents, First Ladies, and kings and queens of industry alike.

Madame's unfinished oil portrait of the Boss ended up gracing the room in which she'd painted it, part of the museum that now resides in FDR's cherished Little White House at Warm Springs.

Anna and I spoke often during these years. Her relationship with Eleanor healed slowly and gently—they never spoke of Lucy again—and she worked tirelessly on behalf of her mother's causes, many on behalf of the United Nations. For the remainder of their lives, I can happily confirm they grew closer than ever before.

Anna also—discreetly and no longer needing Eleanor's permission—kept a close friendship and correspondence with Lucy.

• • •

Within weeks of FDR's passing, the house called Springwood lay vacant. No one would ever again call it home. Franklin had already told his children he would leave it to Uncle Sam to preserve. None objected, and his wishes were observed.

In late April I was helping Eleanor sort his vast library—over ten thousand books now preserved next door—when she happened across the first watercolor Mme. Shoumatoff had done of Franklin in 1943. I made no comment and neither did she, but I watched her studying the canvas.

Anna told me later what then came to pass. Let me offer this, a closing argument attesting to her mother's character.

A week later the watercolor arrived, without a note, at the estate of Lucy Mercer Rutherfurd. Cousin Daisy had mailed it after Eleanor gave her instructions to do so. Lucy wrote a kind and gracious thank-you to Eleanor—Anna has this letter now and shared it with me—the first she'd written to her former friend and employer since 1916. In which she gracefully acknowledged how much Franklin's friendship had meant to her and her husband, both during his long decline and loss, and after.

"I send you, as I find it impossible not to, my love and deep sympathy, as always, affectionately, Lucy Rutherfurd."

Lucy followed this soon after with a loving letter to Anna, which she'll cherish to the day she dies. For, sadly, Lucy left us only three years later; leukemia. The poor woman had also in that year lost her mother to age, and her beloved sister—to suicide—and it's my observation that a pure heart in this world can only take so much.

A sorrow Anna would soon also bear: Her marriage to John Boettiger dissolved in 1948. I wasn't privy as to why, but she remarried—as did John, more hastily. The root cause may have been the black dog that plagued John all his life—we call it depression now.

You see, John, that sturdy, reliable Midwestern soul, only eighteen months after his marriage to Anna ended, sadly took his own life.

• • •

I stayed in my new/old job long enough to enjoy watching my new boss beat Buster the All-American Boy, again, in 1948. You may have seen the photo of the beaming president holding up that immortal headline: "Dewey Defeats Truman."

I thought the world of Harry Truman. A good, kind, and thoroughly decent man, one who served us faithfully and well as a fair and effective leader.

My thoughts on the person and presidency of FDR are on the record now. Any leader can best be seen through the lens of the times in which they serve. In fairness to both, I will only say this: Mr. Truman possessed in his way as fine a character as my prior boss, and that a more diametrically opposing personality would be hard to conjure.

I turned seventy as we entered the 1950s. My health grew slowly, steadily less than sturdy. I tried to resign my post often during my last years in the White House, at least three times I can recall. Each time Harry, kindly but firmly, talked me out of it.

By the end of his term in 1952, I'd learned my lesson: When President Truman announced he would not run for reelection, I put in for my pension and repaired to the old family homestead in Vermont for good.

Before Harry could recommend me to Ike.

Postscript

Through my role in the growth and guidance of the FDR Library, I remained fortunate down the years to spend many days in the company of the woman we now referred to, rightfully, as First Lady of the World.

Many of these memories and emotions moved through me that rainy day in 1962, when I stood alone after her memorial in the Rose Garden, beside the graves of Franklin and, now, Eleanor.

Nearby stand two modest stones for other members of their family: Chief, their loyal German shepherd, and his successor, the noble Scottie, Murray the Outlaw of Falahill, the good boy better known as Fala. He lived in contented retirement at nearby Val-Kill Cottage with Mrs. Roosevelt until his passing in 1952.

I studied the gleaming white marble monument to this man and woman. Carved with only their names and years. Eleanor had, respecting his final wishes, decided not to add the words she'd suggested might grace his resting place.

I can't help recalling words from them both that come to my mind whenever I see that stone, and think of them:

The only thing we have to fear is fear itself.

We must do the things we think we cannot do.

I've told their story as best I can. Like both my bosses, that job is done. Confession, so we've always preached in my tribe, is good for the soul. Perhaps time will offer me more insight into this eternal puzzle. I only know that as shadows lengthen, I find myself increasingly grateful for my memories of those spacious Hyde Park days.

I've borne witness to enough challenge and struggle through my days to know that each new generation, each of you, will face your own. My wish for those who find such unasked-for advice useful is this: May knowing something of the lessons our times gave us provide a measure of strength when you most need it, lend hope should yours falter, and strike a spark of light to hold back the deepest dark.

So may your own days, gentle reader, bring wisdom to master the fears that come your way. Let them never keep you from the fulfillment of whatever gifts the mystery of existence has seen fit to grant you while you're here.

I leave you with words my friend made part of his Second Inaugural, when the Boss had, in that mystic way of his, managed to see not only our time's future but—an old man's hope—the one awaiting you as well:

"There is a mysterious cycle in human events. To some generations much is given. Of others much is expected, but this much is clear:

"Each generation of Americans has a rendezvous with destiny."

W. D. HASSETT
Northfield, Vermont
June 6, 1965

Acknowledgments

In chronological order:

To my Great-Uncle Will, for the talismanic gift he gave me as a child that I've carried ever since.

Which led, five decades later, to a remarkable conversation at Fenway Park with America's Roosevelt scholar emeritus, Doris Kearns Goodwin.

Which led me, seven years later, to Clifford Laube, William Harris, and the entire staff of the FDR Presidential Library and Museum. (A visit belongs on your bucket list.) Special thanks to Park Ranger Kevin Oldenburg, for an unforgettable private tour of Springwood, which brought its ghosts to life.

Generous contributions of my dear friend Emily Mann and an outstanding community of actors allowed me to distill this sprawling saga over time into purpose and coherence.

My resolute agent Jay Mandel reunited me with all my friends of a quarter century at Flatiron Books. Chief among them my wizardly editor Zack Wegman, whose eagle eye allowed me to shape and sculpt the tale into its final form.

Finally, to my loving family and friends with whom I've shared the journey of this lifetime. Special thanks to my cousin Sean Rosemeyer for sharing her trove of Uncle Will's papers and possessions.

Every book is a journey, too. At this point it finds you, the reader, whose faith in the power of the printed word makes what we all do and love still possible.

Keep the faith. It's not just what we accomplish in life. It's what we overcome.

Courage.

About the Author

Mark Frost is an American novelist, screenwriter, director, and film producer, best known as a writer for the television series *Hill Street Blues* and the cocreator of the television series *Twin Peaks*. His books include *The List of Seven, The Paladin Prophecy*, and *The Secret History of Twin Peaks*.